S.B. ALEXANDER

COPYRIGHT

1

SAM

I winced, feeling a sharp pain in my lower back that vanished when I thought of Layla. Fuck! I held my breath as I crawled to my feet and listed to one side. I oriented my vision and sharpened my vampire senses.

Mangled metal, smoke, fire, dust, and debris created a dystopian scene in the hospital's boiler and electrical rooms. The wall between the two areas had crumbled.

The last thing I heard from Layla was her screaming my name. I growled low, yanking a piece of metal from my leg and another from my back.

"Layla!" I shouted.

Sirens trilled. Or maybe the blaring noise was the loud ringing in my ears. After all, the fucking boiler had practically blown up in my face several minutes ago.

Roman Brown would be a dead vampire when I got my hands around his throat. The bastard was the head of a blood cartel and on the most wanted list by my government. Roman was also one of many on our growing list of enemies.

How the fuck did Roman know we were at the hospital? Layla and I didn't even know we would be in the ER until she'd found blood on her panties. I'd never been so fucking scared in my life, and truth be told, not much frightened my immortal ass. Hellfire would rain down if anyone laid a hand on Layla or did anything to hurt our unborn babies. *Oh fuck.* We were having four little ones. Four freaking kids. I couldn't process that right now. I had to find Layla.

I shouted her name again, then listened. That damn ringing was masking everything. Maybe my sharp senses were off. I'd only heard two fetal heartbeats last night when I'd been drifting off to sleep. I hadn't heard four. Maybe the aftermath of the chip malfunctioning had compromised my hearing. Throw in the explosion…

Regardless, if she was dead, I would die right beside her. My life had no meaning without her.

I navigated through the mess, feverishly retracing my steps from the parking garage to the electrical room. I checked my watch. Only minutes had passed since the explosion. But that did nothing to ease the gut-wrenching pain in my stomach. Layla could be under a pile of burning metal.

Think, man. That was the problem. I couldn't wade through the fear overpowering my senses.

I stopped in the middle of the room, took in a huge breath, and concentrated.

Before the explosion, I'd run into a hairnet dude toking on a cigarette as he'd waltzed out of the laundry area. He'd seen two men with short blond hair and fangs and a bald dude with a scar on his face. Scarface had been chasing Layla. And my comrade Lane had been chasing Scarface.

Lane! Oh man. I'd found his head on the road behind the hospital. I would put money down that Scarface was responsible. I clenched my fists, my heart hurting. Lane had been a good soldier and Layla's bodyguard. But I was to blame for Layla getting away. I was the one who fucked up.

Layla and I were sprinting toward the waiting room when two men bull-dozed out from radiology.

A blond giant tackled me to the ground. "Get her," he said to his scar-faced comrade.

"Run, Layla!" I shouted as I pushed my attacker off me. Before he could react, I lifted my hands, the electricity sizzling in my palms, and swung one fireball at him.

He squealed like a pig, the scent of burning flesh permeating the air. Then he stumbled, swatting at his face to put out the fire.

"Sam!" Layla shouted in a petrified tone.

I bolted, my palms out, my head down, primed to burn the fuck out of the bald, scar-faced moron on Layla's tail until Hawk crashed into me. Then I lost sight of Layla.

I pushed the memory from my mind and refocused on the hairnet guy. He'd seen two women run through the laundry area. Hope hit me upside the head. Maybe Layla and Jordyn were in that part of the hospital.

I checked the pockets on my cargo pants for my cell and came up empty. When the boiler exploded, I had it in my hand. I spun around and backtracked, searching the debris-covered floor as I went over to the massive water pump I'd landed against.

Bingo. My phone had slid under a collection of pipes. I picked it up and tapped the cracked screen. My niece's picture came into view. Abbey was standing outside the science museum in Boston. I grinned at the sight of her winning smile, her deep, sparkling blue eyes, and her mane of black hair—until a gruesome thought gripped me with tension. I would bet Roman was in town for Abbey. *No fucking way.* I ground my teeth together. The two most important people in my life in the hands of my enemy! My gut cinched in fury.

Roman was probably casing out the naval base, biding his time to see if he could snatch my ten-year-old niece. She was on his most wanted list—a special human with magical powers, who was worth millions to the right buyer. He'd tried once before, unsuccessfully, but the criminal vampire wasn't giving up.

Then I thought of something Layla's cousin Junior mentioned to us in my apartment that morning. Layla's grandmother, Harriet Aberdeen, was quite excited to meet Abbey. She'd probably sent Roman to snag Layla, her sister Jordyn, and Abbey. The Aberdeen matriarch was itching to lock up Layla and Jordyn until she could brainwash them away from people like me. Plus, Harriet had recently learned that Layla and her sisters had vampire blood running through their lineage. Armed with that newfound information, Harriet believed the Aberdeen sisters would be prime candidates for genetic engineering and to lead her army of supernatural creatures.

As far as what Harriet had in mind for Abbey, I wasn't sure. But Junior had also relayed that Harriet thought Abbey could be the key to Intech's success. I would bet my vamp ass she would have to fight Roman to death for my niece. Both of them would have to tango with me first. Not to mention Abbey's adoptive parents—my sister, Jo, and her husband, Webb.

I shook all that off and called Layla, holding my breath. The line rang several times until her voice mail kicked in. "You know what to do." Her siren voice did nothing to ease the panic gripping my throat. I struggled for air, feeling like someone was squeezing the life out of me.

Death was imminent. Not for me but for any fucker who dared to lay a hand on Layla.

"Baby doll. Please call me."

Clutching my cell, I tempered my rage as much as I could and went in search of my vampire huntress. She had to be here. I searched high and low, in and around pipes, industrial equipment, and remnants of the falling pieces of ceiling and other piles of rubble. I listened. No heartbeats. I sniffed. Not a whiff of Layla's sweet cherry fragrance or even Jordyn's vanilla scent.

I was about to punch an electrical panel when my phone rang. My fucking heart sputtered like a cold engine in freezing temperatures until I saw Olivia's name. Not that I wasn't fond of my SEAL team comrade, but the only person I wanted to hear from was Layla.

"Hey, Olivia."

"Shit. You're alive. Thank God." Her voice cracked. "After that explosion, I was worried."

I gripped the phone, almost crushing it. "Lane didn't make it."

"I know," she said. "I was coming to look for you and found his head in the middle of the fucking road. I put his remains in the back of your Jeep."

That was one image I wouldn't be able to erase. "Have you seen Layla or Jordyn?" During my last conversation with Layla, she'd told me Jordyn was bleeding. I was assuming they were together.

"Sorry, man. No sign of them out here. Where are you now?" she asked.

"At ground zero. Electrical area where the boiler blew up. But I'm on the move. I have to find Layla. Some dude saw her entering the laundry room. He also saw a blond vamp, which I'm sure was Roman. Do you have him in custody? Tell me you do." My gut knew otherwise. Luck wasn't on my side as of late.

"Negative," she said as other voices in the background grew louder. "Look, it's chaos out here." She raised her voice. "Media everywhere. People telling reporters their stories of seeing vampires, particularly a cop who described you and told some bullshit story about how you killed his partner. Whatever you do, don't show your face. Ben and I will do another sweep around the outside of the hospital."

"Did you get Fred Emery, the human who'd been chasing Jordyn?" I wound my way deeper into the bowels of the hospital, leaving the explosion area behind me.

"We have him in custody," she said.

Thank fuck. Maybe my luck is changing.

Someone called to Olivia, sounding like Tripp. "I have to go," she said. "Your Jeep is in the alley still. Duck out and head back to base. Ben and the rest of the SEAL team can handle this. In fact, your father is trying to put out fires with the reporters here."

I couldn't give a fuck about the media. "I'm not leaving until I find Layla." I entered what looked to be a storage area.

Blue-and-white fifty-five-gallon drums of chemicals lined the wall to my right, along with pallets of rock salt and stacks of boxes that contained other supplies. The explosion hadn't affected this part of the hospital. Maybe Layla was fine.

"Sam, please. The cops are seconds away from hunting you down," she pleaded.

"Give me the phone," I heard Tripp say to Olivia. "Sam, get your ass back to base. That's an order. If you disobey me, I'll throw you in the brig. Are we clear?"

I knew they were saying this because they cared, but I growled my annoyance. "The fuck we are. Have you forgotten Layla is pregnant?" This wasn't the time to share the news that she was having four babies. The number wasn't essential anyway. "So, no. I'm not doing as I'm told."

I'd never been one to listen well, although I was a soldier trained to take orders. But this was life and death, for fuck's sake. Drastic measures were necessary to save Layla. No one, including the Council of Elders or anyone else within my government, would order me around, including my old man. He was also an elder and our version of the Secretary of the Navy, so he had all the power with the Vampire Navy SEAL team. But I would rip off my uniform and go rogue if I had to. No one was tying me down or locking me up—not even my father.

"Look, Sam," Tripp said. "I can't imagine what you're going through. We've already cleared out the hospital except for the basement. Do a sweep. Then head back to base." His tone was less commanding, sounding as though he thought Layla was a lost cause.

I refused to believe Layla wasn't nearby. "Are you saying Layla is gone?"

Heart-stopping silence stretched over the line.

"Tripp!" I shouted. "Tell me."

"We can't confirm it, but we have a witness who saw two men in black gear. One was carrying a woman in his arms. The description fits Layla's. They also saw a blond-haired man talking to them outside the hospital's laundry area right before both vehicles sped off."

One of my fangs punctured my lower lip. "Are you sure it was Layla?" Maybe it was Jordyn.

"Auburn hair and pregnant was what the witness told us."

"Fuuuuuck!" I fisted my free hand at my side as my heart practically pushed its way out of my chest. "What about Jordyn?"

"Don't know," Tripp returned. "We'll sweep the basement for Jordyn. Just get your ass in your Jeep and leave." Then he hung up.

I wasn't leaving until I confronted the hairnet dude I'd talked to before the explosion. I was certain he was the eyewitness. Maybe he'd gotten a license plate number or something that would give us a clue or a place to start.

My phone buzzed, and air rushed out of my lungs when I saw the name on the screen. "Hey, baby doll," I answered. "Where are you?" My soul started to mend as I waited to hear her sultry voice.

A deep laugh resonated through the line. "Baby doll, huh?" Roman's voice scraped along my skin. "Kind of fits, since she's pregnant."

Several swear words shouted in my head as the blood drained from me.

"Now, why would you want to kidnap her?" I asked in the calmest voice I could muster. "She has nothing you want."

"That's not exactly true," Roman returned. "I could use her as a toy to fuck with you. But… her grandmother has a hard-on for Layla and, I might add, Abbey. Harriet is dying to meet the little magical goddess. As am I."

Keep your shit together, man. He's only firing you up.

"So how did you know we would be here?" I had ideas. I mean, he more than likely had his goons watching the naval base—similar to Viking II, our sister SEAL team—surveilling him and his men at the chip manufacturing plant, although Roman hadn't been spotted in Cleveland. Or we had a mole in our ranks. Junior Aberdeen came to mind—not that he was part of my team.

"We aren't doing anything different here in Massachusetts than your men are in Cleveland. I know you've been watching us. The question for you is did you and the SEALs know I was in town?"

Fucker. I'd been in a damn coma for weeks, so I couldn't answer that. But if Roman was hiding in the shadows around base, I was sure we would know. We had guards on rooftops and patrols around the perimeter. Unless Roman had been holed up in one of the homes one block from the base. We didn't search homes or bother the locals.

"So, what's with the bomb? You could've killed Layla."

"I didn't know she would be anywhere near the electrical room. Come on, Mason. You know the drill. Take out the power, distract, empty the hospital, grab the victim."

"Are you saying you have a heart?" I highly doubted that. "And what the fuck are you doing, Roman? What is in this for you besides money? Or being Harriet Aberdeen's bitch."

A crazed laugh came through the line. "Sam Mason, you know what I want."

I gritted my teeth, grabbed a pipe above my head, and yanked it out. I knew *who* he wanted, and it would be a cold day in hell before he got his grubby hands on Abbey. "I love to disappoint you. You will never get near my niece."

"Oh, but I will," he said with surety. "When I do, she'll be all mine."

I tore out another pipe, and that time, water sprayed out. But I had to kick my emotions to the curb. The immediate issue wasn't Abbey since she was behind an impenetrable fortress not far from the naval base. Victor Costner, Alia's dad, had his estate fortified tighter than a maximum-security prison. Abbey was staying with Alia. For one, Alia was her tutor. Two, since Roman's escape from our prison at the vampire administration building in Boston, Webb and Jo had taken precautions.

"Where are you taking Layla?" I knew he wouldn't tell me, but fuck if I wasn't going to ask.

"Mason, you'll never see her again," Roman said in an even tone. "And when her grandmother learns she's pregnant—" He whistled. "I can see the money pouring down from the sky. Your little one has got to be worth millions. More than the price on your head, or maybe even Abbey's."

"Let me guess. You want a piece of that pie?"

He guffawed. "I'm not one to turn down cold hard cash or the chance to meet Abbey. Hence the reason I'd taken the job when Harriet needed someone to fetch Layla and her sister. I'm sad I didn't snag Jordyn. The payout was big if I kidnapped both, but

Layla's pregnancy should make up for the money I lost and support the plan I have brewing."

I shoved a hand through my hair. "What? To build your own vampire army? Take over the world? You want power?" Men like him lived for power, money, and control. He ran a thriving blood-smuggling business that we had yet to take down. But we would. Of that much, I was certain. "Let me guess," I snarled. "You're one of the investors in Adam Emery's fucked-up scheme to create super soldiers."

"Maybe. Maybe not." His voice dripped with sarcasm.

"You didn't answer the question," I bit out, though I knew he wouldn't tell me shit.

"You'll find out everything soon enough. But I will throw you a bone. We've cleared out the chip manufacturing plant."

That wasn't a bone. "Let me talk to Layla." I sensed he was about to hang up on me.

"Sorry, dude. She's not with me anymore."

I clutched another pipe, ready to crush it. Tripp had said there were two vehicles. "Why do you have her phone?"

"Partly to fuck with you."

I clenched my fists. "There's a reason you called me, so get to the fucking point."

"I have a message from the grand matriarch of the Aberdeen family. You know, she's a piece of work. I thought *I* was evil. Man, she takes the cake. Anyway, if you value Layla's life, you won't come for her," Roman said. "Harriet's exact words."

The fuck I wouldn't. Harriet didn't strike me as that stupid. Or maybe she was trying to incite me to lure me in. That made more sense. I had escaped from Intech, and I was sure they weren't done with me. "Why can't she give me this message herself?"

"She would've, except she collapsed right before we departed for your beautiful city. Before you ask, I don't know what happened."

I clenched my teeth. "You know I'm coming for you, and I'll find Layla."

He chuckled. "Do what you must. I would do the same." He sounded as though he could feel my pain, but I doubted he had an ounce of emotion in him. "Oh, and one more thing. I'm a patient vampire, Mason. I always get what I want, and Abbey will be mine." Then the line went dead.

Rage consumed me as I stalked out into the waning daylight with one purpose in mind—to murder Harriet Aberdeen first.

2

SAM

Twenty minutes later, I marched down the hall to the men's barracks, primed to strangle Junior Aberdeen. The timing of his arrival the day before wasn't a coincidence. He probably fed Roman the intel after Layla and I had left for the hospital.

Petty Officer Cole Dawson rounded his amber gaze on me, audibly swallowing as concern washed over him.

He stood at attention, lifting his chest. "Sir? What happened?"

I was sure I looked like I'd just walked out of an apocalypse. I was covered in debris from head to toe. "You'll find out soon enough."

My name and ugly mug would be prime-time news and splattered over every media outlet coast-to-coast. We would have paranormal junkies, the kind who filmed those documentaries, camped outside the main gate before long. The Council of Elders would have coronaries. Hell, I was certain my father was having one. We had kept our existence in the shadows for centuries with only a small number of humans in the know. But nothing stayed buried forever. Case in point: At a fundraiser years ago, my sister had allowed her emotions to get the best of her right about the time a cameraman was snapping pictures at the event. The next day, the local newspaper article was titled "Beautiful Creature

Changes Her Appearance in the Blink of an Eye." Underneath the headline were two pictures of Jo—one of her with her human silver eyes and the other with purple eyes and fangs hanging over her lips.

But the situation now was much worse. Jo hadn't been accused of killing a cop.

I stifled a laugh. I was sure my ass would be in front of the council at some point. Still, maybe it was time the humans knew we walked the earth along with other supernaturals, like shifters and witches. Maybe then we could live as one big happy fucking family. *Not a good thing, man. You'll have more vampire hunters tracking you down.* Fuck if that mattered. I was on the most wanted list anyway.

"Open the door," I ordered through clenched teeth.

Petty Officer Dawson did as I commanded.

The minute I stepped in, Junior flew off the bed, his blue eyes bugging out and fear oozing from his pores. "What's wrong? What the fuck happened?" He stumbled into the wall beside the twin bed.

My fangs clicked into place. "You tell me." I wasn't a mind reader, so the only thing I had to go on was his emotions, and since I was an empath, his trepidation was flying at me like a swarm of bees.

My father was supposed to read his mind, but when Layla found blood on her panties, everyone dove into action, and Junior's vetting had fallen by the wayside.

I got in his face. "Are you working with your grandmother? Did you alert Roman Brown that we were on our way to the hospital?" I was ready to carve out his carotid artery. Fuck, my bloodlust was burning a hole in my throat. "You lied to us. You led Layla right into the viper's hands." I gripped his throat. "Layla is gone. Where is she? Start talking, or I'll gut you right here, right now." I snarled every fucking word as my elemental powers took over.

Glasses on the counter near the sink clinked together. The table and chairs slid along the tiled floor.

"Sir," Petty Officer Dawson said behind me before he tried to pull me away from Junior.

Normally, guards didn't question our motives. But the new

recruit, who had recently passed Navy SEAL training with flying colors, had huge fucking balls.

"Back the fuck off, Dawson," I spat over my shoulder. "Or I'll make sure you sit in the brig for eternity."

Once again, Petty Officer Dawson grabbed my arm. "He's human."

I should be proud and reward him for his bravery and sticking to our motto that we didn't harm humans. But he didn't understand what I was going through.

Ignoring him, I returned my glare to Junior. "Start talking."

Junior struggled to pry my hands from his throat as his face deepened to red. "Ease up, man." His voice was strained.

"Sir, stand down," Cole bit out. "Control room, come in."

The radio crackled. "Go," the dude on duty returned.

"We have a situation in the men's barracks," Cole said.

I released Junior and rounded on Cole. "You have some fucking gonads." I stood toe-to-toe with him, breathing fire.

He didn't back down as he stuck out his chest. "I do. Do you want to see them?" His fangs lowered.

I laughed, albeit not nicely. I wasn't in the mood to deal with someone like me. "Your job is to stand guard, not tell me what to do. Get the fuck out." My voice boomed.

He stood his ground. "I'm not going anywhere. I need to protect the human." He glanced briefly at Junior, who was rubbing his throat.

I hardened my jaw. "You want to protect a vampire hunter?"
Cole flinched.
Junior sat down on the bed, the color in his face slowly returning to normal.

"That's right," I said. "This man will carve you into pieces in your sleep, then string you up over a firepit and watch you burn, all the while enjoying a beer and laughing."

"True." Junior found some courage to admit it. "But I'm not stupid enough to fuck with the enemy on his turf."

Footsteps clamored, sounding like a herd of bulls, before Webb burst in. His blue eyes morphed to vampire black. "What the fuck?" Lines creased his forehead.

Cole snapped to attention, eyeing his commanding officer, who was also my brother-in-law.

I silently scratched my head. I'd thought the entire SEAL team was at the hospital.

"Petty Officer Dawson, return to your post," Webb demanded, keeping his focus on me.

Cole nodded once. "Yes, sir." He hurried out like his ass was on fire.

Webb swung his gaze from Junior to me. "What's going on?"

I glared at Junior. "This human set us up."

Webb—cool, calm, and collected—regarded Junior. "Is that true?" My commander was as stoic as ever.

As for me, I wanted to sink my fangs into Junior.

Junior raised his hands. "How could I have done that while sitting in this room with no phone? Remember, Tripp took it."

Well, fuck. I'd forgotten about that.

"Are you saying my grandmother kidnapped Layla? Jordyn too?" Worry seemed to be erasing the fear Junior exhibited a minute ago.

I paced close to the wall between the small kitchen nook and the twin bed. "Roman nabbed Layla."

"Not good," Junior murmured.

I snarled at him. "Ya think?" I fisted a hand, itching to punch him. "It's your fault."

"The fuck it is," Junior returned.

I wanted to blame him, but the only thing I could hang over his red crop of hair was his Aberdeen name.

Webb took one step closer to me. "Both of you, calm down. Tripp radioed in. They found Jordyn behind a clothes dryer in the laundry area. She had a broken nose, a lump on her forehead, and a gash over one of her eyes. She'll be fine."

"That's supposed to help me?" I shouted, even though I was happy Jordyn was okay. "Layla's gone, man." I punched my fist through the Sheetrock and growled like an animal in the wild. The lights flickered above us, and everything in the room shook. If no one knew of my elemental abilities, they would think we were in the middle of an earthquake.

Webb grabbed my arms from behind me. "Sam, take it down a notch."

Whirling around, I saw a sea of red. "The fuck I will. And how soon you forget you went on a rampage when Edmund took Jo. AWOL, if I remember correctly. My dad threw you in the brig." I didn't give a fuck what Webb or my father tried to do to me. I wasn't about to listen, sit around, and strategize—or wait for intel or a lead. Fuck that shit. The only way to keep me down or stop me was to put me in a coma or cut off my head.

I pulled on my hair and paced like a madman. "The one person we feared now has Layla. And my unborn babies." I was suffocating as my brain spun out of control. "We're not having twins. We're having quadruplets."

Not much shocked Webb, but his jaw came unhinged.

Silence except for my heavy breathing ticked for a beat.

Frozen, Junior stared at me like I'd lost my mind, as did Webb.

Yeah, I'd had the same reaction. Actually, I would've passed out if it wasn't for Olivia announcing Roman's arrival at the hospital. "I'm as shocked as both of you." Twins would've been normal, since they ran in both the Mason and Aberdeen families, but quadruplets were unheard of.

Still, I wasn't one to cry—like, at all. But I was a second away from bawling my fucking eyes out. "Layla needs blood. She won't survive, and neither will my babies." I pressed a hand to my chest to quell my racing heart along with the pain in it. I felt like someone was driving a dagger through me.

I wore a hole in the floor while silence dropped like a heavy boulder from atop a high mountain. Back and forth. One step, then two. *Breathe, man. You'll find her before it's too late.* I would love to believe that small optimistic voice in my head, but a day without blood wouldn't bode well for my beautiful huntress.

Fear simmered beneath Webb's shock. He wasn't afraid of anything except losing his wife.

I would like to think Harriet Aberdeen was a weak opponent, but that wasn't true. The human had a side of her that would make our former enemy, Edmund Rain, look like a pussy. I hadn't seen what Harriet could do, but during the short time since I'd met her, I recognized that she would wreak havoc exactly like she'd bragged. Plus, she had a strong team behind her. Roman was a formidable adversary and so was Adam Emery. Though Adam was human with no magical powers, he had the backing of the human government, which could be more detrimental than fighting a vampire. Whether it was the Department of Defense or the CIA or the FBI, it didn't matter. All of them had the means to give us a run for our money. Case in point, the chip in my head—a weapon of mass destruction if the rice-grain-size device turned on.

To make matters worse, Harriet thought Layla and her sisters Jordyn and Rianne would make suitable test subjects to become creatures of the night, since the Aberdeen sisters had supernatural blood running through their veins.

"Did you hear me, Sam?" Webb's voice penetrated through the hell I was living in.

I stopped in my tracks. "What?" I snapped.

"Tripp said you spoke to Roman. Fill me in." Webb crossed his arms over his chest as he stood in the middle of the room at modified parade rest.

I'd called Tripp when I'd been speeding through the city streets after I left the hospital. "Not much to tell. Roman bragged about meeting Abbey. He made it clear that she's his end goal."

Webb whipped out his cell and had Jo on speaker in a flash. "Hey, angel. You're with Abbey, right?"

"Of course," my sister replied. "Why?"

Webb whisked a hand through his shoulder-length brown hair. "I'll fill you in later. Stay put and don't leave the Costner estate." He sighed as he hung up.

"I'll call my dad," Junior said. "I'll see if he knows anything more about my grandmother."

I leaned against the wall beside the hole I'd punched into it.

"According to Roman, she collapsed, but he didn't know much more than that."

Junior straightened. "Collapsed as in dead?"

Don't I wish. "We aren't that lucky."

"Man, this is a shit show," Webb mumbled.

I gritted my teeth. "This is all my fault. If we didn't rush to the ER, Layla would still be here."

"Sam, don't go there, man." Webb shook his head. "It was necessary."

I knew that. Dr. Vieira didn't have the vaginal ultrasound machine to examine Layla.

I pushed off the wall. "I can't sit around." Time was of the essence. What if we couldn't find her, ever? My heart split into a million pieces.

Webb's phone rang. "It's your father." He put the phone on speaker again.

It seemed like maybe Webb knew my acute vamp hearing wasn't working that well. Despite the ringing in my ears subsiding, I made a mental note to talk to Dr. Vieira about my hearing.

"Is Sam there?" my father asked in a tone that would frighten a bear.

"Yes," Webb said. "We're in the men's barracks with Junior, and you're on speaker."

"Junior, call your father. I want a location on your grandmother. I don't care what you have to do to find out. I want answers."

"Steven," Webb said, "Sam found out from Roman that Harriet collapsed before she was scheduled to come here to Massachusetts. That could mean they rushed her to the ER. As soon as we hang up, I'll have Sawyer scour hospitals. We'll start in Cleveland, since we know she'd been heading east from Chicago given that Roman's men had taken over the chip manufacturing plant."

"Roman said they cleared out of that plant," I added.

"I'll check in with Viking II," Webb said. "They haven't relayed that to us."

Maybe Roman had been lying to throw us off track.

I grabbed the back of my neck. "Also, I asked Sawyer to see if he can get a location on Layla's phone." I'd called him on my way here. "Although I'm sure Roman threw it away." The vampire was intelligent enough to know we would track it. However, he did like to play games. So maybe he would use it to continue to fuck with me in some way—lead me in the wrong direction.

"Sam, don't you dare leave the base," my father ordered. "I have fifty fucking fires to put out with human authorities, the media, and the Council of Elders over the chaos at the hospital. I don't want either you or Hawk in public until I can ease the panic of these humans."

One of Roman's men had snapped Hawk's neck while he had his fangs down, which would keep him incapacitated for a while longer. But while he was out, the entire ER waiting crowd had gathered around him, snapping pictures.

"Do you hear me, son?" my dad asked, sounding frustrated.

He knew me well. We had many things in common, and jumping into action was one of them.

"I can't promise anything." I wasn't about to lie or beat around the bush. For fuck's sake, Layla was missing.

I knew my father. He certainly wouldn't obey orders. We were alike in many ways. He'd gone rogue several years ago when he was searching for Jo and me. That was a long story for another day.

He sighed instead of ordering me to stand down or yelling at me not to disobey. "I understand the need to find Layla and that time is critical, but we need a plan. Are we clear?"

"For now, Pops." That was as far as I could go with my promise. "We should scour the city for Roman." He had probably gotten the hell out of Dodge, but the conversation we had about Abbey wasn't sitting well with me.

Webb acknowledged my suggestion with a nod.

Junior rubbed his neck. "What about Jordyn? Is she on her way back?" He sounded genuinely concerned for his cousin.

"She's with a medic. But she'll be fine," my father said.

Junior lowered his shoulders as relief visibly washed over him.

"Webb, set up a meeting in the war room for two hours from now. We'll hash out a plan from there." Then my dad hung up.

Silence descended for a second before I shoved a hand through my dirty hair. "I need a shower."

"Dawson," Webb called in his commander tone.

The newbie SEAL scurried in, focusing on Webb.

"Take Junior down to the interrogation room in the command center. Set him up with a secure line for him to call his father. Under no circumstances do you leave him alone while he makes that call. Are we understood?"

"Yes, sir," Dawson grunted out, not looking at me.

Petty Officer Dawson and I would have words at some point.

Junior rose without a snarky retort or any pushback.

Webb gave Junior a stern look. "Tread carefully."

A crease dented the space between Junior's eyebrows. "I'm on enemy grounds. It's not like I can do anything."

Until either Jo or my father read his mind, I wouldn't trust him.

I started for the door. "I'll be in my apartment."

Webb caught my arm. "Not so fast." He stuck his head into the hall, then closed us into the men's barracks.

I laughed. "Are you about to read me my rights?"

I wouldn't mind tangoing with him. He was powerful in his own right. Most of the Vampire Navy SEALs could wield at least two of the elements. At one time, the elders had mandated that any vampire who wanted to become a Navy SEAL had to have elemental powers. It was rare for a vampire to have anything more than normal strength, sharp senses, and compelling abilities. So, three years ago, the elders lifted that requirement, since our population was dwindling, and those with special powers were hard to find.

Regardless, Webb could manipulate water, earth, and fire. The only people in my world who had the power to control those three plus air were Jo, my father, and me. No one could read minds except Jo and my father, and no one could compel like me. Which was why members of the Mason family were considered the most powerful vampires around, and with more Masons on the way, my kids could reinforce that truism. Even over someone like Abbey, who was becoming quite powerful as she aged into becoming a vampire.

Webb waved a hand in front of me. "Dude, you're losing your shit."

Understatement of the century.

I dropped down onto the bed, drowning in heartache as I thought of Layla. "I might never see my babies born." The fucking tears were ready to spill.

He joined me. "You can't think like that, man."

"How did we not know Roman was in the city?" I asked. Even though I knew Roman was masterful at hiding, I had to throw the question out there. "Don't answer that. I know. I'm pissed as fuck I wasn't more attentive."

"Stop blaming yourself, Sam. We will pull out all the stops to find her, I promise you. But we have to be smart about it. Otherwise, we won't succeed."

He was absolutely right. But I couldn't wait for him or my father to pack us into the war room and hash shit out. Time was of the essence, and I had to find Layla—like, *now.* Otherwise, she wouldn't make it, and not because of her grandmother. She needed blood for those babies to survive.

A plan was forming in my mind, but neither Webb nor my old man would like it.

3

SAM

At one point in my life, I would've gone off half-cocked. I'd never listened to anyone. Growing up in foster homes shaped me into an untrusting, hard-core individual who would react without thought. I had no choice. I was forced to protect myself and my sister. Otherwise, we would both be dead today. Of that, I had no doubt.

I felt like I was right back in hell, only now I wasn't human. I had powers that could decimate a city, burn a person alive, create the perfect storm with water, air, earth, and fire. I had yet to unleash all four at once, but with the fury burning through my veins, I was a ticking time bomb.

Taking in a slow and steady breath, I swiped a hand over Layla's pillow, basking in her cherry fragrance that lingered in the bedding. "I will find you, baby doll. If I have to die to bring you and our little ones home, then so be it." I plucked my phone off the mattress where I'd placed it near me.

During the last hour, I'd showered, packed the essentials for the road, and thought through my plan.

Earlier that day, Layla had set Carly Aberdeen's number on the coffee table. Apparently, the piece of paper had been in the cargo pants I'd had on while I was a prisoner at Intech. Junior's wife had to have slipped it into my pocket when I was passed out. Why? I had no idea. I'd called her that morning, but she hadn't answered. Junior thought Carly might have perished in the fire when she'd run back into her lab to retrieve her notes on DNA mapping sequence, but I wasn't a believer in that theory. Junior and his father, Jack, had spotted Harriet, Rianne, and Noah, another of Jack's sons, coming out of Carly and Junior's house in Chicago with Carly's clothes and her computer bag. That told me she wasn't dead.

What I was about to do was suicide—but I didn't give a fuck. I valued Layla's life and those of my unborn babies more than mine. The only way I knew how to rescue her was to walk into the enemy's lair. Harriet, Carly, and Adam wanted me as much as Harriet wanted her granddaughter, and sitting around, meeting, planning, and waiting for a lead to fall into our laps wouldn't save Layla. I had a better chance of finding her if I was in the hands of my enemy. My plan was weak at best. They would want to pump me with drugs and keep me sedated while Carly used me as a lab specimen. But I wouldn't agree to anything until I laid eyes on Layla.

I called Carly first on the off chance she would answer. I could convince her quicker than I could Roman if he still had Layla's phone for me to call him on. He wasn't naïve enough to believe I would hand myself over without a way out. Sadly, I couldn't devise an escape route until I knew the layout of their hiding place. But I was getting ahead of myself.

Carly's voice mail kicked in. I didn't bother leaving a message. Then I called Layla. Again, Roman had probably dumped her phone since he knew we would trace it.

The line rang twice before it connected, and my pulse went haywire. Maybe my luck was turning. Maybe I'd given Roman too much credit. Or maybe he held true to his nature and was about to fuck with me once again.

"Hello." While I waited for a response, I stared at the picture hanging on my wall. The ocean scene outside my sister's house in Maine brought back memories of Layla and me standing on the sand that early morning a couple of months ago. That was the day I'd told her I loved her. "Is anyone there?" I checked the screen. The call had dropped.

I tried again, and that time, a giggle blasted in my ear.

"Who the fuck is this?" I asked through a growl.

"Sierra. It says on the phone your name is Sam." Sierra sounded young—a teenager, if I had to guess. "Roman Brown gave me the phone. He told me to answer it if you called." Her tone gave me the impression she knew Roman.

"Is that so? And did he give you a message for me?" I couldn't wait to hear this.

"He said to tell you he knows where Abbey is," she said. As I suspected, Roman wanted to fuck with me.

Truth or lie. Game or not. I pondered that for a second, even though my blood gelled. Yet, I couldn't discount the message.

Could my fucking day get any worse? Webb had checked to make sure Jo and Abbey were safe at the Costner estate, or rather, compound. Victor had the best security outside of the military, so I shouldn't be worried. But again, Roman wasn't an idiot. He had men, but he also had the backing of Intech, a corporation that specialized in computer programming for the Department of Defense. That meant they had the means to find anyone or hack into a tightly secure system like Victor's. Fred Emery, Intech's head of security, came to mind. We had him in custody, although he probably wouldn't talk.

I needed to alert Webb.

"Where did you meet Roman?" I asked Sierra. "And do you know him?"

"I was just getting home from cheer practice at Durfee High School, and he was leaving my house. He knows my dad."

Victor's estate was close to the high school. But before I went ballistic, I asked, "Where do you live, Sierra?"

"Not far from Durfee," she said.

Motherfucker. Abbey. He definitely knows where she is. I shouldn't be surprised. Roman probably had contacts in and around the city of Fall River, feeding him information for a nice fee.

"Sierra, what's your last name?" I would need to know that to look into the situation.

"Dupont," she said.

"Can you do me a favor? Keep the phone close to you. I'll need it back, but I'll call you when I have a chance to pick it up."

After she agreed and we hung up, I tried calling Webb. When he didn't answer, I bolted out of my apartment. I called my sister, but no luck there either. Maybe neither of them had picked up because they were talking to each other, but the boulder in the pit of my stomach told me something was very wrong.

Two minutes later, I was flying into the command center—or control room, as we also called it. A flurry of activity peppered the space. I stood on the landing platform overlooking the maze of numerous cubicles where vamps were hard at work, talking on phones, typing on keyboards, and conversing about whatever task they had on their plate.

"Webb," I said, raising my voice over the hum of noise. He'd said he would be here until the meeting with my father. "Anyone see Commander London?"

Harley, Webb's assistant, popped up from near Sawyer's desk.

I flew down the steps.

Harley rushed up to me, tossing her strawberry blond locks over her shoulder. "Oh my God, Sam. I'm beside myself about Layla." Tears clouded her blue eyes. "I can't imagine what you're going through." She threw her arms around me.

I didn't have time to wallow, and I didn't want to be an ass and bite off her head either, so I eased away. "Thanks. But right now, it's urgent I find Webb."

"He's in the interrogation room." She stabbed a finger behind her. "He's talking to Junior and Jack Aberdeen."

I blew past her and came to an abrupt halt when I laid eyes on Petty Officer Dawson standing guard outside the room.

He glared at me.

I held in my anger at the newbie and burst into the room.

Junior and Webb were sitting at the table across from each other with a multiline telephone between them.

"We don't know yet, Dad," Junior said.

Webb jumped up. "What's wrong, Sam?"

I flicked my thumb out the door. "I need to talk to you. Now!"

I hurried out and waited beside Sawyer's cubicle for Webb. As I began to pace, Harley watched me intently, her blue eyes filled with worry.

Webb addressed Dawson. "Go inside and keep an eye on Junior." Then Webb came up to me and crossed his arms over his chest. "What has you rattled?"

"Roman knows where Abbey is," I rushed out. "He's in the Highlands. He knows."

Webb shook his head. "Impossible."

"No, dude. When it comes to that asshole, nothing is impossible." I told Webb about Sierra Dupont and the conversation we had. While I was talking, Webb was trying to reach Jo. "She's not picking up."

"I know. I tried her on my way down here. We need to get over there."

"Harley," Webb said. "Call Victor and tell him we're coming."

On a sigh, I glanced past Webb at the large monitor hanging on the wall. The news was on, and a young female reporter was interviewing the cop who'd accused me of killing his partner. Then my attention bounced to a smaller screen next to the larger one. Another newscaster was talking to the young boy who had pointed me in Layla's direction. I scanned the screens. Each one had different TV stations on, including the national news.

For fuck's sake. My father was right. Tension seeped into my shoulders, irritation riding me hard as my picture and Hawk's, as well as photos of a couple of Roman's men, were plastered on the bottom corner of the screens with our fangs on display. But when I returned my attention to the main monitor, I lost my breath as a burning rage seared my veins.

"What the fuck?" I slapped Webb on the arm with the back of my fingers. "Dude, look at the monitor. Is that who I think it is?"

Webb jerked his head at me. "Is that Wyman?"

That piece of shit. Former CIA agent Wyman, alias Dowell, was the man who'd hired Layla to capture me for his own sick revenge. I'd wiped his memories five years ago during our war with Edmund when Wyman and his partner, Thomas, had been close to making a deal with Edmund. I would tear each strand of thinning brown hair out of his head and feed them to him. Then I would wipe every fucking memory he had—permanently, this time.

A growl barreled out of me. "Isn't he supposed to be working for Victor Costner? I didn't know he had free rein to roam the city. Why was he at the hospital? He's working with Roman. He has to be. How else would Roman know where Abbey is?"

"You don't have to erase his memories," Webb fired back. "Human or not, he's a dead man."

Excitement exploded in me. Webb was talking my language. "Let's get this party started." Maybe Wyman had seen Layla. Maybe the fucker knew where she was.

4

SAM

My nerves were making me itch as I raced through the city streets. Webb had been calling Jo with no luck. He tried Alia and her father, Victor. Still no answer. Both of us were on edge. My mind was running amok with the idea that Roman had taken Abbey. I was about to self-combust from rage that had me almost crushing the steering wheel. First Layla, and now Abbey. The two most important people in my life other than my sister and father. I wasn't sure I could make it through the rest of the day without killing someone.

Webb appeared to be feeling the same way, judging from the muscle that ticked in his jaw. He was staring at his phone as if willing it to ring. He must've called Jo twenty times since we'd left the naval base only ten minutes ago.

I dodged red lights as best I could. Luckily, there wasn't much traffic for seven in the evening or any cops around. The last thing we needed was more media attention on us, but that was a minor complication in my book. My father wouldn't agree, though.

I slammed on my horn and waved my hand at the pedestrian in front of us to hurry the fuck up as he crossed the road. The dude threw me the finger. I didn't fault him, since he had the right-of-way, but time was ticking by, and each second that passed only served to stop my heart. Webb looked ready to vault out of his seat and through the roof of my Jeep to snap the pedestrian's middle digit.

Once the guy cleared the street, I banked right and gunned it up the steep hill leading into the Highlands. Anytime I ventured into this part of the city, memories of my teenage years gave me chills. Jo and I had gone to Durfee High when we'd been human. My best bud, Ben, had grown up in this neck of the woods, and Jo and I had lived with him after our foster dad stabbed Jo.

I slowed down at a four-way stop sign, checking the cross street.

"Don't stop," Webb bit out as his cell chirped and he put it on speaker. "Victor, fuck. Is everything okay?" he rushed out on a heavy breath.

"How the fuck did Roman Brown find Abbey?" Victor yelled as though he were her father. Abbey had been spending a lot of time at his estate, so I imagined he'd become attached to her.

Webb shoved a fist against his chest. "Fuck, tell me he didn't take her."

My body went rigid as I pressed on the gas.

Victor growled. "My men are scouring the property."

Webb punched my dashboard, putting a huge dent in it. "Is that fucker Wyman there?"

"I'm searching for him now. I saw him on the news. Where are you?"

"Sam and I are two minutes out." Webb's jaw was hard as stone. "Where's my wife?"

"Burning one of the intruders alive," Victor said with excitement.

Webb sighed, although lightly, knowing Jo was okay. Hell, I pushed out a long breath myself, grateful nothing had happened to my sister. I couldn't take much more pain. I should be used to the kidnappings, the battles, the wars, losing teammates, loved ones, and being hunted like I was a rabid animal who needed to be put down. Yet as powerful as I was, I wasn't immune—not physically or emotionally. Layla had said to me recently, *"Even the best can fail."* I was stupid to believe otherwise. But for fuck's sake, why couldn't we live in peace? With my family growing quickly, I had to find a place where no one could find them. Yet, nowhere on this planet was safe. There was always a mole or a way in, a back door, or some crack in our armor that allowed our enemies to penetrate through.

After Webb hung up, he punched my dashboard again. "Son of a bitch!"

My headlights bounced along the dark side street as we took flight over a speed bump. The damn streets were laden with them—for safety, according to Alia. I always swore like the sailor I was whenever I came to the estate. Tonight wasn't any different.

I shouted several expletives in my head. "There's no way Roman captured Abbey. Jo would never let that happen." I had to say something to calm my nerves more than appeasing Webb's rage.

He was practically breathing fire. "Like when there was no way *you* were taken? How soon you forget about the drug-filled darts."

I couldn't argue. Instead, I careened left, and the Jeep fishtailed as I drove up to the wrought iron gates that were wide open. A man lay on the ground outside the guardhouse. The scent of his human blood drifted in through the open driver-side window.

I slammed the gas pedal and navigated the winding driveway that was lit up by the landscape lights. Before I screeched to a halt in front of the Colonial-style mansion, Webb jumped out. With vampire speed, he flew into the house, not taking any notice of another guard who was out cold on the stone steps.

Once I cut the engine, I hopped out, snagging my gun from my holster. I could use my elemental powers, but tonight I was in the mood to shoot a vampire or two until their hearts burned to ash. Cobalt was our kryptonite, and I salivated to pump several rounds into my enemies and watch them die slow deaths. Unless it was Roman. Then I would rip off his head with my bare hands.

With my weapon at the ready, I searched the sprawling property comprised of manicured shrubs and trees of all sizes. Most were on the verge of blooming. Spring was slow to kick off, since we'd had cold temps and a light dusting of snow at the beginning of April, which wasn't unheard of in New England.

A dose of vampire blood, tangy and smelling like iron, carried on the light wind. We had a more distinct aroma than humans. Maybe that was because we drank the processed crap made with human blood that was days, weeks, or even months old that we bought from our supplier.

I darted my gaze to the tunnel of trees surrounding a brick path that led to Alia's cottage.

I jogged in that direction, keeping my senses on high alert. I came to an abrupt halt at the edge of the lighted path. Four feet in front of me was a head that had been detached from a male body. A clean cut and Victor's MO. The vampire was a Viking in battle with his sword as his weapon of choice.

But as I approached, joy made me smile when I realized that the head belonged to Scarface. The same asshole who had been chasing Layla out of the hospital and probably the same vampire who had torn off Lane's head. Karma was a bitch. I had to thank Victor if in fact he'd been the one to kill Scarface.

A branch snapped, and I jerked my attention to the right, ready to fire, until a quick sniff put me at ease. My sister's lavender fragrance announced her arrival before she came into view.

"Sam." Jo sounded relieved to see me as she hurried over, searching in all directions.

I followed suit, my senses on high alert.

She flicked her black hair from her forehead, her inhuman violet eyes sparkling beneath the rays of the moon as she stopped in front of me, seemingly calm. "I'm okay," she said, reading my mind. "Abbey is too. She's in Victor's safe room."

I had to love her mind-reading abilities at times.

I blew out a relieved breath. "Safe room, huh?"

Her violet eyes returned to their normal silver as she hugged me. "Yeah. We're fine, brother. Abbey's with Alia. We got them in when the alarms went off."

I released another sigh, this time loudly. I probably woke the birds. "Thank God." I didn't know what I would do if Abbey had been taken. Still, my insides were a pile of mush, knowing Layla was in the hands of our enemies.

She unleashed me from her grasp and set her worried gaze on me. "They took Matthew though."

I reared back. Alia was going to freak the fuck out. Her son had been a product of my uncle Patrick's experiment—a successful one. He'd turned into a full-fledged vampire with ease. Matthew was human with vampire blood running through his veins. Alia had chosen not to turn because she wanted kids, but her father, Victor, was one of us.

"She won't take this well," Jo said. "And neither will Victor."

He would no doubt set the world on fire to find Matthew. I sure as hell hoped so. Our ranks were diminishing in number. Sure, we had new recruits in Hawk and Dawson, but they were novices.

"I suspect Roman wants to use Matthew as leverage," Jo added.

I raised an eyebrow. "For what? Abbey? That doesn't make sense. It would mean more if you were taken, since you're Abbey's mom." Adoptive mom, but her mom nonetheless. Given that Jo was a vampire, she couldn't have children, so after Abbey's birth mom, Rachel, was murdered by Abbey's father, Edmund, Webb and Jo stepped up to become adoptive parents. If Abbey had any relatives on Rachel's side, we weren't aware of them. As far as Edmund went, he had a brother and a sister, but he never spoke to them, at least not since my father had known him. Still, my dad wasn't about to hand Abbey to anyone related to Edmund. We couldn't risk Abbey's life if Edmund's siblings turned out to be as evil as he was.

She shrugged. "You might be right." She scanned the area as though she'd heard something.

Fuck. I didn't. I honed my hearing but came up empty, my gun at the ready.

But then a faint sound of heavy footsteps filtered into my ears before a tall, broad-chested dude took shape.

I was ready to fire when Jo placed her hand on my gun and then pushed it down. "It's Alex, one of Victor's men."

Alex spoke into his earpiece. "Sir, I found Jo. Copy that. Yes, the compound is secure. Roman's men are gone. I'll round up the bodies. Yes, sir." Then he regarded Jo. "Your husband is in the house. Library, to be exact."

She let out a breath, walked over to him, and gave him a hug. "Thank you for your help in taking Abbey into the safe room." She tossed a look over her shoulder. "Come on, Sam."

I nodded at Alex as I passed him.

As we headed into the house, Jo asked, "Did you know Roman would be here? And how does Roman know where Abbey is?"

The answer to the first question involved a long story. The other one I couldn't answer, but I had ideas.

"Did you see Roman?" I asked.

"No," she said. "I think it was just his men."

After we climbed the steps onto the porch, Jo ran through the open front door and into the sprawling mansion. I followed her, skirting the staircase, going down a narrow hall, and heading into a massive room that rivaled the size of my apartment. Books galore, a leather couch, and two chairs, family pictures, and cherrywood tables decorated the room.

Jo launched into Webb's arms, and he caught her with ease. The two hugged for a long moment.

Victor, tall and formidable, stood by the fireplace, glaring at the frightened human tied to a chair in front of him.

Wyman's shoulders were hunched up to his ears as fear soaked him down to the bones.

He *should* be scared out of his mind, especially of me. Although Victor was also a force to be reckoned with.

I covered my nose with the back of my hand as I joined Victor's side. "Did you piss your pants, Wyman?" I didn't have to look to know he had. The urine stench was about to make me gag.

Jo untangled her arms from her husband. "Abbey is okay."

"I know. Victor checked the safe room when I came in," Webb said. "We'll get her and Alia as soon as we're done with this asshole. I don't want Abbey to witness this."

Victor looked at his sword leaning against the stone fireplace, the blood glistening along the blade.

"Did you cut off Scarface's head?" I asked out of curiosity.

Victor stuck out his chest. "You know I did."

"Thank you," I said. "He was the fucker who chased Layla, and I believe he also killed Lane."

Fear swam in Wyman's brown eyes as he watched Victor and me intently.

I crossed my arms over my chest. "How did you know Layla and I would be at the hospital?" I asked Wyman. "I saw you on the news."

He regarded Jo and Webb standing next to me. "I overheard Jo talking to Webb." Then he turned his attention to me. "I told you from the beginning. I feel responsible for Layla. I owe it to her dead father to watch over her."

Admirable, but it wasn't his job. "Or maybe you're working with Roman Brown," I said.

He raised his chin. "I promise you, I'm not."

"He's telling the truth," Jo said.

Man, I would trade my empath ability for mind reading just for situations like these.

"Then how the fuck did Roman know Abbey was here?" I asked.

Jo eyed Victor with a wary expression. "Maybe it wasn't Abbey he came for."

Roman's goal was to take Abbey but maybe Matthew too.

Victor's brown eyes bled to black as his face reddened. "Are you saying it was for Matthew? They took my grandson? Why would they do that?" He stalked over to a waist-high bar and picked up his cell that was sitting next to a decanter of whiskey. "I don't believe you." He called his grandson while pinning his hard gaze on Jo as if it was her fault.

She hooked her arm in Webb's. "I'm sorry, Victor. I didn't have time to tell you before now, since I was in the middle of fighting off attackers, but I saw them taking Matthew, and I couldn't stop them in time." Sadness washed over her.

Victor's fangs descended, slow and deadly. "He's not answering. I will massacre Roman Brown. And what the fuck is going on? Don't answer that. I know. I've been privy to the meetings with the Council of Elders."

Victor was a prominent figure in our world and went out of his way at times to do the council's dirty work or help however he could.

Victor retracted his fangs. "Webb told me that Roman gave Layla's phone to Sierra Dupont and that her father, Nathan Dupont, knows Roman. I don't believe that. Like us, Nathan wants to protect humanity."

Webb scraped a hand along his jaw. "Are you two close friends?"

"I wouldn't say close," Victor said. "His wife, Carmen, and my daughter, Alia, are good friends. The Duponts have been here for dinner."

"Do they know Abbey has been staying here?" Jo asked, still tethered to Webb's arm.

Victor bobbed his head. "Sure. Carmen adores Abbey."

I growled. "They had to be the ones who alerted Roman. They know him somehow."

Webb held up his hand. "Easy, Sam. Maybe they do. Maybe they don't. Roman is probably surveilling every part of this city. He could have someone trailing Abbey from the base to this property. If I'm right, he could've also seen the Duponts leaving the estate. Maybe Roman confronted Nathan and brokered a deal to alert him when Nathan knew Abbey would be here."

"Okay," I returned. "But that doesn't address how Roman's men breeched the compound. Isn't this place fortified? That's why we chose this spot to protect Abbey."

Jo pinned a hard look on Victor. "Sam's right, Victor. What happened? The way I see it, Abbey was lucky I was here."

I was preparing for a fight. Victor had an ego and was proud of his security and his team of men. He looked briefly at Wyman.

Jo pursed her lips. "Wyman didn't leak anything or let them in. But line up your men, and I'll find the mole, if there is one."

Victor nodded, acquiescing instead of jumping down Jo's throat for even suggesting he had a leak in his organization.

I grabbed Victor's sword to do something with my hands when a thought zipped through my brain. "Are the Duponts vampires?"

Victor sighed. "No. But Carmen comes from a prominent

vampire family. Like Alia, she chose not to turn so she could have children. Why?"

I walked up behind Wyman. "Those of our kind who have chosen not to turn, like Alia, for example, are the ones who are in jeopardy. Or humans like Matthew who have vampires in their family. Let's face it—Matthew was the only true full-fledged vampire to come out of my uncle Patrick's experiment, which was why he was taken. At least, I believe Carly figured out that puzzle piece. Considering they took Matthew, I'm banking that she has. She does have my uncle Patrick's notes, which I'm sure include his formula for the serum he used on Matthew and probably identified Matthew by name in those notes."

"So, you think Roman is targeting Carmen or Sierra?" Victor asked.

"Possibly," I said. "I'm not a hundred percent sure, but Harriet believes the Aberdeen sisters would be model subjects for genetic altering because they have vampire blood running in their mother's family."

"They probably targeted Matthew to study his DNA makeup," Jo piped in.

"Exactly," I returned. "If I'm right, then Sierra might be on that list." Maybe Alia and Carmen also. Hell, anyone who had vampire blood in their family history.

"If Intech's experiments are a success, then others like Sierra will be prime candidates for their army," Wyman said. His CIA mind was working through scenarios, and I liked that. He might prove to be valuable after all.

"Implant a chip into them, and Intech has control and super soldiers," I added.

Webb pinched his chin. "We do have Intech's head of security in our custody. He probably won't tell us a lot, but we'll try to pull out as much info as we can."

"I'll talk to Nathan Dupont," Victor said.

"I can hack into Intech," Wyman offered as he wiggled his tied hands. "And also their sister company, Camden Industries."

I was sure Sawyer and his tech team were working that angle.

Regardless, Wyman was returning to the base with me. I didn't want him out of our sight until we could trust him. Roman's men could've followed him from the hospital to Victor's house for all we knew.

Webb kissed his wife on the temple. "Since I won't be murdering this asshole"—he pointed at Wyman—"why don't you retrieve Abbey?"

My sister left in a flash.

I dragged the tip of the sword along the back of Wyman's neck. "If you so much as sneeze in the wrong direction, I'll use this sword to slice your skull from the rest of your body. Are we clear?"

He tensed so hard he was shaking. "Crystal."

Using the sharp blade, I severed his ties.

He flew out of his chair and stumbled, almost falling headfirst into the blazing fire. "Thank you," he squeaked out as he righted himself and faced me.

"Heed my warning, dude," I said through clenched teeth.

Wyman rubbed his wrists. "I promise, you can trust me."

We would see about that. Besides, he had some mad computer skills that might serve us well. Nevertheless, Roman could've been scoping out the high school for that very reason and contacting parents of teenagers who carried the vampire gene.

Webb swiped a hand over his brown hair. "We have a ton of moving parts. There's Intech, Camden Industries, and the Aberdeens, who now have Matthew and Layla. Not to mention, Roman is gunning for Abbey. Sam has a chip in his head, as does the shifter Dane Gray. We know the players are Carly Aberdeen, Harriet Aberdeen, Adam Emery, and Roman Brown. And we now have the Duponts and maybe a leak in Victor's staff."

Victor poured whiskey into a glass. "One thing I'm confused about, Sam. If Carly has Patrick's data, why did they take you?"

I tucked a hand into the pocket of my cargo pants. "She needs fresh DNA to whip up the serum, and Patrick's success was with Jo's DNA and mine."

"So you think that Matthew is the last piece of the puzzle?" Wyman asked.

I nodded. "I do. Carly has DNA from Dane and me. Now she needs to study Matthew's DNA mapping sequence. Once she has both, she might have the secret sauce to perfect makeshift supernatural creatures. Add to that the chip to control said creatures."

Victor growled. "My daughter is going to have a nervous breakdown."

If I knew Alia, she would. Her son was everything to her. But she wasn't my concern. Layla was, and I had to get my ass in gear if I wanted to see my huntress ever again.

5

LAYLA

My head throbbed and nausea swirled in my stomach. The van was moving at high speeds. I'd been in and out of consciousness. For how long? I wasn't sure. I licked my dry lips before swishing saliva around in my parched mouth. That familiar burn in my throat began to grow hotter and stronger. Blood. I needed Sam's blood. Oh my God. Sam. He must be out of his mind with worry.

I swallowed thickly, hoping my pulse would slow and that burn would go away. But I knew it wouldn't until I drank the sticky red stuff. I raised my head from the dirty floor, blinking several times. Darkness spilled in through the windshield as the lights from the dashboard glowed. I squirmed out of my fetal position as the van banked around a sharp curve, causing me to roll and slam against the inside wall behind the driver's seat. With trembling fingers, I frantically pulled on the zip ties around my wrists and ankles, but I wasn't strong enough to break the damn ties.

Breathe, girl. Don't panic. Easier said than done. My heart was in my throat.

From what I could see, thick trees lined the road. That told me we were in the middle of nowhere. Maybe I was wrong. *Please show me I'm wrong and that civilization is nearby.*

"Where are you taking me?" I asked in a barely audible voice.

The man in the passenger seat turned to look at me. "Somewhere you'll never be found." His brown eyes glinted with a truckload of happiness. He'd had that same look just before he jabbed a needle into me at the hospital while the other SWAT man with him had tried to contact Fred Emery.

Then I'd lost consciousness, but I remembered every detail leading up to my kidnapping as things had gone horribly out of control.

Sam sat in the exam room in the ER, processing the shocking news that we were having four babies. "Last night, as I was drifting off to sleep, I heard two heartbeats, not four," he said.

I was about to say something to calm him down when my phone rang. I fumbled to find my cell in one of my coat pockets. By the time I fished it out, the ringing had stopped, but Jordyn's name brightened the screen. I called her immediately, anxious and excited to share the news. Though she probably wouldn't bat an eye, since she thought Sam had magic sperm and had said that morning she wouldn't be surprised if I had a litter.

I giggled. Maybe Jordyn had unique foresight into the future. We had vampires and witches in our ancestry.

But as the line connected, two things happened at once.

Sam jumped out of his chair, pressing on his earpiece as Jordyn shouted into the phone, "Layla, run!"

Sam barked into his comm, "Motherfucker. Are you sure, Olivia?" He flicked his chin at me. "Put Jordyn on speaker."

I swallowed a ball of fur, obeying his command.

"Talk to us, Jordyn," Sam said.

"Fred Emery from Intech is chasing me," she said, breathing heavily.

"Where's Hawk, your bodyguard?" Sam asked.

"I think a vampire snapped his neck," she said.

"Where are you?" I asked my sister.

"I'm hiding behind a car in the parking garage on the third level. I think I lost that creep."

Sam pressed on his earpiece again and relayed the info to Olivia. "Can you or Ben get to Jordyn? Copy that? Layla and I are leaving now." Once Sam ended his communication with Olivia, he said to Jordyn, "Hang tight. Help is on the way."

I inhaled the musty odor floating in the vehicle as a chill skittered up my spine. Help never came. Instead, Fred Emery and his merry fuckups from Intech converged on the hospital along with Roman Brown and his team of vampires. Maybe the whole fucking world wanted Sam and me.

I knew Harriet Aberdeen, my grandmother, was behind my kidnapping. She wanted to lure me away from Sam. Maybe, if I were in her shoes, I would do the same. After all, the Aberdeen family hunted and killed vampires. They didn't fall in love with one, and they sure as fuck didn't have their baby—or rather, babies. Part of me was eager to see her face when her eyes landed on my belly. The other part of me sent waves of fear coursing through me. I would like to think I knew what she would do, but I didn't.

I rested my conjoined hands on my stomach. *Don't worry, little ones,* I told them silently. *I'll gut her if she so much as tries to hurt us.*

As if the babies heard me, that familiar tingling in my belly wormed its way into my chest. Ever since I'd learned I was pregnant, I'd been experiencing a fluttery feeling that had begun as a light tickle, and as each day passed, the feeling grew stronger. I was changing. In what way? I didn't know. What I knew was that the pregnancy had some magical effect on me. I was beginning to believe Dr. Vieira could be right. My babies would be born either witches or vampires or both.

I adjusted my body into a sitting position and leaned against the cold metal wall. "So, are you two men in line to become vampires or shifters?" My throat was scratchy, and I sounded as if I had a ball of phlegm stuck in it.

Carly Aberdeen, my cousin-in-law, was the mad scientist behind the genetic engineering. The company she worked for, Intech, had taken Sam and an alpha shifter, Dane, to extract their DNA for her experiments on humans. These guys were probably hoping to become the next test subjects.

"You know you'll die if you do. It's been tried before, and

hundreds of humans perished in the experiments." I wasn't lying. If they wouldn't tell me where they were taking me, why not tell them what they were up against? At the very least, maybe I could convince them that they were murderers like Intech. "Think about what you're doing. Do you have kids? A wife? A family? Do you want to see them die?"

The man in the passenger seat flinched. He had a loved one. I was sure of it. I couldn't see the driver since I was behind him. Still, I'd hit a nerve.

So I pressed on. "My grandmother wants to use me as a test subject. Did you know that? She'll kill my baby." They didn't need to know I was having four. What I had to drill into them was that an innocent unborn child's life was at stake.

"Gary," the driver said to his partner. "Shut her up."

I stared at the muscle ticking in Gary's scruffy jaw. "Even if you know what the endgame is, you'll still find yourself dead. If I were you, I would run fast and as far as you can. Because in the end, you and the people you're working for will be burned to a crisp." Sam's elemental powers would cut a swath of mass destruction in his path in his efforts to find me. Then he would torture anyone who had a hand in kidnapping me.

"Shut her up," the driver practically shouted.

I laughed. "What's wrong? Are you afraid of the truth?" I was in no position to be cocky, but I had nothing to lose at the moment. They wouldn't kill me.

Gary shook his head at his partner. "She's right, Rick. I didn't sign up to die."

Hallelujah. I was getting through to one of them.

"What are you, a fucking crybaby?" Rick asked. "You knew what you were getting into."

"No one said we would have a hand in killing a pregnant lady or her child." Gary's jaw was stone.

"Too late now, dude. We're in deep."

Hope sprouted, and I sighed. "There's still time. You can let me go. Otherwise, you'll end up dead like your boss, Fred Emery." I didn't know if I'd killed him or not. When I'd found him smashing

Jordyn's face into a parked car, I saw red as rage drove my actions. I rammed a dagger deep into his back repeatedly until he collapsed. If he wasn't dead, then maybe he was paralyzed.

Rick's laugh sent a shiver down my spine. "That's supposed to scare me?"

"Maybe not you. But Gary is shaking in his seat," I said with a smug grin.

Gary glared at me. "Shut the fuck up."

I rolled my eyes. "Your funeral."

I had no idea if we were close to our destination, but I wasn't giving up the fight. As a soupy silence filled the inside of the van, my mind worked to figure a way out. I firmly believed what Gary had said. I would never be found—if only because I knew my grandmother would do everything in her power to ensure I never saw Sam again.

I was screwed—doomed—and so were my babies. I banged my head against the wall. *Think, Layla.*

"I have to pee." A classic excuse for an escape. But I had to do something, or I would never see Sam again. I would never marry the vampire I was deeply and hopelessly in love with. Yet, I didn't care about that as much as I wanted him with me when and if the babies were born.

"Then pee," Rick said in a sharp tone. "Because we're not stopping."

I scrunched my face in a fake attempt to look like I was in pain. "Just pull over then. It's not like I can escape out in the middle of nowhere." I would probably die if I tried to hightail it into the woods. I did not know the temperature outside, but even if it was above freezing, spending hours in the chilly night air could be deadly. On top of that, coyotes and wolves were probably out there somewhere.

Gary looked at me before he gave Rick a sidelong glance. "We should stop. If she tries to flee, she won't get far."

"She can wait," Rick bit out. "We're almost at the compound."

My nerves on edge, I held my hands so they would stop shaking. I had to do something. "I can't wait," I said through clenched teeth.

Both men went mute, ignoring me.

I was not giving up. I raised my voice. "Pull over."

Rick shouted, "Shut the fuck up!"

Pinpricks of anger poked my skin like someone had stabbed me with a thousand needles at once. I managed to turn my body so that I was facing the driver's seat, then jammed my feet into his chair. "I said pull over." My voice was bordering on an epic scream.

Rick grunted. "Subdue her."

Gary was unleashing his seat belt when that familiar tingle instantly overpowered my senses. Before I could stop myself, the banshee in me took over, and I screamed at the top of my lungs.

6

LAYLA

We were on a fast track to hell. Gary passed out, his body slamming into the dashboard as the van swerved and picked up speed, which told me that the driver was also out cold.

No. No. No. Why did I scream? What the fuck was happening to me? It was almost like someone had taken control of my body. My heart was in my throat.

"I'm sorry, Sam," I said as I smashed into the back of the driver's seat, which meant we were sailing down a hill or embankment.

I fought for purchase, something to latch on to, but I had nothing. I was tossed around like these assholes had thrown me into a clothes dryer.

I closed my eyes and braced for impact when a familiar voice whispered in my head. *You'll live. But run,* the young boy with a lisp said.

My psyche froze as my hands caught on to something. How the fuck was I hearing the little boy from my dreams? The same boy who claimed to be my son. I swallowed down the fear and every other emotion as my dreams played out in front of me. A dark road. Dead of night. Fire. An ominous truck. All of that was stuff from my recurring dreams. Maybe I was dead already. Maybe I was living in hell.

The sound of crunching metal blared in my ears and snapped me out of my panicked state as the van rammed into what I suspected was a tree.

I labored for breath as I jostled around. My face was mashed into the back of the passenger seat. I squirmed to get free, but my hand was pinned beneath the seat. For a second, I breathed a sigh of relief. The boy was right. I was alive, or at least I thought so. I had no time to analyze the freakiness of what had just happened.

I dragged my head down along the leather seat, and I found I was hooked on to one of the rails that slid the seat forward and backward. A ray of hope made me smile. I might be able to get the fuck out of here and run like the boy had told me I should. I rubbed the plastic restraints against the metal rail fast, furiously, and as hard as I could. This had to work.

Little by little, I could feel the ties loosening. As I continued to free myself, that overwhelming power encompassed me once again. I felt like someone had shot me with a large amount of epinephrine. My heart rate increased, and as I pulled against the force, the zip ties broke free.

"Thank you," I said to no one or—if the boy was listening—to him. *Oh fuck.* I was severely losing my shit.

Now I had to deal with my ankles. I slid between the two seats and discovered Gary wasn't there. Fear gripped my chest—not because I was afraid he was dead but that he could be alive and out in the darkness, waiting for me. I shook that worry off. With the blood on the windshield and the gaping hole in it, he had to be hurt. The driver, on the other hand, was slumped over the steering wheel.

My breathing ramped up in fear the dude might suddenly come to. But when I felt along his waist next to the holstered gun, he slumped against the door. I held in a squeal until I found a pouch next to the gun. That time I squeaked out a noise, yanked the blade from the pouch, then hurriedly sliced the plastic ties on my ankles. Once free, I snagged Rick's gun and bolted out, only to fall. I landed on my side, my shoulder taking the brunt of the impact against a rock. Pain shot down my arm, but I couldn't worry about that. So I stood on shaky legs and waited a beat to make sure I could walk—or, rather, run. The headlights beamed ahead, highlighting the densely wooded area.

I glanced up the hill but couldn't see squat. Slowly, I skirted the van and went up to the driver's door. As soon as I opened it, Rick fell out, but the seat belt stopped him from hitting the ground. I cut the belt, and he tumbled into the thicket as branches snapped beneath him. I knew he was dead, but I checked for a pulse anyway. Nothing.

Blood seeped from a gash on his forehead and also trickled out of his ear. I suspected it was the impact that had killed him and not my banshee scream. But I couldn't worry about how he died. The bottom line was, I'd killed him. No question about that. I was racking up the dead bodies. At the abandoned airport in Illinois, I'd shot one of the SWAT guys who had a hand in Sam's kidnapping. I'd also played a role in my uncle Ray's death.

But my feelings about my actions could wait. I was at war, a damn big one. Enemies were multiplying—Carly Aberdeen, Harriet Aberdeen, Rianne Aberdeen, Adam Emery, Roman Brown, and whoever else was part of their scheme to take down Sam Mason and me. Then again, maybe their plan was to annihilate the entire Vampire Navy SEAL team. I could see Roman salivating to gain power within the vampire government. My family's goal was to make sure I never saw Sam again.

I stripped the rest of Rick's gear—flashlight, another knife, two clips full of bullets, and his bulletproof vest. Then I searched him for his cell and came up empty. After a quick scan inside the van, I struck out. It was best I didn't find it—tracking devices and all. Besides, we were in the mountains, so cell coverage had to be nil. Even if I called 911, I couldn't tell them where to find me. I didn't even know what fucking city or state I was in. We'd been traveling for hours, so I was certain I wasn't in Massachusetts or anywhere near the naval base.

After slipping on the vest and loading the gear and the weapons into my coat pockets, I climbed down the hill a few feet and gasped when I laid eyes on Gary.

"Help me." His dark eyes, wide with fear, glinted in the beam of the headlights. He hung on to a branch, the lower half of his body dangling over the side of a cliff. The enormous chasm below him didn't bode well for him.

I shook my head. "I'm sorry. I don't have the strength." That was the truth. I would fall over with him, and I had babies to protect. Besides, even if I could save him, I couldn't trust him. "Where are we?"

He struggled to pull himself up. If he was husky like his partner, he might succeed, but this dude had a slender upper build, and his biceps weren't as big as Rick's.

"Are you going to answer me?"

His features pinched. "Please. I'll help you. I won't take you to them."

I squatted down and gave him a sad smile. I believed he was telling the truth. "I can't. You know that."

Tears pooled in his eyes. "Then do me a favor."

I shrugged. Why not? The dude was about to plummet to his death. I should feel bad about that, yet I couldn't muster up any feelings at the moment. "I'll try."

"My name is Gary Hutchins. I live in Naperville, Illinois. I'm a single father. My son is staying with my brother and his family. Can you tell my son, Owen, that I love him?"

Damned emotions hit me, clogging my throat. I could feel his pain as if it were my own. "I'll try." I didn't know if I ever would or could.

He slipped a little. "I'm sorry about what's happening to you. I was only doing the job to pay for Owen's hospital bills."

A deep feeling of regret blanketed me.

"We're not far over the border in West Virginia. The place we were taking you is fortified behind cement walls. I've only been there once, but I was serious when I said you wouldn't be found. Even if your people had been able to figure out where you were, they would never get past the walls."

Maybe a human wouldn't, but a Vampire Navy SEAL, and a powerful one at that, would. "Best way out of here?"

He tipped his head to my right. "Go back the way we came, but stay off the road. The van has a tracking device, so it won't be long before they show up." He inhaled a large breath, then let go, saying, "I love you, Owen." His voice echoed as he slipped into the abyss.

Shuddering, I thrust the sad scene from my mind and focused on my own plight as I ran back to the vehicle and rummaged through it for any other supplies, like water and maybe a blanket. The temperature wasn't freezing—I would guess it was in the forties—but that was still cold and could be a problem over a long period of time. The moon sat high in the star-ridden sky. My guess was that it was around midnight. That meant I had to stay warm until the sun came up, but I couldn't build a fire. That would give me away. Before I put my survival skills into practice, I needed to move.

Aside from a bottle of water, I didn't find much else. So I zipped up my coat, turned on the flashlight, and started my trek through the woods. Whether I would make it out alive or not, one thing was certain—I wasn't going down without a fight.

7

SAM

I laid my weapons out on the bed in Jo's guest room. I couldn't bring myself to stay in my apartment last night. Layla's fragrance drove me mad and only punctured another hole in my heart. Not quite twenty-four hours had passed since she'd been kidnapped, but it felt like eons. I barely slept, trying to figure out my next move. My plan to walk into the arms of my enemy was proving more difficult than I expected. I'd tried calling Carly several times, but to no avail. I didn't have Roman's number, and I doubted I would ever find it. The vamp used burner cells. I couldn't blame him. If I were a criminal, I would do the same.

Regardless, we had no leads on where to begin. As much as I wanted to tear up the planet, I needed a place to start.

After we returned from Victor's estate, I'd gone through videos of the news segments that Sawyer's team had downloaded off the web, looking for a clue—a van, license plate, or something to give us that one tiny ray of hope that we could track Layla. I'd even grilled Wyman, since he'd been at the hospital, but the thorn-in-my-side human hadn't seen her.

The tech team was still scouring the cameras around the city, surveilling hotels, rental homes, and even the Indian reservation.

49

When I'd first met Layla, Roman had forced her into doing his bidding. He'd held Jordyn hostage until Layla could glean any info from me on Abbey. The phone Roman had used to call Layla led us to a warehouse on the reservation on the outskirts of the city. In the end, it hadn't panned out. The fucker had been one frustrating step ahead of us—an intelligent adversary, for sure.

As far as the meeting with my father went, he had to postpone it until further notice, which was fine by me. We had several moving parts, and it was best to schedule a time to meet when he had all the facts and feedback from our sources in the field.

Regardless, my old man might not be available for several days. The Council of Elders and our human governmental partners were up in arms over the mayhem we'd caused at the hospital. At some point, I was sure I would stand in front of the council as they chewed out my ass before they threw me in the brig for a few years. Most humans were oblivious to our existence, and our laws punished those who outed our kind. Neither Hawk nor I had done it on purpose, but the council wouldn't accept that excuse. The rules and regulations that governed my world were strict, and for a good reason. Anarchy would erupt if humans knew about our existence— if it hadn't already, that was. My mug was on every fucking news station from one coast of the country to the other.

I snagged the sheath that contained my dagger and was wrapping it around my leg when Abbey's strawberry aroma drifted in. I lifted my head to find her standing in the room.

I was relieved that she'd been in the safe room at Victor's when Roman's men converged on the estate. To our dismay, though, no one had spotted Roman in the chaos.

I grinned at my niece. "Are you a ninja?"

She rolled her bright-blue eyes that sparkled, framed by her stark black hair. "You didn't hear me?" The light in her eyes vanished as she blanched.

I shook my head. "I smelled you." Before I did anything else, I had to see Dr. Vieira. "I think the explosion compromised my hearing." Or the chip. The fucking thing needed to come out. I should've heard her heartbeat long before now.

She pursed her lips, her gaze rounding on the carpeted floor. She had one of those looks that sent an army of nerves to clutch my stomach. An expression that screamed that she'd had a vision or a dream either about me or Layla. Hell, she'd seen Rianne killing Layla. Maybe it was too late.

My heart came to a screeching halt. "Abbey, what's wrong?" *For fuck's sake, please don't tell me Layla is dead.*

She sat on the mattress at the end of the bed, fidgeting with one of her fingernails.

I moved my remaining weapons out of the way and joined her, closing my somewhat trembling hands into fists and resting them in my lap. I could feel her anxiety so strongly, I almost lost my breath. I hated and loved my empath ability, but this was one time I didn't want to feel Abbey's emotions.

My ten-year-old niece shouldn't be carrying the world on her shoulders. She was an extraordinary human. She was born to a vampire father, Edmund Rain, and a human, Rachel. Both were deceased. Still, Abbey was slowly changing into a vampire as she aged, which was unheard of among our kind. Her DNA had started shifting when she was just two years old, along with her ability to see into the future. But that was only one of her remarkable powers, and if the prophecy proved to be true, then Abbey would become the only female vampire in our existence to procreate if she chose to when the time came.

Silence hung over us for a beat as her fear and trepidation enhanced mine to the point that sweat beaded on my forehead.

"You can tell me," I assured her. Abbey disliked sharing her visions with anyone, and I couldn't blame her. What she saw in the future was hardly ever good.

She shuddered and picked at a piece of lint on her black leggings. "Roman will capture me, Uncle Sam. I've seen it."

I lost the ability to breathe. She didn't mention Layla, but I set that aside for the moment, as my niece meant the world to me. "No, he won't" was all I could say despite my gut agreeing with her. "Your visions have been off lately." That had been true about two months ago, but I wasn't certain if it was still true now.

She darted her worried blue gaze up at me. "Maybe they have. But the recurring dreams of Roman tells me he'll capture me. I just don't know how or when."

I swore my heart stopped cold. Roman needed to die and soon.

I draped my arms around her, then tugged her into my chest. "You know we won't let that happen. Your mom and dad will burn down Earth before they allow Roman to take you. I will too." I kissed the top of her head, desperately wanting to erase all her bad memories so she could enjoy her youth.

She sighed. "You can't stop fate, Uncle Sam."

Wanna see me try?

I held in a growl, knowing she was right—hating that she was right. "What else is bothering you? Is that what you came in to tell me?" I didn't think it was though.

She pulled away, then placed her small hand on my face. It was her way of seeing into my future and how she sometimes confirmed what she'd seen in one of her dreams.

A veil of blackness dropped over me for a split second before she let go and jumped up, anxiety dripping off her, her big blue eyes wider than ever.

Fuck. This isn't good.

I caught her wrist before she darted off. "Hey, whatever you saw won't come true." Those were the only words I had. "You can tell me. I won't freak out." At least not in front of her.

Her gaze was downcast before she raised her chin and blinked. "I... saw you as a monster." A tear cascaded down her rosy cheek.

I knew she wasn't referring to me as a vampire, even though humans would call my kind monsters. Still, I didn't know how to respond. My sweet and precious niece had frozen my brain cells.

She shuddered. "I can't explain it, but you won't be Sam."

I tucked wispy strands of her hair behind her ear. "You know I love you." Not that my statement would erase her vision—but it was helping me temper the fear that was cinching my heart.

She bit her bottom lip. "Yeah. But I'm afraid for you. I saw you attacking..." She swallowed as more tears pooled in her eyes. "Layla. You don't want to, but you won't be able to stop yourself."

It took all the restraint I had not to lose my shit. "The chip," I mumbled. I would bet that fucking device was to blame. I wrapped her in my arms. "I won't do that." I had to believe my statement— but given my recent actions, I wasn't so sure I could.

Two days ago, when I'd woken up from my coma, I'd learned I'd been the very monster Abbey was probably referring to.

"Son, do you know you attacked Peter?" Dad asked, changing the subject, no doubt feeling Layla's edginess.

"I've never seen this man before in my life," I returned.

Peter touched the vein in his neck. "You bit me."

Layla interlocked her fingers in front of her and rubbed one thumb over the other. "You've been asleep for over a month, Sam. Carly Aberdeen put a microchip in your head to control you, but the stupid thing malfunctioned, which is why you've been in a coma. Then Jo and Webb found Peter. He's the scientist who originally designed the technology, although he invented it to help the handicapped. When he came in to analyze the program, the chip rebooted, and you..." She shivered. "Then Jo stabbed you to distract you from Peter, and you attacked her."

"We thought you were going to hurt Layla," my father added. "You don't recall any of that?"

"Uncle Sam?" Abbey's concerned voice filtered into my ears. "Did you hear me?"

I blinked and zeroed in on my niece. "I didn't." I was in hell.

She gave me a sad smile. "You have to fight as hard as you can to not hurt Layla because you're the only one who can save her."

I squeezed her closer to me to stop my body from shaking with anger and so many other emotions. The chip had to come out. Like, now. I would kill myself if I laid a hand on Layla.

"I'm sorry, Uncle Sam."

I leaned away and searched her face. "It's not your fault." I moved one of her pigtails over her shoulder. "Never think you're responsible for the things you see in your visions. And never be afraid to tell me." The only reason my heart wasn't breaking into a million pieces was rage. Pure rage. Not at Abbey but at the situation, my enemies, and the whole fucking world. It seemed I couldn't catch a break. But I shouldn't be surprised. Supernatural or human, I'd been dealing with shitheads and savages since I'd grown up in the foster system.

Regardless of my past, magical abilities were both a curse and a blessing. Jo hated reading minds, I despised being an empath, and although Abbey never complained about her visionary gift, it wasn't difficult to see she didn't like her otherworldly powers.

I kissed her on the forehead. "I promise I will be fine." I was talking out of my ass again, but I had to ease her anxiety as well as mine. "Sometimes knowing what's ahead can help to stop it." Not that we had done anything of the sort yet.

She eased out of my hold and pouted. "I hope so."

Jo called Abbey's name before coming into the room. "It's time to leave for your tutoring session with Alia."

"I have to get my book bag," she said as she breezed past Jo.

Victor's daughter Alia had returned with us yesterday while he assessed the breach that had allowed Roman's men to storm onto his estate. As all of us suspected she would be, Alia was distraught that her son had been kidnapped, but she was confident in her father and trusted that he and my SEAL team would find Matthew.

We'd also dragged Wyman back with us. I'd been tempted to throw him into a cell, but I suggested Sawyer give him a cubicle and put him to work since the tech team was low on bodies.

"As long as you don't give him access to our top secret information," Webb had said. "Have him take over where Jordyn left off on the dark web."

My sister leaned against the doorjamb. "Jordyn should be released from the infirmary today," Jo said, reading my thoughts and beaming like she was proud of me.

"What's with the smile?" I was certain her happiness wasn't over Jordyn or the fact that Doc wanted Jordyn to stay overnight for observation. But ever since I told my sister Layla and I were having quadruplets, she couldn't stop smiling.

"I still can't believe I'm going to be an aunt to four little ones." She tucked a hand into a pocket of her black jeans. "Dad will flip when you tell him."

I pushed to my feet, grinning. I couldn't help but share in her excitement, just as I refused to believe I wouldn't get Layla back. "He will, but he's probably heard already." The news had gone around the SEAL team quickly. Tripp, Sawyer, Harley, Olivia, and Ben couldn't stop congratulating me when I'd returned from Victor's. Although the last I'd heard from Webb, my old man was locked in a conference room with the elders in Boston, hashing out how to deal with what went down at the hospital.

"How's Alia this morning?" I asked.

"Not sure yet," Jo said. "I'm swinging by one of the transient homes to pick her up. Any news from Victor about whether he spoke to the Duponts?"

"No." I collected my weapons. "I'll call him."

My phone buzzed with a text.

Doc: *I need you to meet me in the infirmary.*

Me: *Copy that.*

Perfect timing. I wanted him to check my hearing. I kissed Jo on the forehead and hightailed it out. Maybe Doc had good news about the chip. If he did, then I wouldn't become the monster Abbey had seen in her visions.

As I hopped into my Jeep, an evil laugh roared in the deep recesses of my brain, and the hackles on the back of my neck shot to attention.

Not a good sign.

8

———————

SAM

Thirty minutes later, I was walking into the infirmary. Doc's home away from home served as a research facility as well as a mini hospital. A pristine white-tiled floor punched a path down the middle, separating waist-high lab benches that traveled the length of the room on two sides.

I stopped and listened, testing out my hearing. Normally, when I entered, I could hear the soft whir of the overhead exhaust fan as though I was standing next to it. I concentrated on the large piece of equipment against the left wall, but only a faint hum trickled into my ears instead of the usual loud engine-type sound.

Doc came out of one of the patient rooms that banked the wall to my right and swung his brown gaze my way. "Sam, I'll be a few minutes." He sauntered over to Peter Landon, who was hunched over a laptop on one of the lab benches.

The scientist responsible for developing the chip—not for the reasons Adam Emery had but to help the handicapped community —flicked salt-and-pepper hair from his forehead as he regarded Doc. The two started chatting.

I was curious if Peter had any answers on how to remove the

rice-grain-size device. Since he'd managed to shut it down, he'd been studying the programming code.

While I waited for Doc, it was a perfect time to talk to Jordyn. She might be able to shed some light on Layla's kidnappers other than Roman.

I'd started for her room when the double doors behind me opened, and a whoosh of air blew in. The aroma of wet dog wafted in the air. At least my sense of smell was still on point.

I tossed a look over my shoulder. Dane Gray, alpha to the Gray Pack, strutted in, wearing a scowl the size of the state of California as he narrowed his russet-colored eyes. He seemed like he wanted to bash my head in for some reason. To my knowledge, I hadn't done anything to provoke the alpha despite us not liking each other.

I sneered. "Who pissed in your dog food?"

He threw me the finger with one hand and swiped the other through his unkempt white hair. "Still a dickwad, I see." He stabbed a finger at Doc and Peter. "They better have good news."

"Or what?" I mashed my lips into a thin line, keeping my fangs tucked in as best I could.

He let out a low growl, his eyes flashing red. "I'm going on a killing spree."

My fangs shot out of their own accord. Maybe because I was ready to murder someone—anyone—if I didn't find Layla soon.

"Dude, I'll join you," I said.

As we stared at each other, something Tripp had said the other night hit me. Dane's brother, Ross Gray, had a hard-on for Layla. He'd kept blaming her for his pack's involvement with Roman, Intech, and mainly for the death of one of their own.

Our trek down chaos lane had started at the vampire club two months ago when I'd met Layla. She and her sisters had never intentionally set out to kill anyone that night, which was odd for hunters whose family had been murdering my kind for centuries. Their job was to capture me by luring me out into the open and to shoot a drug-filled dart into me to knock me out. But in the process, they killed a woman—a shifter from the Gray Pack who'd been dating, of all people, Roman Brown.

"What's wrong?" Dane asked. "Do you have a stick up your ass?"

Even though Dane and Ross were brothers, I didn't see the resemblance. Ross was bald with hazel eyes. Maybe he had white hair before he shaved his head.

"Actually, I do," I returned.

Dane snarled and stepped into my personal space, his disgusting breath snapping me out of my funk. "Then spit it out."

We were about the same height—well over six feet. We had the same build, and I would like to think I would win if we ever had the chance to fight. Maybe the time to air out our differences was now. It was clear we were both harboring some pent-up emotions—anger and frustration, to be exact.

"You and I need to go a few rounds," I said through clenched teeth.

His nostrils flared. "No question about that."

"You need to tame your second-in-command. If Ross lays one hand on Layla, I'll gut him."

Dane jerked back. "What are you talking about?"

I angled my head as something occurred to me. "Is Ross working with Roman or Intech?"

Dane threw his head back and laughed. "Did you inhale some vampire crazy juice? Fuck no. Remember, Roman set me up. He was the reason I was on that table beside you in that lab."

"That doesn't matter. I understand Ross has it out for Layla. Maybe he helped kidnap her." Maybe Roman got to Ross. Or the other way around.

Dane's thick eyebrows disappeared into his hairline. "You're not making sense. And someone took Layla?" Surprise colored his tone. "Let me guess. Roman?"

"Bingo, dude."

A muscle ticked in his unshaven jaw. "My brother hates that asshole as much as I do. He would never work with him."

"Do you know that for sure? You've been away from your pack for as long as I was in a coma. A month is a long time, man. Ross might've taken things into his own hands. He blames Layla for the shit we're in."

He whisked a hand through his hair. "Are you forgetting I do too?"

I fisted my hands. "Maybe you're in on his deal with Roman. You know, I find it odd that your compound is in the Catskills. The same area where we speculate Intech has set up shop. And let's not forget, you were Roman's bitch when he stormed the base a couple of months ago."

His canines lowered as he got in my face. "Bloodsucker, you are reaching for straws and pissing me off."

I dragged my tongue over one of my fangs as adrenaline spiked through me. "Do you want to punch me?" *Please say yes.*

His claws, black and sharp, grew out of his fingernails. "I want to strangle you."

I laughed, sticking out my neck. "I dare you."

The tension skyrocketed between us.

He reached out with his sharp talons, about to either strangle me or scratch out my eyes. I pushed him, beating him to the punch.

He went flying through the double doors. The minute he fell on his ass, he was on his feet.

I marched toward him, ready to unleash my elemental wrath—fire. Light him up like the Fourth of July.

He charged me. "I should end you here and now." He tackled me to the floor and swiped his talons down my face.

The sting only served to incite me even further as fury twisted and snaked through me. Heat traveled down my arms to the palms of my hands, my fire element primed to singe the white hair off his head.

His bones began to snap, crackle, and pop—a sign he was shifting. But when fire erupted from my palms, he rolled off me.

I jumped to my feet. "Come on, mutt. Let's see what you got." I'd never fought a wolf before, but I was eager to.

Doc rushed out and positioned himself between Dane and me. "Gentlemen, this is no place to fight." His tone permitted no argument as he held out his arms as though he could stop a massive wolf and a powerful vampire. Maybe he could. Doc had a few vamp strengths of his own, but he had no elemental powers, which put him at odds against us.

Dane shook off his wolf, retracting his claws and canines. "Your bloodsucker started it." He sneered at me.

"What are you, six years old? I don't care who started it," Doc said with a growl. "This is my facility, and I will not have you two tearing it apart. Take your asses down to the gym if you want to see who has the bigger ego. Now, both of you get inside. Peter and I want to go over what we've found on the chip's data so far." Doc waved a hand toward the infirmary. "After you two."

We both obeyed like we were afraid of Doc.

But the asshole side of me had to say one last thing. "Dude, I swear if your brother is involved—"

"He's not," Dane bit out. "And make all the idle threats you want. We don't harm women and children."

While I believed him, I didn't trust him—and his brother even less. Vengeance blinded people and corrupted their morals, no matter what. I'd almost killed my foster dad when I'd found him attacking Jo. Five years later, I still harbored the itch to murder the bastard.

"My threats are real, Dane. She's carrying four babies." He didn't exactly need to know the latter, but I had to drive my point home. "If Ross has a hand in why she's not standing beside me, I'll eat him alive."

Dane came to an abrupt halt, his eyes glowing red. Shifters were like vampires in that their emotions caused their eyes to change colors. Dane was part shocked and... whoa! Dare I say fearful? I could feel what he was feeling. For the little time I'd known Dane, he'd never shown any emotion other than anger.

"Men," Doc said behind us. "I warned you."

Dane continued to stare at me, and for some reason, a chill skittered down my spine.

The double doors burst open, shattering the tension of whatever had Dane spooked.

Ben rushed in, carrying a blond woman who was out cold.

9

LAYLA

The sun had come up twice since I walked away from the van. That meant I'd been trekking through the mountains of West Virginia for two cold and tiring days. At night, I'd found refuge with tree boughs and brush to rest my aching body on and temper the wind. During the day, I hiked as long and far away from the dead kidnappers as my weary legs would take me. I'd made great strides —at least I think I had, since no one had found me yet. But that was a poor indication. The terrain was rough, but it had changed. Who knew? I might be heading directly into the enemy's lair. But I had yet to see anything with cement walls like Gary Hutchins had described.

Blue-and-orange hues peeked over the treetops as dawn was about to light up the sky, which meant day three of the misery was about to commence.

My legs and lungs burned, I couldn't feel my feet and fingers, and nausea had set in. I wouldn't be surprised if someone found me dead soon. A person could only survive without water for three days. The bigger issue was my need for blood. I was craving it like a starving vampire. If I didn't find any soon, I wasn't sure what would happen to the babies. I might consider ingesting blood from a rabbit or other wild animal if I came across one. So far, the only signs of wildlife had been owls and birds. I should be grateful that I hadn't run into a wolf or coyote.

I moistened my chapped lips with my tongue and adjusted the tree boughs that were poking into my ass. I squirmed to find a comfortable position against the prickly bark. But it was no use. Instead, I hugged my knees to my chest, blowing my hot breath into my hands as I glanced out at the huge chasm and prayed I would find my way out of these godforsaken mountains.

I was deep in the heart of tall firs, evergreens, and deciduous varieties of trees, and I was pretty damn sure I was miles from the smashed-up van. I had to be. I had to believe I was close to finding some type of life other than my grandmother or her counterparts.

I growled at the thought of Granny—a seemingly sweet and innocent older lady who had sharp talons and canines glued to her teeth. She was far from sugar and honey. Oh, she talked like she was the nicest woman on the planet, but Harriet Aberdeen was a viper waiting to strike. Maybe she'd assumed I'd plummeted over the cliff to my death like Gary had. If I was dead, then she'd won. On the other hand, she thought I would make a good candidate to turn me into a supernatural creature. If she was desperate enough to lead an army of supernaturals, then she might do whatever was necessary to hunt me down. She might even consider using my babies for her army too. Unless she was satisfied with my sister Rianne, who was raring to take the plunge as Carly's lab rat.

I shook off thoughts of my evil grandmother, recalling that Gary had told me we were just over the border in West Virginia. He'd also advised me to stay off the road. I wasn't sure I could anymore, though I was so deep in the forest that I had no idea which way the road was. I did have a good sense of direction, since the sun had been my guide. But so far, I hadn't found any signs of human life. Even if I did, I might run smack into one of my enemies. Plus, I was hundreds of miles from Sam. Without a way to contact him, I was royally screwed.

Buck up, missy. Get on your damn feet and keep walking.

I growled at my inner voice. Where the heck was the little boy

I'd heard when we crashed? He had words of wisdom for me. Like *run*. Well, I had done so, but now what? I kicked out my legs and rubbed my belly. *I'll get us out of here, little ones.* I had to. But I was afraid that without food or blood, I wouldn't be able to walk another mile.

Maybe if I just slept for an hour, it would fuel my energy. I closed my eyes and sighed. My body began to give in as sleep tugged at me hard. Just a catnap—a few minutes of shut-eye would take the edge off. The area was eerily quiet except for the faint sound of the river below. Slowly, I relaxed, and just as I was about to drop into a dreamlike state, a branch snapped.

I hopped up, whipping out the gun and searching left, right, and behind me. My pulse pounded in my ears. I hoped my grandmother hadn't found me, but my desperation for a warm bed and food was overtaking my fight to flee. I wanted to believe that her compulsive desire to keep me away from Sam was her only goal and that she had no other agenda. But intuition said otherwise, and my stubborn and feisty side wouldn't or couldn't give in. I was tougher than that weak side of me. At least I wanted to think so. But I couldn't die out here. I had to put the babies first, even if that meant I had no other choice than to give in to Granny.

I aimed the weapon in all directions and listened intently with my heart in my throat and my legs quivering. The longer I listened, the more fear wrapped its tentacles around me. Normally, I wouldn't be so freaking scared. I was a fucking vampire hunter. I'd spent many nights camping and hunting those creatures with my family. But the operative word was family, which meant I had backup. Right about now, I would rather run into a bloodsucker than Harriet fucking Aberdeen.

After several tense minutes of eerie silence, I released a quiet breath and put one foot in front of the other, my senses on high alert. I probably spooked a possum or a squirrel. I wouldn't mind capturing a squirrel. The little rodents weren't the best type of sustenance for the babies, but something was better than nothing to satisfy the hunger and blood craving. I hadn't attempted to build a fire, afraid it would give away my location, but tough times called for desperate measures.

I followed a path west with the river and gorge to my left. Dawn glowed brighter, and I was stoked that the sun was about to light up the area. Not being able to see in the dead of night was frightening to the point that even the flashlight in my coat pocket and the bright full moon had done nothing to soothe my nerves.

I swallowed thickly, stopping to dart my gaze in all directions. When I resumed my trek up a gradual incline, I again came to a halt. I blinked several times to make sure I wasn't seeing things. Delirium had come and gone off and on, and the weaker and more nauseated I became, the more I had to question my sanity.

I oriented my vision. I wasn't crazy. A cabin sat atop the hill. Hope whooshed through me until a thought zapped it away. What if the person who lived there worked for Intech? I'd covered a lot of ground, though maybe I hadn't gotten that far away from the fortress Gary had spoken of.

I didn't see any vehicles or a road. Not even a path large enough for any size vehicle. If anyone was inside, they had to have hiked in. Or they could've used an ATV four-wheeler, but I didn't see one of those either. My guess—it was a hunter's retreat and only used at certain times of the year.

I scanned the area several times, listening, searching, and waiting. I had to be cautious, though I was close to giving in. After Dr. Martin had examined me in the ER, he'd said I was in great shape. At the moment, I had to question whether that was still true. In shape or not, I needed rest, and I didn't want to push myself too hard in case that would harm the babies.

Here goes nothing.

I climbed over branches and rocks and weaved in and out of trees until I was several yards from the warm and inviting home. Then I shielded myself behind a tree and peered around it. My spidey sense told me no one was home. Then again, it was early morning, so the occupants could be asleep.

I dug deep for courage, the adrenaline fueling my legs as a tiny bit of hope mixed with caution swirled in my stomach. I inched up to the cabin, then onto the porch with my gun at my side. As I tiptoed over to the window beside the front door, the rickety wood squeaked. I cringed, hoping I didn't alert the homeowner, but then I mentally slapped myself.

Just go up to the door and knock.

I would if I wasn't so damn afraid of running into someone who worked for Intech. The decision was made for me when a deep growl resonated behind me. My heart skidded to a halt.

Like an unpracticed ballerina, I twirled around, aiming my weapon at the perpetrator. I lost my breath as my tired eyes widened at the massive animal baring his canines. The tan wolf's red-tipped ears, glowing amber eyes, and large size wasn't of this world but of the supernatural.

I could shoot him, but what if he could help? Plus, a gunshot would echo far and wide. It might alert my grandmother's lackeys if they were trailing me. I didn't think they were, only because they would've nabbed me by now. Unless this wolf was on her payroll.

I stared at the beast, debating what to do, when a muscle spasmed in my lower back. I winced, and the gun dropped from my hand. I rubbed a knot the size of Rhode Island, tears brimming in my eyes.

Between the impact of the accident and hiking for hours on end, you've done too much.

I had to sit down, so I eased myself onto to the top step, inhaling and exhaling—once, twice, three times.

Suddenly, bones cracked before a naked woman rushed over. Her wavy multicolored hair—mostly brown with blond and red streaks—fell down over her breasts. Her skin was dirty, as though she'd been rolling around in the mud, and she was in great physical shape, with toned biceps and muscled thighs.

"Ma'am, are you hurt?" She sounded genuine and sweet.

But sweet wasn't always a good sign. Harriet came off as sweet, and she was anything but.

I pressed my fingers into the knot and continued to rub. "It's a muscle, I think." It had to be. I didn't feel anything leaking onto my panties, like blood, but I should check just to be sure.

I wanted Sam so desperately. I wanted a warm bed, food in my belly, and to disappear where no one could find Sam or me. I was a strong person—resilient, as my dad had told me many times. I didn't give up on anything, but a person could only take so much.

The she-wolf held out her hand, her amber eyes morphing to a striking golden yellow. "I'm a medic. Let's get you inside." Her voice was silvery and pleasing to the ear.

"Medic?" That sounded military, but that didn't mean she was trustworthy.

Again, I wasn't in any condition to worry about anyone other than myself and the little ones growing in my belly. I couldn't keep running. For fuck's sake—I didn't even know how to find my way out of the mountains. But I had a feeling she did.

She helped me up. "My name is Sergeant First Class Rebekah Whyte. And you are?"

"Layla Aberdeen," I said as she ushered me into the warm cabin. "I pulled a muscle. That's all." I held my hand on that spot as I crossed the threshold. The minute I did, I stiffened.

Trust didn't come easily. I thought I could trust my sister—someone who I'd grown up with, fought with, fought for, would die for, and loved with all my being. And Rianne had turned on me.

"Layla," Rebekah said in a soft tone, "I'm not the big bad wolf."

A nervous laugh broke free. "Isn't that what the wolf said to Red Riding Hood?" Okay, that wasn't how that fairy tale went. Despite my wariness, I was in pain, hungry, thirsty, and so damn tired I could sleep forever. She *could* be the big bad wolf, and I doubted I could run two feet, especially with my back in spasm mode.

As if she knew what I was thinking, or maybe she heard my stomach growl, she said, "There are cans of soup in the cupboard. I'll heat some up for you."

My mouth watered at the mention of food. "Do you live here?" I hoped she didn't. The two-room cabin was depressing. A torn-up love seat sat in front of a fireplace that had a mountain of ash in the hearth. Dust covered the coffee table, and I swore an animal had died somewhere inside. And despite the dirtiness of the place, I longed to sleep on the twin bed directly ahead of us.

She let go of me. "I don't. I'm just passing through. This is an old family hunting retreat that hasn't been occupied in a couple of years." She darted over to a hook on the wall outside the bathroom and grabbed a flannel robe. "Although I think my brother has been here recently. I can smell him." She waved a hand at the bed. "It would make me feel better if you sat down." After shrugging into the robe, she crossed the room and threw a large piece of wood into the fireplace.

"I need to use the bathroom." I shuffled in that direction rather than hurrying, careful not to aggravate my back any further.

Once inside, I removed my coat and bulletproof vest. I'd forgotten I had on the latter. Slowly, I slid my leggings down, then my panties, and sighed heavily when I found no sign of blood. Then I pressed my fingers into that pesky muscle and massaged it as hard as I could. If I was going to hike my way out of these mountains, I didn't have time for injuries.

Maybe a few yoga stretches would do the trick. But the space was too tiny to do anything other than what the bathroom was designed for.

I quickly relieved myself, then washed my hands. As I did, I examined myself in the small round mirror above a chipped porcelain sink. I almost laughed at the woman peering back at me. My dull auburn hair was matted to my head. My blue eyes were hollow. My lips were chapped, and my face was ashen. Oh well. I'd looked worse after a night of killing bloodsuckers.

After combing my fingers through my hair, I grabbed my coat and vest, then found Rebekah at the stove, pouring a can of soup into a pot. She'd changed out of her robe into a pair of fatigues with a tan T-shirt tucked into them. A gun was holstered on her hip, a dagger in a sheath around her leg, and the soles of her flak boots had mud crusted around them.

Her military status conjured images of Sam dressed in his gear, looking mouthwateringly handsome. I would give anything to be in his arms right about now. I had no doubt my hot-as-fuck vampire was flipping out. The possessive, green-eyed creature was having a coronary for sure.

Rebekah pivoted on her booted heel. "Feel any better?"

I threw my coat and vest onto the bed and beelined it for the fireplace. "I'm fine. But if you don't mind, I'm going to do some yoga stretches. I've been hiking for two days, so all my muscles are feeling it." I moved the coffee table out of the way and eased down onto the dirty wood floor. Actually, it was cleaner than the tree boughs I'd sat on for the last two days.

"Go right ahead," she said. "When you're done, I would like to examine you, all the same."

I wasn't about to argue. I would love it if she listened to the heartbeats. Knowing my babies were okay would give me that boost of energy I would need to find my way home.

I kicked out my legs and bent over, holding the stretch and breathing evenly. The fire felt wonderful and, hopefully, would help loosen my tight muscles. "That would be great. Um… were you tracking me earlier?" Maybe she'd been in the shadows when I'd heard that branch snap.

She went over to her bag on a chair next to the love seat. "I picked up your scent last night." She pulled out a stethoscope and came over to me.

Little by little, my defense shield lowered. I didn't think someone as nice as her would be working for my grandmother. Unless Harriet ordered her to treat me with kid gloves—if Rebekah found me.

I stuck my hands on my hips and arched my back. "Do you have a phone I can borrow?"

She moved her high ponytail over her shoulder as she knelt down. "No cell coverage in these parts, but I do have a way to communicate in emergencies. I would like to check you out first, then we can come up with a plan on how I can help."

Even though my situation was dire, I understood that she needed more from me. Military folks liked to assess things before they acted in order to make sure they weren't jumping into a fire without a plan. Case in point: when Commander Webb London had scolded me in a recent conversation at the hotel outside of Chicago. His exact words were imprinted on my brain: *If you're not trained to know your surroundings right down to the speck of dirt on the ground, you'll get yourself killed."* Rebekah knew the mountains. She could guide me out. Besides, the babies were my priority.

I tucked my legs underneath me, then pressed my hands into the floor behind me.

She proceeded to listen to my heart, lungs, then belly, concentrating heavily on my stomach. After a long minute, surprise washed over her. "I hear four heartbeats."

I shuddered, smiling, and almost hugged her. "I know."

She grinned, her golden-yellow eyes glistening. "Congratulations. You know, quadruplets occur in about one in seven hundred thousand pregnancies."

"I didn't know that." *I haven't had time to think about my pregnancy. I've been running from my enemies.*

"Where did you pull that muscle?" she asked.

She definitely gave me the vibe that she was a good person.

After I showed her the spot, she felt along my lower back, then massaged that knot. "Your muscles are tight." She continued to knead and rub for a long minute. "The yoga stretches will help."

I was already feeling less pain.

I studied the pretty woman, who looked like she was in her twenties. Maybe she was twenty-three, like me. "Thank you for helping me."

She smiled warmly. "No thanks is necessary. I live to help those I serve."

Call it fate or destiny, but I felt like she and I were meant to meet. For what reason, I wasn't sure, but I was grateful and lucky. However, until I was safely in Sam's embrace, I wasn't ready to celebrate.

10

LAYLA

Ten minutes later, I sat at the dining table, staring out the window at the trees swaying in the wind while Rebekah set down a steaming bowl of soup in front of me. Dark clouds were rolling in, and it appeared a storm was brewing.

She went over to the window. "Mm. I was hoping to leave today."

"Do you have a car?" She had to have one parked somewhere.

She returned to the stove for her bowl. "It's at the ranger's station."

Jackpot. "Is it far from here?" I was ready to leave now.

With her bowl in hand, she sat at the table. "Who are you running from, Layla?"

"Is it that obvious?" She was perceptive, although she'd been tracking me, so she'd probably seen me always looking over my shoulder.

"Bad people," I responded as I picked up the spoon. My stomach was growling and my taste buds salivating for the canned soup. Hell, I would eat anything right about now. Sadly, the food wouldn't satisfy that steady burn growing hotter in the back of my throat. Over the last couple of days, it had waxed and waned. Dr. Vieira had never said what would happen if I didn't drink blood.

I could broach the topic with Rebekah. She might understand and give me some of her life's essence. But I wouldn't bring it up until it was absolutely necessary and I felt I could trust her.

She studied me. "Care to elaborate?"

"Not really," I said. She would think I was looney if I told her I was running from my grandmother.

"Okay. How about this? You didn't flinch when I shifted. Are you aware of my kind?"

I didn't have a problem answering that question. "Very much so. I'm a vampire hunter. My family has been hunting the bloodsuckers for centuries. So we're in tune with creatures like you."

Her eyebrows knitted. "When you say bad people, are you referring to vampires?"

She probably wouldn't stop probing until I gave her something of substance. I could lie, but that wasn't me. And if I wanted her help, she needed to understand the severity of my situation. Actually, she might be in danger as well. After all, Carly's genetic engineering involved shifters too. So the only course of action was to start from the beginning.

I hesitated to shovel soup into my mouth, fearful she might've drugged the food. My gut was saying she didn't, but just in case, I should wait for her to eat. "I've been kidnapped by my grandmother," I told her, even though I wasn't one hundred percent certain about that. "The van I was in crashed somewhere in these mountains. The two men who snatched me from the hospital in Massachusetts are dead. I've been wandering these parts for two days."

Lines formed around her pretty eyes. "Your grandmother kidnapped you?" Shock rode her tone.

"I know. It's sounds unbelievable." I puffed out my cheeks. "I'm pregnant by a Vampire Navy SEAL. And my sweet granny thinks I've committed a sacrilege."

She reared back, her mouth gaping open. "A vampire SEAL?"

"Do you know any?" Soldiers stuck together, and as far as I was aware, the supernatural military wasn't as big as the human military.

She clasped her hands together, resting her elbows on the table, not in the least interested in eating. "I do."

My mouth parted. Now I was the one in shock. If she said Sam Mason, I might hug her or punch her. Sam could snag any woman into the bedroom with one look from his panty-melting green eyes. He'd probably fucked a lot of women before I'd met him. But his past hookups weren't any of my business, and it sure wasn't important now—but then, why the fuck was jealousy making me tense?

"A friend of mine, Crysta Evans, has a cousin on the Vampire Navy SEAL team," she said. "Lieutenant Tripp. I've never met him."

Relief coursed through me that she didn't say Sam. Nevertheless, I flinched. I mean, what were the odds of her knowing someone I knew? If I thought she was working for my grandmother, I didn't anymore. Though I couldn't open the entire jar of trust. Just because she was military didn't mean she couldn't be bought to side with the enemy. Yet what I'd shared so far wasn't top secret. My enemies, including Granny, knew everything except the part where I was pregnant and carrying four babies. Even the latter would be revealed when or if my grandmother found me. Hell, my captors had probably revealed that to Granny already.

"I know Tripp," I said. "He's Sam Mason's immediate boss. Sam is also the father of my unborn children."

Awe washed over her as she fixated on me. "*The* Sam Mason. Son to Steven Mason?"

I licked my lips. "You know the Masons?"

"Not personally. But again, it's a small community."

Silence hung over the table.

She was probably ruminating over Sam and me or my situation in general. I was sure she had a thousand more questions. I had a few for her. But when she started eating, that was my confirmation that the food wasn't drugged.

I was tempted to pour the soup down my throat. Instead, I shoveled it into my mouth as fast as I could.

She emptied her bowl quickly. "I'm curious how a vampire hunter hooks up with the enemy—and such a powerful one at that. Were you trying to kill Sam?" Her golden-yellow eyes were alight with curiosity as though she was listening to someone read her a good book.

I grinned, remembering the night at the vampire club. "My two sisters and I were hired to capture Sam. The job was supposed to be simple." I laughed at the idiocy of what had happened. "Or so I thought. All we had to do was shoot a few drug-filled darts into him, knock him out, then hand him off to our benefactor."

"Let me guess. The job didn't go well," she said with a smirk.

I chuckled. "Not in the least." The only good to come out of that night was Sam. He'd stolen my breath and probably my heart, but I'd had no notion of giving him my soul. Oh, how things had changed. "It turns out Sam Mason was a hard vampire to nail." Maybe not in the bedroom, but she didn't need to know that. Nevertheless, heat wormed its way down to settle between my legs. "Anyway, to make a very long story short, Sam and I hooked up. And you see the rest." I glanced at my stomach.

She rubbed her lips together. "So, your grandmother found out about you and Sam. Does she live in these parts?"

Her inquisitive nature and the compassion in her eyes gave me more of a sense that I could confide in her. So, after a sip of water, I continued. "Not at all. My grandmother, Harriet Aberdeen, has some sick plans in store for me. She's teamed up with a company called Intech. The man who owns that company is trying to develop a way to genetically alter humans into someone like you and Sam."

Her jaw dropped as she fumbled for her dog tags and clutched them. It was as if the tags were a talisman used as a calming device. "You're kidding."

I inhaled deeply and after releasing my breath said, "I'm afraid not."

"Genetic engineering?" She sounded horrified.

Join the club, I wanted to say. "I can't fall into the hands of my grandmother, Rebekah. I'll never see Sam again. You said earlier that you had a way to communicate. I believe this is an emergency.

Please! We need to leave. Now!" I didn't care if we traveled in the pouring rain, but thankfully, the dark clouds hadn't opened up yet. "How far is the ranger's station?"

She pushed to her feet, collected her bowl, and placed it in the sink. "Five miles. But with the storm coming in and your need to rest, it's not a good idea. We should wait until the morning."

"No. I can make it." I felt like a sitting duck in this cabin. Granted, I wanted to sleep, but I wouldn't be able to.

Her lips pinched together. "Layla, the terrain is rough, the weather isn't on our side, and we're looking at a two-to-three-hour journey, and that's hoofing it."

"I hear you, but I will feel better if we keep moving."

"Do you know where the men were taking you?" she asked.

I swiveled in my seat to face her. "Only that it was close to where we'd crashed. I don't know how far that is from this cabin. Before one of the men fell off the cliff, he told me that the place is fortified behind cement walls. He seemed pretty adamant that no one would rescue me. Since you know the area, do you know of a place like that?"

She leaned her hip against the sink. "The area has grown so much. More homes, cabins, and new businesses."

"You seemed worried. Do you know Intech and what they're doing?" Maybe she did and that was the reason she was here, although the panicked look on her face said otherwise.

Her forehead creased. "No. But my brother, Tucker, went missing two weeks ago. What if…"

I smoothed my sweaty hands down my thighs. What if Intech was looking for me and instead found Tucker? "You said earlier you smelled Tucker and suspected he was here. Why? To hunt?"

"His pack believes he went rogue to marry a human girl. Tucker's alpha contacted me and asked if I'd heard from him. I'm always on missions, so I hardly talk to my brother. I took leave from my unit so I could track his phone up in this neck of the country. I lost the signal before I even got here."

I didn't have the heart to tell her what Carly had done to the alpha shifter Dane Gray—but she needed to know. After I filled her in on my relation to Carly, what her role was with Intech, and what she'd done to Dane, including implanting a chip in his head as well as Sam's to control them, Rebekah rushed over to her duffel bag.

Fishing around inside, she pulled out what looked to be a phone slightly bigger than a cell. "With the storm moving in, coverage can be spotty on this satellite phone. Since the Vampire Navy SEALs have been dealing with Intech since the beginning, I would like to defer to them. Call Sam Mason, and I'll give him the coordinates. Then I need to call my captain."

A ball of excitement had me on my feet as she handed me the phone. I didn't have Sam's number memorized, but I knew my sister Jordyn's. I prayed she was okay and that she would answer. After all, she'd been pretty beat up after her run-in with Fred Emery. Still, Jordyn would do whatever it took to get the message to Sam.

I blew out a breath. "After I speak to him, it's imperative we bolt before the rain starts. If Tucker was taken, then Intech knows about the cabin." Anxiety kicked my elation to the curb at the notion that they could be watching and biding their time before they barged in and took me. Rebekah, even in wolf form, couldn't fight off a group of SWAT-type men, especially if they had drug-filled darts.

"Make it quick," she said. "It's possible to track a Low Earth Orbit sat phone."

If this was the only way to contact Sam, then I didn't care. Worst-case scenario: Sam would have my location even if my grandmother found me.

Hope bloomed like a wonderful spring day—yet why did I feel like my world was about to turn darker than the clouds outside?

11

SAM

I jabbed my fists into a punching bag in the base gym, waiting on Dane to show his ass. After our conversation with Doc and Peter, Dane and I agreed we would meet to knock each other's lights outs.

It was the third day since Layla had been taken, and we had no leads whatsoever. I was one ornery fuck, and if anyone looked at me the wrong way, I snapped. My mind was on overload too. Abbey's vision that I would harm Layla was stuck on repeat, which just added to my overall grumpy demeanor. But my niece's prediction might prove to be true if Peter and Doc couldn't find a way to remove the fucking chip.

Surgery had been out of the question, but Doc had changed his tune. Instead of no operation, he wanted to drill into my skull. *Why* was the million-dollar question. And I didn't have to wait long for the answer.

Apparently, the coding had a self-destruct mode, which meant that whoever was behind the controls could press a button, and kaboom—my brain matter would be scattered and splattered every-where. Yeah, surgery was looking like a walk in the park, but…

There was always a *but*.

After an MRI yesterday, the scan showed that the tiny little fucker decided to swim to other parts of my head. *Ding, ding, ding.* That was the main reason I'd lost my acute hearing. Sure, I wasn't deaf, but as a vampire, I might as well be. I might lose my vision or sense of smell next. That would suck the big one.

Dane didn't want anyone drilling into his head either, though his chip hadn't shifted. Peter kept reiterating that actions and reactions to a device that controls the brain differed in each victim.

For example, I couldn't recall that I'd attacked Peter or my sister with the chip engaged, whereas Dane's mind had remained intact. His problem had been his inability to shift from wolf into human form until Peter shut down his chip the same night I'd come out of my coma. Peter had theorized that Intech programmed Dane to stay as a wolf. If he had, then Dane's wolf would've taken over, and he would've become the predator he was born to be.

On top of all that, Peter was against surgery, especially for me. "Too risky," he'd said. "If the chip keeps moving, we might have a hard time doing anything."

"Then how in the fucknation do you plan to pluck the sucker out?" had been my retort, even though I had to agree with Peter. I wasn't stoked about a surgeon boring several holes into my skull only to fail in the end. Or worse, touch a part of my brain that could render me a vegetable. I had a family who depended on me. I wanted to marry my beautiful baby mama, watch my kids play in the sand, swim in the surf, and build sandcastles. I wanted to teach them how to fight, play sports, if that was their thing, and everything else that came with growing up.

The door creaked open, and Dane strutted in, carrying a boatload of anger that dripped off him. He growled as he pinned his red eyes on me, his wolf on the verge of coming out to play.

I snagged a towel off the shelf, then wiped the sweat off my face and chest. "Who pissed in your cereal other than me?"

He ripped off his shirt and removed his phone from his gym shorts before setting them down on the bench against the wall on the far end. "My brother Cooper has been trying to reach Ross and two of my enforcers. They were scoping out the area where you think Intech might be setting up shop. They left two days ago, and we haven't heard from them since. Vera's heading here to pick me up."

"Dude, our team called in last night. So far, they've found nothing that indicates Intech moved their operation to the area. The power grid lit up because of a new warehouse store."

Kraft, one of our SEALs, and Crysta, Tripp's cousin and a shifter, had been dispatched on a fact-finding mission to the Catskills.

"Do you think that fucker Roman snagged Ross?" I asked.

His claws grew. "Fuck yeah. I'm so fucking tired of this shit. I'm ready to rip heads off."

I was more than anxious to do the same. We were striking out on all fronts. Our sister SEAL team, Viking II, had confirmed that the chip manufacturing plant was a ghost town. We speculated that they'd pulled out along with Roman's men because we were onto them. Roman had been right when he told me we wouldn't find anyone there anymore.

The only somewhat good news—Peter had an idea for chip extraction that wouldn't require a drill. Bad news—it was a long shot, according to him. But he wouldn't elaborate except to say he needed a case of the chips in order to test his idea. So Viking II was picking the place apart before they returned home. My fingers were crossed that they would find a handful at least.

Dane cracked his knuckles when his phone rang. He backtracked as his cell echoed in the room. "What is it, Cooper?" he snapped as he answered.

Cooper Gray was the youngest of the Gray brothers, and I'd been told he'd tried to help deactivate my chip prior to Peter arriving on base. He'd left before I had a chance to thank him.

Dane dragged his hand through his white hair. "What? When? How? Motherfucker!"

I tried as best as I could to sharpen my hearing but didn't have to when Dane hit the speaker button.

"Coop, Sam is in the room with me. Repeat what you said." Dane's features were pinched, and his claws grew even longer.

"Our enforcers returned without Ross," Coop said. "We tracked his scent to that diner where Dane was taken. Apparently, Ross left the hotel room to grab food but never returned. We found his smashed phone near his truck in the diner's parking lot."

A bone snapped in Dane's shoulder as if he was about to shift. "It has to be that fucker, Roman. Coop, make sure no one leaves the compound. Step up security. What's Vera's ETA to pick me up?"

"She just left. So, three hours."

"Call me if you find anything else out," Dane said. After he hung up, he launched his phone at the matted wall across from us and belted out a roar that stung my ears. Maybe now my hearing would be restored to its normal vampire sharpness.

"I was looking forward to jamming my fists into your ugly mug," I told him, "but let's talk to Sawyer. If the diner has security cameras, we might see who took Ross."

Before Dane could respond, Jordyn flew in like a tornado, her brown eyes popping out of her head as excitement and fear washed over her.

Maybe Kendra was awake. Ben had brought in the blond, green-eyed vampire known as Kendra two days ago. She was the same woman who'd been accused of killing Layla's father by her uncles, Ray and Jack.

Layla had insisted on talking to Kendra if Jack ever found her, so when he did, he dragged Kendra to our meeting with him at the abandoned airport outside Chicago. But Layla never had the chance to talk to Kendra. After my father had asked Kendra to wait in the plane, she'd disappeared. However, Kendra's involvement with Layla's father wasn't in question.

After Jo had read the minds of Roman's men who we had in our custody, she'd learned that Roman had been arguing with a woman at a hotel in the old textile district. Ben and Olivia had gone to investigate, and they'd found Kendra unconscious on the floor in her hotel room with several of those drug-filled darts stuck in her chest. Doc thought she would be out for days with the amount of drugs in her system.

"Is Kendra awake?" I asked.

Jordyn was itching to talk to her as much as I was. For my part, I wanted to know how Kendra knew Roman and what her involvement with him was.

She shook her head, stumbling as she rushed across the room, looking like a raccoon thanks to that fucker Fred Emery. He'd bashed her face into a parked car and had broken her nose. "No, she's not." She labored for breath. "It's Layla. It's Layla, Sam."

My heart skipped several beats. I heard her, but... "Come again?" I sized up the petite Aberdeen sister as though she were crazy.

Jordyn dropped her phone on the mat, her hands quaking like a drug-deprived addict. She bent over and picked it up, tapped on the screen, then practically shoved it at me. "She's here."

"Sam!" Layla's siren voice blared in the room over the speakerphone.

Clutching my chest with one hand, I held the phone with the other, swinging my shocked gaze to Dane.

"B-baby doll?" My voiced cracked as my legs wobbled. For once, luck was on my fucking side.

A shudder came through the line. "Fuck! I thought I would never hear your voice again," Layla cried.

That hole in my heart mended as I held the phone with a shaky hand. "Baby doll? Are you hurt? Are the babies? Where are you? Talk to me." My knees were knocking together, so I sat on the bench. Dead, suffering silence ensued as I fixated on the phone, waiting. "Layla, are you there?"

"S-Sam!" Her voice came and in out.

"I'm here," I responded, my heart in my throat. There were four bars, indicating the bad connection wasn't on my end.

"If you can hear me, hold on," Layla said in a frantic voice.

Jordyn gnawed on a fingernail. Dane crossed his arms over his chest as they both hovered around me.

"Sam, can you hear me now?" Layla asked.

I sighed. "Yes, baby doll. Are you hurt? Are the babies? Where are you?" I repeated.

Layla sniffled. "I'm okay. Tired, sore, and I need blood, Sam. I haven't had any since I was taken." She heaved a breath. "I'm worried for the babies."

It was heart-fucking gut-wrenching to hear the despair in her tone as I tried to think of a solution.

"Layla, this is Dane," he said, stepping in, probably because he could see panic on my face. "Where are you?"

"I'm at a cabin in the mountains of West Virginia," she said. "The van I was in crashed. The two men who kidnapped me are dead."

That snapped me out of my funk. "West Virginia. Crash. Are you sure you're not hurt?" Dane, Jordyn, and I swapped worried looks.

Painful silence stretched through the line once again.

"Layla," Jordyn snapped. "Answer us. Did we lose you?"

"Sorry, a storm is coming. I'm fine," Layla said in a distressed tone.

She wasn't, but she was alive, and for the moment, I could breathe. "Jordyn, have Sawyer trace the call. I'll be right behind you." I flicked my head at a retreating Jordyn. "Dane, can you go with her? Fill Webb and Tripp in on your brother." I needed a moment alone with Layla and to calm my nerves before I bolted out of here.

He held up his hand. "I will, but, Layla, are you still with those dead men? If so, you can try their blood."

"I'm not. I'm with a shifter who's helping me. Hold on a sec. I'll put you on speaker."

Again, Dane and I wore *what-the-fuck* expressions. Had the shifter escaped from Intech's clutches?

Once she had us on speaker, Layla said, "I'm with Sergeant Rebekah Whyte. We're using her sat phone."

How the fuck did Layla meet a military shifter? I didn't believe in coincidences. Maybe they were after the same people we were. I'd heard of an elite group of shifters in the army. Special Forces, if I wasn't mistaken. Their role was similar to ours—counterterrorism, manhunts, hostage rescue, and essentially to take down criminals in the supernatural community, like Roman Brown.

"Hi, guys. I'm a medic in the Army Special Forces," Rebekah said. "You might have heard of the Scorpion Angels. If not, I'm sure your father has, Sam. Anyway, we don't have much time. I'm worried someone can trace this phone. We're heading to the ranger's station. In the event that we're separated or something happens to us, my captain's name is Leo Paulson out of Fort Bragg, North Carolina. Layla and I are in the West Virginia mountains south of Morgantown. I'll text the coordinates to this number." She talked as if she was on speed.

Silence stretched over the line for a split second.

"Okay, you're not on speaker anymore," Layla said. "Rebekah is gathering her gear. There's a storm coming. Sam, you—"

The line went dead.

Motherfucker. My growl shook the mirrors on the wall. I tapped in the number of the most recent call. The line rang and rang. Another growl flew from my mouth.

"I'll meet you in the command center," Dane said before he darted out.

I was about to pull a Dane and throw the phone against the wall, but then it rang. I fumbled to answer. "Layla?"

"Sorry. Like I said, there's a storm coming. Look, you need to hurry. Intech is around here somewhere, but I'm not sure if they're tracking me."

I pushed to my feet. We needed the cavalry ready to go.

"I'm coming for you, baby doll." I was out the door in eight strides.

"I have to go," she said. "I love you hard, Sam Mason. Promise me something."

My pulse was beating faster than the speed of light. "Don't say what I know you're about to say."

She sniveled. "You need to know something. And I mean this with every fiber of my being. If anything happens to me, promise me you'll murder my grandmother and Rianne. You have to promise me, Sam. They're not my family anymore."

I had no problem following through on that promise. "Stop talking like I'll never see you again." I gritted my teeth, my tone stern and unyielding. I wouldn't accept anything other than her in my arms, snuggled up against me while I showed her how much I loved her. "I'm going to marry you, Layla." My voice softened. "You and I will live a long life without fuckwads hunting us or trying to use us or our children. Do you hear me? You and I will marry under the stars. We'll make love every day for the rest of our lives. We'll watch our kids grow and teach them all the things about family, love, and how to protect themselves and each other. That's my promise to you, and no one, and I mean no one, will come between us or get in our way. If they do, I will cut out their tongues, chop off every limb, and feed them to sharks in the Atlantic."

She cried and laughed at the same time. "Sharks, huh? I love your vampire ass, Sam Mason."

I closed my eyes briefly, staving off the waterworks, and for fuck's sake, they were about to pour out of my eyes harder than Niagara Falls.

"Tell Jordyn I love her," she whispered.

"You can tell her yourself when you come home."

"Home—that sounds nice. We need to think about the nursery," she said.

That was the least of our worries.

"Baby doll, one more thing. Roman told me your grandmother collapsed right before she was to accompany Roman to kidnap you and Jordyn. He doesn't know what happened. Junior talked to his dad, and Jack doesn't know either. We've checked hospitals around Cleveland and also the Catskills where we thought your grandmother might be headed, but we didn't find anything."

"Shit. Do you think she's dead? Maybe she had a heart attack like my uncle Ray." Layla sounded more relieved than horrified. "You could check Morgantown."

I would definitely relay the info to Sawyer, but Harriet wasn't my first concern, though I would deal with her at some point.

"Look, whether your grandmother's breathing or not, you still need to be concerned about Rianne, your cousin Noah, and Carly. I've been calling Carly, but I'm striking out. Sawyer checked her phone records, and she hadn't used her phone since that day you and I escaped from Intech. Who knows, she might be dead after all."

"I still don't understand why Carly gave you her number," Layla said.

"Million-dollar question, but it's not important. You are."

Regardless, if Carly was alive and I had the opportunity, I firmly believed I could convince her to bat for our team minus the genetic engineering. The way I saw it, remove the queen from the ant colony, and the army would fall—at least for the short-term, until Adam found another scientist. Unless he and the rest of his lot met a sudden and painful death.

"What about Fred Emery?" she asked. "I stabbed him pretty good. Jordyn mentioned he's in the base prison. Is he talking?"

"Negative. He's been in and out of consciousness. And during the times he is lucid, he isn't talking."

"Layla," Rebekah called to her. "I need to call my captain."

"Baby doll, be careful."

"I will. Love you, vampire." Her voice quaked.

I grinned as happiness filled my heart and soothed my soul. "Ditto, baby doll. I *will* find you and bring you home. That's my solemn promise. I don't know Rebekah, but I'm holding her responsible if anything happens to you." With Rebekah's wolf senses, I was sure she'd heard me.

"She's only one person, Sam. She can't fight an army alone. And you need to consider the chip in your head. So *you* need to be cautious," Layla warned.

Fuck that device.

Nothing and no one would keep me from saving my one true love.

12

LAYLA

Rebekah had insisted that we wait until I'd had a few hours of rest before we made the trek to the ranger's station. I appreciated her concern. It was heartwarming that a perfect stranger cared. Sure, her military edict to protect those she served played a role, but outside of the uniform, I could still see she had compassion for others, and my trust in her solidified.

But with the impending storm, it was critical to leave now. Not only that, but I couldn't rest, let alone sleep. My nerves were teetering on the brink of destruction.

I inhaled the crisp mountain air, glancing up at the angry sky. The storm clouds hadn't opened up yet, but the earthy scent right before the rain came down was being carried on the wind. Any second now, we would be soaked and trudging through mud. But I didn't care. The farther we hiked toward the ranger's station, the more my excitement built. I knew it would be hours before Sam arrived, but the thought of seeing the hunky vampire was pushing me to power through the soreness in my muscles. That and his emotional speech of how he would marry me. Under the stars sounded like sunshine and heaven. *Will we get the chance?*

Maybe luck was on my side. Meeting Rebekah was a miracle, in my book. If it weren't for her, Sam would've never known where I was. I owed the she-wolf big time.

"We have to hustle if we want to beat the storm," Rebekah tossed over her shoulder.

We were only thirty minutes into our journey, and according to Rebekah's estimate, we had about two hours to go or longer, particularly if I had to rest. I wasn't planning on stopping, but my body could only take so much. The spasm in my back was still there but dulled. And the only nuisance really driving me crazy was the burn in the back of my throat.

Of course, Rebekah had heard the conversation with Sam and Dane on the topic of blood. After I'd hung up, I'd explained to her why. She'd been quick to cut her palm and squeeze blood into a glass—but the minute it hit my tongue, I'd spat it out. Her musty animal aroma should've been a sign that her blood wasn't compatible, but I'd been desperate to cool the burn. Instead, I ate crackers and drank ice water—anything to take my mind off the cravings.

Sighing, I checked the sky above. We wouldn't make it another five minutes before the dark clouds unleashed their fury.

I tucked my hands into my coat pockets and bowed my head, watching every step I took. "I'm right behind you." The wind was brutal, kicking up dirt and dead leaves. I needed a set of goggles to shield my eyes from Mother Nature.

I picked up the pace and let my mind drift to anything other than the need for Sam's blood or wondering whether my grandmother had people searching for me. Or if maybe she was dead. The news that she'd collapsed was more of a relief than a concern. If she couldn't bark orders, then it was likely no one was searching for me. Rianne didn't care about me. Granny was the only one who had a hard-on to pry me away from Sam.

For now, I focused on something happier, like Sam's emotional speech. Another reason the adrenaline was high, giving me the burst of energy I needed to make the journey. I giggled at his promise to cut off limbs and feed them to the sharks in the Atlantic, remembering something similar I'd said to him about sharks. He and I had been traveling up to Jo and Webb's house in Maine. I'd just found out I was pregnant, Rianne had turned on me, and she and my cousin Noah had unsuccessfully plotted to murder Sam. So my hot-as-sin vampire had been trying to soothe my nerves.

"Layla, let's try and relax for the next two days and not think of your sister trying to annihilate your boyfriend," Sam said.

I snorted out a laugh. "You're my boyfriend?"

"You don't agree? How about partners? Enemies? Fuck buddies? Pick one or two," he said.

"Partners," I fired back. "That's a weird one. I'm going with enemies. Just don't ever call me your baby mama because I will cut off your balls and feed them to the sharks." I pointed at the Atlantic Ocean as we drove by.

The more our relationship grew, I was finding he and I were similar in a lot of ways. We were both stubborn, strong-willed, fought for those we loved, and thought along the same lines. I wasn't enamored with his other pet name of baby mama, but it had grown on me, and regardless, he loved me. I loved him. I couldn't wait to say I do and promise him my soul beneath the stars. I felt we had that undying love that only happened once in a person's lifetime. We could live in a cave or a hut with no running water or electricity. As long as we were together, building our family, and we were safe, nothing else mattered. More importantly, like him, I wouldn't allow anyone to come between us.

I'd wanted to tell Sam all that on the phone and more, but I'd gotten choked up during his speech.

A raindrop fell on my head, pulling me back to hell.

Rebekah spun on her heel. "I'm going to check out the terrain over the hill and get my bearings. It will take me a second. Stay here. These trees will provide cover." She darted off.

Rain began to fall at a steady and heavier rate. The wind howled and kicked up leaves and rustled branches as icy fingers tiptoed down my spine.

I reached into my coat pocket and wrapped my fingers around the handle of the gun just in case I needed to use it. I would give anything to have my uncle Jack's flamethrower right about now. I swore that if I got out of these mountains, I would beg Sam to lock me up and throw away the key, at least until these babies were born.

As if the babies heard me, an intense tingling snaked into my chest—a sign my banshee was ready to release the scream of the century. Laughing, I squinted and swiped rain from my eyes once again. My scream didn't affect an immortal. As Steven had described the effects, their eardrums might be damaged for a bit.

Rebekah returned. "There's an open path we can take that should lead to the ranger's station." She glanced at her compass.

The military woman was prepared for anything. The bag she had slung over her body contained several weapons, camping gear, and MREs or Meals, Ready-to-Eat.

I had taken one step when she held her finger to her lips and stiffened.

Fuck me. No. No. No.

I carefully searched around us, holding my breath, but jumped a freaking mile when thunder boomed.

Get your shit together, Layla. You've been here before. You've traipsed through woods in the middle of the night and faced vampires who had the strength to end you in a nanosecond. You're a survivor. Pregnant or not, you're not a wimp.

My inner shrink was right—if I wasn't tired, craving blood, and my legs didn't feel like they were about to detach from my body.

"What is it?" I asked as we huddled between two fat tree trunks.

She tipped her ear slightly toward the ground, holding up her hand, her nostrils flaring.

I squeezed the handle of the gun tightly.

Then her golden-yellow eyes transformed to a luminous amber, and her canines clicked into place. "We have company."

My banshee was ready. "Can you hear them?" I knew she had impeccable hearing, but the sounds of Mother Nature made it feel like we were sitting next to the speakers in the front row of a concert.

She nodded. "But it's their scent, too, and the wind is my friend right now. And one of them is breathing quite heavily, almost panting."

"Shifters?"

"Mostly humans. I don't know how many, but more than two."

Well, fuck. We had the weapons and her otherworldly abilities, but even still, we couldn't take on a group of them.

She slid her hand into the side pouch of the bag strapped across her chest and pulled out two phones. "In case we get separated, take these. With the heavy rain, the sat phone might not work. Coverage can be spotty in storms. My pass code on my cell is 3330. You should have cell service about a half mile from the ranger's station. Call for help."

I gritted my teeth, hating that I couldn't fight like I wanted to. That just pissed me the fuck off. I could shoot a weapon, so that wasn't a problem. But to physically engage with the enemy wasn't the smartest move for me. I felt like a damsel in distress—weak and dependent on others. That wasn't me—but this wasn't about me.

"You keep the sat phone," I said. "I'll take your cell. If anything happens to me, then go for help. You're faster than me, especially your wolf. Don't try to save me. I can handle my grandmother."

I hoped I could. Maybe since I was carrying a Mason, she wouldn't follow through with her twisted plan of changing me into a bloodsucker—at least not until the babies were born. Then she would not only have me, but she could raise and mold my children to one day lead her army. If she decided on that, then it would buy time for Sam and the SEALs to rescue me. It wasn't as if I would deliver tomorrow. I knew it was long shot at best, since Harriet didn't want more bloodsuckers in the world.

"Promise me you'll go for help. If Intech captures you, you'll lose yourself to your wolf. Then you won't be able to save your brother," I added, knowing Rebekah had a bad feeling that Intech had Tucker. "You can help the SEALs." I doubted they would bring an entire SEAL team with them. Some had to stay behind to protect the base, especially since Roman was a threat and had been successful in blasting through the gates in his attempts to snatch Abbey.

"I don't like this," she said.

Neither did I. "There's one thing I haven't told you. I sort of have a magical weapon." I'd filled her in on a lot of things but not on my banshee scream.

Her amber eyes glowed liked lanterns in the stormy forest as her forehead furrowed.

"I caused the accident I was in with the van. I have a banshee scream that knocks out humans. If I'm successful in using it now, I'll be right behind you. Sam's dad said it hurts his ears, so you shouldn't be close to me."

She shoved the phones into her bag, then wrapped it around me. "Save your scream. They might not hear anything in this storm. Once I shift, follow me. If I have to take any of them out, keep running. Clear?"

She had a point. The sound of raindrops hitting the forest floor competed with the howling wind, and I was having trouble hearing my own voice.

In a flash, she began to shift. Her chin jutted out as her animal snout came into view, and hair grew from her face before the rest of her body followed suit. Her clothes ripped in the process as more bones cracked and took the shape of a pretty she-wolf.

Eerie to watch but cool at the same time.

Once the animal was standing next to me, she pushed her snout into my arm as if to say *be careful*. Then she bounded up the hill. Adjusting the heavy duffel bag over my body, I hurried behind her.

My nerves were singing as I inhaled a huge gulp of mountain air and rain fell into my mouth. Damn fucking weather always seemed to be an omen. We'd fought Roman Brown in a blizzard. Sam had been strung up over a firepit in Montana during a raging thunder-and-lightning storm, I'd been kidnapped by Intech as snow piled up at an abandoned airport, and now the howling wind and torrential rain was about to fuck with me.

When I crested the hill, the wide dirt path gave me a sense of hope. All I could think about was *follow the yellow brick road*. But my excitement died when Rebekah stopped and sniffed. Then she jerked her head to the left, gave me a quick glance as if to say run, then dashed between two trees.

I held the gun with two hands and broke out in a run as I continued searching around me. But the fucking rain was impacting my vision, and something didn't feel right.

Then a yelp rented the air, and I froze.

"Rebekah!" The sound of my pulse beating in my ears drowned out the peal of thunder as I swallowed a damn elephant. For some reason, my legs wouldn't move, but that familiar tingling in my belly came out of nowhere. It was as if the babies knew I was desperate for help. I had no time to think, and I couldn't control the urge to scream if I wanted to. A swirling sensation whooshed from my belly into my throat in less than a second.

Lightning cracked, and thunder roared.

The gun dropped from my hands as I held out my arms, closed my eyes, and welcomed Mother Nature in all her glory. On a deep inhale, I unleashed my weapon that could knock out any human from West Virginia to California. The high-pitched scream echoed, sounding like a sonic boom. Whether or not anyone heard me, I wasn't sure. When I pushed out the last ounce of breath and energy I had, I opened my eyes and stumbled backward.

I tried to speak but couldn't. I had no words as my eyes grew wider than the gorge I'd seen the other day.

My sister Rianne was dressed to fight a war—black jeans, flak boots, weapons strapped around her waist and legs, bulletproof vest, and a ball cap that had the initials EML on the front. She smiled broadly as she puffed out her chest.

Standing next to her was none other than my cousin Noah. His blackish-brown hair curled around his ball cap. The pompous ass smirked as his dark eyes filled with victory and something else I couldn't put my finger on. He wore the same outfit as Rianne. The only difference between them was that Rianne was holding a dart gun and Noah had a sword, his weapon of choice when we'd hunted as a family.

I shouldn't laugh, but I couldn't help myself. How times had changed. Now I was no longer the hunter but the *hunted.*

I laughed even harder when Rianne pulled out earplugs. The witch knew my secret weapon.

But her condescending grin faded when her gaze dropped to my stomach.

I gave her a blinding smile as though I had the upper hand, and for fuck's sake, I didn't. Especially not when a man dressed just like the stupid duo came up behind Rianne, aiming his dart gun at me.

Raising my hands, I kept smiling because Rianne was still staring at my belly. I shouldn't be acting like this was a joke or some fun game. But I couldn't help myself. The shocked look on her face was priceless.

Rianne snapped her fingers. "Noah, take her to Carly. If she fights, cut off her head." She eyed her guard. "You—with me. I want to find that wolf. She's hurt, so she can't have gone far."

If I had any love left for my sister, it instantly vanished. But one thing was certain: she might've won this round, but she wouldn't win the next.

13

LAYLA

Noah kept pushing me as we trudged through the woods. I wasn't sure how long we'd been walking. Maybe minutes. Maybe hours. To me, it sure as fuck felt like days. My body was about to give out, my legs especially. My brain, on the other hand, was running rampant with questions galore. But one stuck out brighter than the lightning zipping across the sky. Would my cousin follow orders and cut off my head? Possibly. Noah was enough of a hothead to do something as cruel as kill his own kin—particularly one who was in bed with the enemy. Even more frightening was how easily Rianne had spit out the order. It gutted me that our relationship as sisters was over. I didn't see how we would ever recover or return to the days where she had my back and I had hers.

The immediate issue was my bastard cousin. I itched to strangle him. If I wasn't pregnant, I would, despite the sword in his hands. I'd always been quicker on my feet than Noah. I'd also bested him three times, although he had filled out more since he was eighteen. Plus, he had the type of attitude that packed more of a punch than his fists.

The rain poured down, sparking memories of that stormy day in Montana when I'd sprinted to save Sam from the clutches of

Noah and Rianne. A wild, nervous laugh escaped me. Now I was the one who needed to be rescued. I had no doubt that Sam would move mountains to save me. However, I worried that the chip in his head might throw a wicked curveball into the mix.

I was also concerned for Rebekah. Hopefully, Rianne didn't catch her. Not that Rebekah could take down Intech on her own, but I liked the she-wolf. She also knew the mountains and would be a great asset to Sam.

Noah shoved me up an embankment. "Move!" he shouted above the blaring storm.

My arms flew outward to break my fall, and one of my knees hit a dead branch. The pointy piece of wood was sharp as it punctured through my leggings.

Anger as hot as the sun on a humid summer day barreled through my veins. I pressed my hands into the muddy soil. When I did, I grabbed a rock that was lying near my right hand.

"Get up!" he shouted.

I wasn't supposed to despise family, but the hatred I had for Noah scorched my insides, and a wild need to kill erupted.

I pushed up until I was on my feet, then climbed the hill a foot or two, the road in my sight. The idea of freedom came to mind.

Run like the wind, Layla.

I wanted to, but first I had to slow him down or hopefully knock him out with the rock in my hand, then take the sword and slice off his head. I scrambled up to the road as fast as I could, then glanced both ways. A van with its back doors open was parked about twenty-five yards from where I stood. No way was I getting into another fucking van unless I was the one driving. Maybe they'd left the keys in it for a quick getaway.

"Go ahead and run, cousin," he said. "I'll catch you."

I threw the rock with a somewhat steady hand. When it hit Noah's head, he floundered, losing his footing, His arms pinwheeled as he fell backward. The sword dropped to the muddy earth as he tumbled down, fighting for purchase, trying to find something to grab to stop his downward trajectory—but gravity was a beautiful thing as he tumbled and rolled.

I watched, smiling broadly as his body was about to ram into the large evergreen behind him. Just before it did, I ran toward the van, hoping the keys were in it. If not, I could hot-wire it. I'd done it before when Jordyn had lost the keys to our dilapidated Nissan.

I huffed and puffed, running for my life. The moment I reached the driver's side door, the van shook and then there was a boom.

Stymied, I walked backward into the middle of the road and glanced up. It sounded like something had landed on the roof. Shock stole the breath from my lungs as I froze until a peal of thunder boomed and jarred me out of my stupor. What the fuck in tarnation?

Peering down at me, the monster smiled, showing fangs.

My hand flew to my mouth as I shook my head. "Noah, is that you?" I was surprised I could speak.

An Aberdeen with fangs? A vampire hunter with canines that were long—extremely long—and deadly? No fucking way. If his parents could see him now, they would shit their pants.

He opened his arms and laughed. "One and the same, cousin. Like the new me?"

Um… fuck no. "What are you?" Disgust came through my tone loud and clear.

His red eyes were brighter than a full moon in a dark sky. His cheekbones protruded outward as if he was trying to shift, and his nails curled around his fingertips. He looked like a cross between a shifter and a vampire but only because his fangs weren't thick like the wolf shifters.

Holy nutso. Carly had whipped up some type of new beast. My guess was she'd combined Dane's DNA with Sam's.

He jumped from the rooftop, landed on two feet with ease, and feigned a pout. "Not a fan of my new look?"

As despicable as he was, I couldn't look away. "Fuck no."

He closed the distance between us and sniffed my neck. "You smell delicious."

I pushed him, and he flew backward and hit the van. How did I have the strength do that? I glanced at my hands as though they held the answer.

Noah belted out a laugh. "Seems someone else has some powers. Must be that vampire blood that runs through your mom's family."

Or I was getting help from my four little ones—but he didn't need to know that.

He stalked toward me. "Now, you can either fight me or be a nice girl and get in the van."

I would love to tango with my cousin, but the only weapon I had was my banshee scream, and he was wearing earplugs. Not to mention, he had claws and fangs. If he was truly nonhuman, then my scream wouldn't affect him. Above all that, I was cold, covered in mud, and soaking wet. I hadn't slept but maybe three hours, if that, in three days. I was hungry for food and craving blood like no one's business, my body ached, my legs were saltwater taffy, and the only thing keeping me sane other than rage was knowing Sam was on his way.

"Aren't you supposed to cut off my head if I got out of line?"

He retracted his fangs. "Rianne's not in charge. Granny is."

Oh joy. It was my lucky day. Well, I had two questions answered. Carly was alive, and so was Harriet. Damn the bad luck.

I raised my hands. "Lead the way, cousin."

If Noah had taken the plunge into monster territory, did that mean Rianne had too?

As he ushered me into the back of the van and handcuffed me, I wanted to ask, but he slammed the door in my face.

14

LAYLA

I stood in front of a floor-to-ceiling window that overlooked the lush green treetops that spanned the landscape for miles. The same thick wooded mountains that I'd trampled through for the last two and half days. Noah had brought me into the belly of the beast hours ago and handed me off to a guard who escorted me to this room. What time of day was it? I couldn't tell since storm clouds covered the sky.

So far, no visits from Harriet, Carly, or Rianne. I bit a nail, wondering if Rebekah had gotten away or if enough time had passed that Sam was in the area.

I shuddered as the rain outside pinged off a metal railing that rimmed the perimeter. I was on the fourth or fifth floor or maybe even higher. Numb was the word to describe how I felt for a variety of reasons, but none of them disoriented me more than seeing what Noah had become. To say shock had me immobilized was an understatement. It would be even more of one if I found out Rianne had followed through on giving up her humanity.

I still couldn't wrap my head around my sister's decision. Then again, she probably didn't understand mine either.

The other thing that had me rattled—this room and view. Both were eerily familiar, as though I'd been here before, which, in a way, I had—in one of my nightmares I'd had at the hotel outside of Chicago that day Intech had taken Sam.

Lush green treetops spanned the landscape for miles. For a beat, I struggled to figure out where I was. When I spun on my heel, my surroundings changed once again.

The expansive room was sterile, the air cold, and I hugged myself, shivering. The lights were bright, almost blinding, but something in the distance caught my eye. I slowly walked in that direction, squinting to read the three letters within the red circle stamped on the wall. The first letter was a capital E *followed by a capital* M, *but the third one vanished when a shiny object to my right caught my eye. My pulse went haywire when my gaze landed on a stainless-steel table. But it wasn't the table that had me sprinting over to it.*

No. No. No. My bare feet slapped against the tile floor that felt like a slab of ice. I pumped my legs hard, my arms in sync like I was running the 100-meter dash in the Olympics.

Lightning shattered the sky, throwing me out of my reverie, and I jumped a mile when the clap of thunder boomed. I was afraid to think of what would come next. If my dream was playing out right before me, then I was in for one death-defying ride.

I scanned the grounds below. The fortress was exactly like Gary Hutchins had warned me it was—high cement walls that seemed impossible to penetrate, although C4 would do the trick.

As much as I knew Sam would do the impossible to rescue me, I had to start thinking of my own way out. I was confident Sam wouldn't fail—but I couldn't shake the thought of the chip in his head.

Screaming wasn't an option. On the way up to this room, I noticed that the guards wore earplugs. The security panels posed a problem. Unlocking a door required a pair of eyes, not fingerprints. It was easier to cut off a thumb than gouge out an eyeball.

The door to my room opened. "Ma'am," Barnes said.

I could see the blond giant's reflection in the window. The man was tall and burly, and the black uniform golf shirt he wore was entirely too small for his chest. He was the guard who Noah had handed me off to. The same one who'd bitten off Noah's head for manhandling me like I was some sort of river rat. I wondered if Barnes could be a friend or if he was a die-hard foe.

He set a tray of food down on a metal table near the bed. "You should eat."

I should but couldn't. My stomach felt queasy, and I was craving blood more than food at the moment.

"Take it away," I said, not turning around. "It's making me want to gag." Whatever was on the plate smelled rotten.

His boots scuffed the tiled floor as he approached, looking at me through the reflection in the window. "You should also change out of those damp clothes. You've been in them for hours." He sounded like he cared.

I pivoted on my heel and swayed.

He reached out and steadied me. "Please, you need to rest." He guided me over to the cot that had a thin mattress and a flat pillow.

I didn't protest, yet I was afraid that if I sat down, I wouldn't be able to get up. Or that if I fell asleep, I would wake up on a table in a lab.

Once I was seated, he picked up the clothes from a chair by the door and set them on the bed. "You'll need to change into these before I take you to Carly. She doesn't want any dirt in the lab."

I full-on laughed. "Fuck her. If she wants me to clean up, then she can tell me herself. And I want to talk to my sister Rianne." *Or murder her.*

Not that she could help me, but my curiosity was boring a hole into me, and I wanted answers. I had to know if she wasn't human anymore. Not that I could reverse the process or do anything to help her. As many times as I'd tried to reason with my stubborn sister, she never listened. I was smoking dope if I thought she would now. I'd asked Noah several questions on the way here, and my asshole cousin only laughed and followed up by saying, "All will be revealed soon enough."

I rubbed that pesky knot on my lower back. "How long have I been here?" With no phone, watch, or clock in the minimalistic room, I had no idea.

"About ten hours. Give or take," he said.

Sam had to be close to arriving at the ranger's station. Unless the fucking storm delayed flights. I didn't think Sam would drive. Flying was faster. If I knew Sam, he would take the fastest route.

"Do you know if a lady by the name of Rebekah was brought in after me?" I'd heard her yelp right before I'd run into Rianne and Noah. "What about my grandmother, Harriet Aberdeen? Is she here?" Noah had said Granny was in charge, but that didn't mean she was on-site. She could be in a hospital close by if what Sam had said was true and she'd collapsed for some reason. Heart attack, hopefully.

Barnes studied me, seemingly debating whether he should tell me all the secrets inside these walls.

I gave him a sad smile, hoping he was the type to feel sorry for me.

He had opened his mouth to speak when footsteps clamored in the hall.

Rianne marched in like a soldier ready for war.

Let the games begin.

No matter how tired, angry, depressed, and worried I was, it was time to do battle with words rather than fists. Or maybe fists would come later.

Regardless, my jaw hit the floor as the air left my lungs.

She had a dagger in her hand and was pointing it at me. "If you scream, I'll gut that baby right out of your stomach."

Barnes slid between Rianne and me, his large frame blocking me from the woman who was no longer my sister. "Ma'am, I would put that weapon away."

"Barnes, get the fuck out," Rianne barked.

The giant, who looked as if he spent his free time lifting weights and taking steroids, crossed his bulky arms over his broad chest. "Not happening. I don't take orders from you."

"I'll handle Carly." She sidestepped him, but he swiped the dagger from her, then her gun.

She bared her teeth but kept her mouth shut.

I had to hand it to her—she had some female balls. Barnes could squash her in an instant. Then again, she was an

Aberdeen, so she was headstrong and didn't take crap from anyone.

"I'll be right outside." He regarded me with soft hazel eyes, then he closed the door behind him.

A vicious silence filled the room.

I needed to thank Barnes even though he was operating on orders from Carly. Still, I suspected the man had a heart. Or maybe he didn't agree with what Intech was doing. Gary had been desperate for the money to pay medical bills for his son. Maybe Barnes was faced with something similar.

She stood just inside the door with her feet shoulder width apart and hands behind her back, outfitted in a uniform consisting of a white golf shirt with her last name sewn in red on the left side of her chest. She wore black leggings tucked inside her spit-shined military boots, and she'd shaved her head. Her long wavy brown locks were history. Our mom would cry if she saw Rianne now. She wasn't the same person I'd grown up with. I guessed I wasn't either.

She angled her head, studying me as though I was the most interesting person on earth to her, which I couldn't possibly be. "Tell me how your scream knocks people out."

I snorted. "Don't know." In truth, I really didn't. Dr. Vieira and I suspected the babies were giving me magical powers. Like hell I was about to share that with her.

She cupped her hands in front of her. "Is it because of Mom's vampire lineage?"

I picked at dirt in my nails. Upon closer inspection, I was filthy. My hands looked like I'd been digging for a bone.

"Maybe," I said, though considering witches were part of our history, that might be a reason as well. "You look pretty." Bald head or not, Rianne was beautiful. Her new look, if she was still human, brought out her high cheekbones and big brown eyes.

She flinched at my compliment. "And you look horrible," she was quick to add in a condescending tone.

Her crass jab at my appearance should've made me angrier than I already was, but I didn't have the energy to attack back. "Why am I here, Rianne?" I was pretty sure I knew, but I wanted to hear her say it. "You and Granny must know you can't brainwash me into jumping on board with your sick plan."

She snapped to attention, her brown eyes flashing with challenge as if to say, *I dare you to cross me.* "You're here to refresh your memory about why the Aberdeens have killed bloodsuckers for centuries. You'll see that what we're doing is good for humanity."

Fuck me. Talk about brainwashed. Rianne was so far gone.

Using her finger, she twirled an imaginary circle around my stomach. "But that thing throws a wrench into our plans." The repulsion in her tone had me balling my hands into fists in my lap.

"Sis, aren't you stoked that you're about to be an aunt?" I couldn't help my sarcasm.

Her jaw tightened. "If it were up to me, I would carve that demon out of your stomach."

The interesting response led me to think that maybe Granny wouldn't touch me. Why not ask? "Are you saying Granny wants her grandkid to be born?" No way was I clueing her in that I was having quadruplets.

She flicked her chin at the T-shirt and pajama bottoms next to me, ignoring my question. "Change into those clothes."

I plastered on a smug grin. "What I'm wearing is just fine. I won't be here long."

Her nostrils flared. "You think you're smart enough to escape? Or are you banking on that bastard of a boyfriend to rescue you?"

"Sam doesn't know where I am." I was lying, of course. Sam and the SEALs needed the element of surprise.

"He will." Her ego sprouted as she puffed out her chest. "He'll come freely when the time is right. You and I know he'll do anything to save you and now that thing in your stomach."

I raised an eyebrow while shivers blanketed my body. "When is the right time?" I didn't want to know the answer, and yet I did.

"When both of us are reborn," she said so easily and with excitement in her tone.

The hairs along my arms stiffened, and a sudden pain gripped my chest at the reference to *us*, which meant I was included. Yet she could be using the whole reborn thing as a scare tactic, since she'd given me the impression a moment before that Granny or maybe Carly didn't want to touch me because I was pregnant.

Nevertheless, I couldn't bank on what-ifs. While I waited for Sam, it was more important than ever to find an ally like Barnes to help me. I could use my pregnancy as a way to coax him to help. He seemed like he cared.

"You want to look like Noah?" I asked.

She crossed her arms over her chest. "Fuck no. But I won't. And neither will you. Our DNA markers show signs of vampires in our bloodline. Granny is confident that we will make the change seamlessly, won't resemble Noah, and will have more abilities than he does."

I belted out a laugh. "In whose universe do you think we can become an exact replica of someone like Sam? We might have similarities to the bloodsuckers in our genetic makeup, but we don't carry the gene."

Rianne mashed her lips into a thin line. "You're not the scientist here."

I could speak for myself though. I didn't carry the gene, according to the tests run by Dr. Vieira. I wasn't sure about Rianne or even Jordyn. As siblings, we shared about fifty percent of the same genetic coding. And just because I had the right blood type to get pregnant by a vampire, that didn't mean Rianne and Jordyn did. Truth be told, Rianne and Jordyn had more traits from our mother —brown hair and eyes and the same shaped nose. As for me, I resembled my dad with auburn hair, blue eyes, and freckles. If I was a gambler like my uncle Ray had been, I would bet Jordyn and Rianne probably had more of the vampire DNA markers than me.

"You said Granny is confident about your foray into monsterhood. Does Carly agree?"

She sneered. "Carly will do what Adam tells her."

Rianne and Carly didn't appear to see eye to eye. I might be able to use that to my advantage.

"Once you go down that route, there's no turning back. You'll never be human again. Are you sure that's what you want?" I asked in an even tone.

She stuck out her chin, that defiant side of her rearing its ugly head. "I've never wanted anything more. Think about it, sis. Immortality. Powers to control the weather." She waved her hand at the window. "The ability to compel someone. The list goes on. But the best part? I would have the power and strength to fight Sam on an even playing field."

I rolled my eyes. "Why do you hate Sam so much?"

Revulsion swam in the deep depths of her brown eyes. "Hate is too weak a word to describe how I feel about that asshole vampire." Disgust was stamped on every word. "He doesn't deserve you. You're too good for someone like him." Her voice softened. "That day he compelled me into a vegetative state, I vowed I would kill him. Then, after I found out you slept with him, I knew I'd lost you, and that only confirmed what I needed to do."

I could feel my eyebrows squishing together. "But you came around after he saved your life from the explosion at our rental house. If I remember correctly, you even threw yourself at Sam and thanked him." My voice hitched.

"None of that changes the way I feel about him. But if we're laying our cards out on the table, then here's the truth." She flashed a softer look my way. "I loved you once, Layla. I would've died for you. You, me, and Jordyn could've changed the world. But you and Jordyn and your desire to live with and fuck vampires is wrong. Jordyn's excitement to work alongside the Vampire Navy SEALs was revolting. While you were sick, she wouldn't shut up about them. She kept talking about Sam like he was a god and saying how you were in love with him. And when Noah overheard Jordyn one day, he went nuts. So I told him everything. Noah didn't brainwash me. Granny isn't doing that either. I am my own person. You and Jordyn go against everything the Aberdeen name stands for. It's just wrong for you to love a vampire." Her face had turned red.

The more we argued, the more a nagging pain in my chest intensified. "If you had known Mom's family history while she was alive, would you have murdered her?"

Granny and Uncle Ray would have, although maybe not my uncle Jack. He hated bloodsuckers as much as Rianne, but Jack wasn't the type to kill a family member. If he had it in him to do just that, then he would've tried to end my life. As for my dad, I would never believe he could or would have laid one finger on the woman he loved. He might have struggled with her history, but there was no way he would have killed her.

She stuck out her chin. "But she isn't alive."

I blew out a breath, hoping to ease the chest pain. "That's not an answer."

A strained silence bounced between us.

The adrenaline that had kept me on my feet was gone. I was beginning to feel extremely tired, my sore muscles throbbed, and the spasm in my lower back was competing with a new one in my neck. Above all else, I missed Sam terribly.

"Here's one for you," she said. "As long as you're with that bloodsucker, you'll never be my sister. And you can't have that baby. The world doesn't need another Mason. They have too much power and arrogance, and I'm going to stop that."

I was stuck on *you can't have that baby*. "You want to kill an innocent unborn child? Because it's Sam's?" I flew at her and got in her face. "Over my dead body." I would become the Queen of Death if she or anyone dared to try.

She practically pressed her nose into mine. "Save your energy, sister. You and I will have our chance in the ring. But first, you're going to witness my rebirth. I want you to see a phoenix rising from the ashes. It's time the Aberdeens ruled humanity. It's time to show the vast population of bloodsuckers that they can't kill humans for sport or hunger. Either they bow down to us or we eat them for breakfast. Once my rebirth is complete, I'll watch yours. Afterward, we'll be sisters again, fighting side by side."

Rage definitely drove people to do horrifying and unspeakable acts, and I wasn't immune. I was also like Rianne in many ways, letting my ego and fury take control.

She barely blinked when I grasped her throat with both hands and squeezed until her face turned deep red. "Fuck waiting for our chance in the ring. You need a wake-up call, sister. You see, anyone who tries to touch this baby will die a slow death. You think my scream is the only surprise I have up my sleeve? Think again." I didn't have any other abilities that I knew of, but my ego was having a field day. "And if Carly tries to inject me with that crazy juice, I'll be the one burning down this facility." Boy, I was talking through my ass—but that swirling ball of energy was wreaking havoc in my stomach, and I felt alive. It was like someone had shot a high dose of epinephrine into my arm.

She struggled to pry my hands from her throat as her brown eyes bugged out of their sockets.

I knew I wouldn't win this round, but it sure felt fucking good to see her sweat until the pain in my chest sharpened to pinpoints and stole the air from my lungs.

I stumbled backward as the room spun, and panic set in.

I opened my mouth to scream for help, but nothing came out.

Rianne choked, then called my name.

I shook my head, pressing my hands into my chest as my heart beat wildly fast. The pain was beyond anything I'd ever felt before.

"Barnes!" Rianne shouted as she helped me to the bed. "Breathe, Layla."

I pointed to my chest. "I think—" Tears streamed down my face.

Barnes loomed over me. "Rianne, alert Carly. Now!" He lifted me into his arms.

As he carried me out, I barely whispered, "Tell Sam I love him."

A bright light flashed, then darkness pulled me under.

15

SAM

I sat in the passenger seat of the rented SUV while my father drove. I glanced past Dane in the back seat and out the window behind him. The headlights slashed through the rain as Tripp, Olivia, and Ben followed behind us.

The storm raged outside the windshield. Since I'd talked to Layla well over twelve hours ago, I hadn't been able to think, stay in one spot, or breathe well. It felt like an eternity since I'd seen her in the exam room in the ER. I prayed like a motherfucker that she was okay and waiting for me at the ranger's station.

Once she was back in my arms and safely on base, she wasn't leaving, at least not until the babies were born. I was barely keeping my shit together. Webb and Tripp almost had to tie me down after I'd spoken to Layla.

Webb had been in commander mode, wanting to look at maps and shit. *Fuck that.*

Dane tried to stop me from jumping in my Jeep. "You're in no shape to drive, bloodsucker," he'd said in an even tone.

How he'd been so calm when his brother was probably strapped to a table with a collar around his neck and the stupid device on his head that programmed the chip was beyond me. Granted, Ross might be able to break free like Dane and I had, but Layla didn't have any powers other than her banshee scream. For the short term, that ability might give her a head start but not if she, too, was lying on a table.

Man, she's at the ranger's station. You have to stay positive. Believe.

I would be able to do that if we'd left as soon as I'd hung up with Layla. But bad luck was the name of the game. Of all fucking days, the plane had mechanical issues. Not to mention the storm of the century. The pilot warned us against taking off. I would've agreed with him if it wasn't Layla's life on the line. My one true fear was plummeting from the sky in a metal tube. Vampires might be immune to a bunch of things, but burning alive wasn't one of them.

So my father, Dane, Tripp, Ben, Olivia, and I had suited up with parachutes in the event we had to bail. To make matters worse, Doc and Peter argued with Webb to sideline me because of the chip. I had the same concerns, but again, nothing would stop me from rescuing my future wife and the mother of my children. If Peter was right and the chip had a self-destruct mode, then so be it. At least I would die knowing I did everything I could to save Layla.

The final decision came down to my father, and he knew better. He also knew that if the tables were turned, he wouldn't allow anyone to stand in his way. As far as Dane went, he didn't work for us, and there was no stopping him from saving his brother, although we couldn't say for sure if Ross had been kidnapped by Roman or Intech. The diner didn't have any cameras to speak of.

My dad gave me a sidelong glance from the driver's seat. "Son, you have to promise you won't do anything until we can assess what we're up against."

"We already know," I snapped. "If Layla isn't at the ranger's station, Pops, I'm going to find her." We devised a tentative plan on the plane, but before we engaged, we always scouted out the area in the event we had to adjust, which sometimes happened.

Sawyer's tech team had done a bang-up job of locating Intech's location, or rather the colossal landmark, on satellite. We were a hundred percent certain that the thirteen acres comprising buildings, two greenhouses, and a mansion set apart from the rest and surrounded by a brick wall belonged to Intech. The good news—mountains surrounded the property on three sides, which meant no neighbors to worry about. Bad news—the facility was heavily guarded.

We had a skeleton team with us since we were down so many men. We'd lost Lane. Viking II hadn't returned yet from Cleveland. Hawk and Petty Officer Dawson weren't ready for a full-blown mission, and a sensitive one at that. Kraft was still in the Catskills, our other seasoned SEAL was on a scouting assignment, and the one person we desperately needed had stayed behind. Webb wanted to be close to Jo and Abbey in case Roman was watching the naval base.

"Your father's right," Dane said from the back seat. "We can't rush in until we see with our own eyes how many guards there are and confirm the layout and ensure we have a solid plan, as we'd discussed on the plane. I want my brother out of there, but if I'm dead, I'm no good to him."

I hated that he was right. Layla needed me alive. But we were getting ahead of ourselves. I had to believe Layla was waiting at the ranger's station.

Still, my mouth hadn't caught up with my brain. "I want to knock your lights out right about now. I want a rain check on our sparring session."

"Fine by me," Dane said. "Look, man. Hatred aside, we have to be more strategic than ever."

That was just it. I wasn't a strategist. That award went to Olivia. She was even better than Webb, who was a mastermind at plotting and planning. I was more tactical, or as Olivia had once told me, I was an executioner. So I knew what I needed to do—execute, murder, and burn down anything in my way.

The dashboard lights illuminated my father's strong jaw. "Son, we'll bring Layla and my grandchildren home. I don't care if we have to burn our way in."

As an empath, I could feel the love pouring off him as well as his anger, sadness, and worry. He and I *were* father and son, for sure. My temperament wasn't any different. I'd bitten off heads since Layla went missing. Yet the word grandchildren and the conviction in his voice made me want to bawl like a boy who'd lost his mother. *Fuck.* I'd done that very thing when my mom died but not in front of anyone—not even Jo. I'd held her while she'd cried for days on end. It was then that I'd learned I had to be the strong one. I had to protect her from asshole foster dads and bullies at school.

I'd blamed my father for the hell Jo and I had been through in foster care. His reasoning: the foster system was the best place to hide from our former enemy Edmund Rain, who had been hunting Jo and me for the same reason as Intech—to study our DNA. But I couldn't change the past, and he and I had worked out our differences. I was certain he would be a devoted grandfather and protector to my children.

My dad put two hands on the wheel. "So be strong for Layla, son," he said, reading my mind. Normally, my dad had to be touching the person to read his mind but not when it came to Jo and me.

I stared out the windshield, the wipers swishing back and forth at high speed. The coordinates that shifter Rebekah had texted to Jordyn's phone were leading us down a dark two-lane mountain road. But the torrential rain was making it difficult to see three feet in front of us. Thankfully, my sharp vampire vision still worked. My hearing wasn't back to normal yet. Peter thought it would return once the chip shifted again—if it did.

We were about a mile from the ranger's station. My nerves were making me jittery. I was tempted to jump out and scour the area or do anything to keep my mind from spiraling into a tornado of darkness. As it was, an anxious clawing scratched my insides. I couldn't pinpoint why. The only good news so far had been hearing Layla's voice and knowing she was alive. The rest of the day had gone to hell.

I shoved my hands through my hair, then checked my cell. The signal fluctuated from two bars to three. Nevertheless, we were prepared with all our gear—sat phones, computers, weapons, night goggles, a supply of blood, and the special antidote Dr. Vieira had developed to counteract certain sedatives. It hadn't worked on the ketamine that Carly had used in the drug-filled darts. However, I believed the antidote blocked gelsemium, another drug that she'd used to stop my elemental powers from working.

My phone buzzed with Victor's name flashing on screen. I hit the speaker button. "Any word from Nathan Dupont?"

We weren't sure of the connection between Roman and the Duponts or what their role was with Intech. One thing we knew for sure was that Roman's endgame was Abbey.

"Sadly, yes." Victor's baritone voice thundered in the cab of the SUV. "Nathan is dead, and Sierra is missing. Carmen found Nathan's bludgeoned body in his study early this morning. I learned that Roman and Nathan had worked together many years ago at a pharmaceutical company. Send me your location. I'm coming to help. I can't stand by and wait for news on my grandson. This shit has to stop."

No lie there. But if my father thought I was a wild card, Victor was worse. Five years ago, when his grandson Matthew had been human and taken by Edmund Rain, Victor had gone psycho. He'd joined our fight to hunt down Edmund and my uncle Patrick. When we finally had Edmund cornered, Victor became a madman. He'd wielded his sword like a baseball batter swinging for the fence, primed to slice off Edmund's head. But our formidable enemy had been one step quicker. Edmund had dived through a window and disappeared. Nevertheless, Victor was a warrior centuries old and had fought in battles where he'd been one of a handful left standing.

My father eyed my phone. "Victor, do me a favor. I need you there. Take your men and Carmen and head to the naval base. Your daughter is there anyway. We're down soldiers. And I would feel comfortable knowing I have a warrior such as yourself helping to protect our civilians and military. The council will owe you. Can you do that for us?"

He growled through the phone. "Fine. I want updates. I'll have my plane fueled and ready to go if need be." Then he hung up.

The sign we'd just passed indicated that the ranger's station was up ahead. I gnawed on the inside of my cheek, my stomach in knots, excitement holding steady. Just minutes away from seeing

Layla, her gorgeous face, ball-squeezing blue eyes, and a smile that always made my heart fill with love. I couldn't wait to wrap her in my arms and inhale her cherry scent that promised passionate nights and smelled like home.

I tapped my foot on the floorboard. "We could use Victor's sword skills."

"He's even more quick-tempered than you, son. I don't need that right now."

Victor was exactly what we needed, but I didn't press the issue.

All of us were wound tight, especially my dad. He hadn't had a chance to breathe since the chaos at the hospital. He'd been on the firing line with reporters. His response to them had been, "Until I can assess the situation, I have no comment."

But the media and what had happened was the least of our worries. Humanity was in crisis. If we didn't do something about Intech, the world as we knew it would be a dark and dangerous place. First, though, Layla was all that mattered. Once she was safe, then I would do whatever I could to take out Intech, Roman, and Harriet Aberdeen.

My father flipped on the blinker, braking as he finally wheeled into the ranger's station. The minute he slowed, I jumped out into the pouring rain, sharpening my senses, scanning, sniffing, and listening, even though that particular sharp sense was broken for the moment. The rain sounded like a chorus of chaos, and if I had my normal vampire hearing, it would be possible to detect even the faintest of sounds over Mother Nature.

I marched over to the only car in the lot. The Toyota Highlander was empty save for a blanket, a cooler, and a duffel bag that sat on the back seat.

Tripp pulled in alongside my father, both cars shining high beams on the dark and eerie building. An ominous prickle skated along my spine. Something wasn't right.

My fangs slid out, my eyes flashing silver, and my elemental powers on the brink of competing with the thunder and lightning. This was the perfect weather to strengthen my abilities.

Dane sidled up to me. "I only hear one heartbeat. Whoever's inside is in distress."

With quick movements, I wrenched open the door, tearing it off its hinges. The second I crossed the threshold, the scent of blood pierced my nostrils.

Motherfucker.

Absolute panic hurtled through me. "Layla," I called, even though the scent hanging in the air smelled like a wet dog.

Dane flicked on a switch, and the two-room office space was bathed in light—a desk, a couch, pamphlets scattered on a table, and a blood trail that led to what the sign on the door indicated was the bathroom.

"Layla," I called again, my heart about to punch through my ribs as I hauled ass into the bathroom.

I shook my head, blinked, and focused on the unconscious naked woman who wasn't Layla.

Dane pulled me out of the doorway. "Move."

I stumbled back as my mind scrambled like eggs in a frying pan. Where the fuck was my baby mama?

Dane carried the woman out and set her on the striped couch. Her dog scent told me she was Rebekah or another shifter, at least. Unless the ranger was a shifter. But we'd already learned the ranger was a he and not a she.

After Rebekah had given me the coordinates, Sawyer's team pulled up everything on the area—cabins, camping sites, homes, businesses, and all the background information on the ranger. Sometimes the internet had outdated information, so Wyman had called to confirm our findings.

Dane shrugged out of his jacket and covered her. Then he removed the towel from around her thigh and inspected the wound. "The bullet is still in there."

His claws emerged before he stuck his thumb and forefinger into the hole and dug out the bullet. Blood oozed out but immediately began to congeal. He tossed the slug onto the floor, then rewrapped the towel around her leg as her eyes fluttered open.

She swung her gold eyes from me to Dane, then back to me. "Which one of you is Sam?"

Dane stabbed a thumb in my direction. "Bloodsucker."

She sat up, wincing. "I'm Rebekah. I'm so sorry. They took Layla." She touched the wound on her leg. "We were outnumbered. And after I shifted, I spotted a gunman with his rifle trained on her. I was close to attacking him when I got shot. I managed to circle around to the spot where I'd left Layla, but it was too late. She was surrounded by another man with a rifle and two others—a woman and a guy named Noah. I didn't see their faces. But the woman told Noah to take Layla to Carly. She's the scientist Layla told me about, right? I think those people also kidnapped my brother."

Well, Carly was alive. One question out of the way.

"I assume that's why you're here," I said. "If so, where's your unit?"

"I called my captain before Layla and I left the cabin. My unit is on the way," she said. "I took time off when my brother's pack got worried about him. I tracked him to these parts."

My dad rushed in out of the rain. "Layla here?"

I didn't have to answer. I shoved both hands through my hair and yanked on the strands. Otherwise, I would be unleashing my wrath. I needed to save every ounce of energy for my enemies.

He was reading my mind as he growled.

Tripp, Olivia, and Ben came in, loaded down with bags and gear. They each took one look around, and horror washed over them.

Then Tripp began barking orders. "We need to go through our plan one more time. Before we do, Olivia and Ben, suit up. It's time to take a ride to Intech and do some scouting. The rest of us will set up our gear."

Ben clapped me on the shoulder, pity steeped in his reddish-brown eyes. "Sorry, dude. We'll get her back."

I didn't need sympathy. I wanted them angry as hell. I knew they would have their soldier hats on once we were in position.

Olivia gave me a nod, then said to Ben, "Move, hybrid." She was one of our better scouts. Ben wasn't far behind.

I returned my attention to Rebekah. "Was Layla okay when she was with you? The babies? She was in a van that crashed." I needed something to keep me sane.

Rebekah batted her pitiful golden gaze at me. "When I found Layla on the porch of my cabin, she was super pale, tired, and hungry. I examined her. The babies' hearts are beating. All four of them. She tried my blood, then spit it out, but she's a strong woman, Sam."

Layla certainly was. My concern wasn't for her stamina but over the fuckwads like Harriet. If Carly was alive, then why wasn't she answering her phone? She'd been the one to give me her number for some odd reason.

I fished out my cell from my cargo pants and called her again. The line rang once, then her voice mail picked up. "Carly, why the fuck did you give me your number if you're not going to answer? This is Sam." After I left my number, I hung up.

The jaws of life had its teeth around my neck. "I need some air. I'm not going far, Pops. I promise." I had time, since Ben and Olivia were investigating the scene before the shit hit the fan.

He nodded, then opened a telepathic connection. *Son, clear your head. I want you focused and being the soldier you were trained to be. Layla will need every ounce of energy you have, including your elemental powers.*

Copy that, I returned.

The storm was the perfect venue to absorb every ounce of Mother Nature that I could. I would be in tip-top shape and ready to unleash my wrath.

16

SAM

The canopy of trees provided a shield against the rain as I bounded into the woods behind the ranger's station. I settled at the edge of a cliff and looked out over the gorge as lightning flashed, followed by a rumble of thunder. I opened my arms, glancing skyward, and roared out my frustration, rage, and tension, absorbing Mother Nature in all her glory. As if the gods above had me in their scopes, a bolt of lightning zigzagged downward to touch my foot. I sucked in air as an electrical current hurtled up my legs and spread throughout my body, making me shake harder than the highest magnitude earthquake.

"Give me all you got!" I shouted to the gods.

As if my wish was their command, another bolt hit in front of my feet. This time, the charge spread out through the forest floor, the earth rumbling beneath me.

The wind howled, blowing leaves and snapping branches. The smell of wet pine and moist earth floated around me. Then, for a mere second, the rain slowed, and the ringing of my phone echoed in the night.

My eyes widened at the caller ID on my screen. "Carly

Aberdeen," I said her name as I answered. "If you so much as touched Layla——"

"Save your threats, Sam," she volleyed back, irritation in her tone coming through loud and clear. "I don't have much time. When you called, I was talking to Junior. He told me you were in the area. Not surprised about that either. In fact, Adam and the others, especially Rianne and Harriet, were banking on your arrival, although not this soon."

"That bastard," I mumbled. There went the element of surprise.

"Junior is helping you. So save your disdain for my husband." She said the word *husband* as if she was proud of Junior.

"There's a greenhouse outside the lab building on the northwest corner of the property. It's 9:00 p.m. Meet me there at ten thirty sharp. The only way in is over the wall. The cameras sweep the area every five minutes. You won't have much time."

I wasn't concerned about cameras. Wyman, the great hacker that he claimed to be, would be our ace in the hole when it came to shutting down the power.

"Where's Layla?" I demanded, gritting my teeth.

"I'll be frank," Carly said. "I didn't sign up to use pregnant women. Layla doesn't belong in this fight, Sam. She almost coded. Her heart is weak."

Dizziness hit me faster than a plane at Mach speed. Carly wasn't pulling my leg either. I could hear the urgency in her tone. "Did you inject her with whatever the fuck it is you're whipping up?" My nerves went haywire as nausea crept into my throat.

"No," she said emphatically. "I've managed to stabilize her. She needs the help of your vampire experts. If I'm correct, she's carrying a nonhuman. That and the stress of what she's been through the last few days has caught up with her. I'll do what I can to help you get her out of here. I would bring her to you, but Harriet, Rianne, and Noah are hovering."

A savagery that I'd packed away in childhood rose from the depths of my soul, provoking the beast who'd been dormant for many years.

Growling, I stomped my foot on the ground, calling Mother Nature to fill me to the brim once more. The earth shook, trees swayed, and the energy thrashed about like a caged animal struggling to get free so that it could hunt down Harriet, Rianne, and Noah and annihilate them.

"Sam, are you still there?" Carly asked. "I promise, Layla is fine. Do you want my help or not?"

"She'd better be the fuck okay," I bit out. "And I don't *need* your help. Have you forgotten what I can do?"

"You do need me." Her voice sizzled with confidence. "You have a chip in your head. I can make sure it doesn't engage."

I believed her about Layla but not so much about the chip—though maybe I was too outraged and not thinking clearly when it came to Layla. "Why should I believe you?" I demanded, though her answer didn't matter. One way or another, we were bringing my huntress home tonight—with Carly's help or without it.

"I've always liked Layla. And I'm trying to help you, Sam."

"Then I also want a vampire by the name of Matthew Costner and two shifters, Ross Gray and also a recent victim of yours whose name is Tucker."

"I have no idea who those people are. They're not here," she said matter-of-factly. "Look, Sam. There are different agendas at play here. I'm not privy to everything Adam, Roman, or Harriet have up their sleeves. I have to go."

"Wait. One more question: Why did you slip me your phone number?"

"Because I need you, and I knew your curiosity would get the better of you. I didn't have a chance to add my name to the note because Adam came in. I'd cut the feed to the cameras in the glass room, so he thought something happened."

"Need me? For what? More of my DNA? And if you were certain I would call, why shut off your phone?"

"A story for another day, Sam. Time is ticking away. Ten thirty sharp." Then she was gone.

I was inside the ranger's station in a flash and practically nose to nose with Rebekah. "Why didn't you tell me Layla's heart is weak?"

Dane pulled me away from the pretty shifter with the multicolored hair. No longer naked, she was now dressed in army fatigues.

Rebekah pushed off the desk she'd been leaning against. "Layla's heart was fine when I examined her. I promise."

Tripp and my father surrounded me as I glared at Rebekah.

"What happened, son?" my father asked, placing a hand on my chest and urging me to take a step backward.

Growling through a sigh, I crossed my arms over my chest. "Carly called. Layla almost coded. Her heart is weak. Layla's stable for now. Carly wants me to meet her at the greenhouse outside the lab building at ten thirty." I regarded Dane and Rebekah, who stood next to each other by the desk. "Carly says Ross and Tucker aren't there."

Confusion crossed Dane's face. "Then Roman has Ross. Fuck!"

Rebekah's expression matched Dane's.

"Carly did say there are different agendas going on," I added. "Ten thirty is too fucking long to wait." I wanted to blow the roof off the ranger's station as desperation and fury commingled into an explosive energy ticking away inside me.

Tripp went over to his laptop and pulled up a satellite image of the facility. "If Carly is helping, we need to revise our plan slightly."

"Son, are you sure you believe Carly, and it's not a ploy to barricade you behind those cement walls?"

"She's telling the truth, Pops. I heard the urgency in her voice. Look, it doesn't matter if she is jerking my chain. We have a strategy. We keep to it, and as Tripp said, we can adjust slightly. I'll scale the wall. Go in quietly. Once I'm in, I'll give you the signal. We can have Rebekah communicate with Wyman on when to cut the power."

The woman was Army Special Forces, so she could do just about anything.

"I can do that," she chimed in. "I saw an all-terrain vehicle out back. We can use it to chauffer Layla once you get her out. Unless you have another way."

"That's a great idea," Tripp said from where he was sitting in front of his computer at the table adjacent to the desk. "As it stands, our vehicles will be a good distance from entry points. You can transport Sam and Layla to one of the vehicles."

"That frees up Ben to team up with Olivia," I said. "Tripp, you can take me to the drop-off location before you get in position." Tripp and I were supposed to cover one exit along the wall. We'd strategized on the plane ride, and the original plan was to blow each of the exit sites just as Wyman cut the power. Which would still happen, but not until I was inside.

"Basically, you'll have a head start," Tripp said to me. "Maybe luck is on our side tonight."

I sure as fuck hoped so.

My dad was texting on his phone when it rang, and he answered. "Webb, anything wrong?" he asked. A muscle ticked in his jaw. "You think they're headed here. We'll keep an eye out. Talk to you soon." He lowered his cell. "Junior and Jordyn are gone. Webb thinks they're on their way here."

"I agree," I added. "Carly talked to Junior before she called me. I'm sure Junior is dying to see his wife." I couldn't blame him as long as he wasn't leading Jordyn into the hands of her grandmother.

"If they are," Tripp said, "they won't be here for hours, since they're driving, so we need to stay focused on the mission."

My dad nodded in agreement as he gripped my shoulder. "Son, if Carly fails and your chip engages, you have to fight with everything you have not to allow it to pull you under." Worry was evident in his green eyes.

"I got this, Pops." My tone was confident until I remembered what else the chip could do—self-destruct. *Boom.* My brain would be burnt toast.

17

LAYLA

I woke to bright lights and an uncomfortable silence. I had an IV in me, electrodes stuck to my chest, and a blood pressure cuff around my right bicep. I was dressed in the T-shirt and pajama bottoms Barnes had brought into my room, and the only sign that I'd wandered the muddy forest terrain was the dirt beneath my nails.

After a quick glance around, I gulped in air and flew into a sitting position. Blood was splattered on the white sheets covering the row of empty beds across the aisle and on each side of me. As if that was the spark to light the fire, the inferno in my throat came to life. I needed to sate my craving like an alcoholic needed a drink. I rubbed my throat and swished saliva around in my mouth, but it was no use. I couldn't focus on that right now though. The important obstacle in front of me was to find a way out of this godforsaken place, especially when the conversation between Rianne and me came soaring back.

You can't have that baby. After we're reborn, we'll be sisters again.

Fear and panic seized my breath. I whipped my gaze to the IV bag and the yellowish liquid inside. *Oh my fucking word.* Surely, they didn't inject me with the crazy juice. Normally, there was clear saline in IV bags.

Inhale. Exhale. Breathe, girl. Think. Run. Do something other than lie there.

I ripped the needle from the back of my hand as terror had me laboring for breath. I tore the rest of the medical crap from my body and examined myself, feeling my face and checking for fangs. As far as I could tell, I was still human.

On a long sigh, I refocused and hiked my gaze from one end of the spacious room to the other. Aside from the beds, IV stands, and heart monitors, I counted two exits. Where was Carly? Rianne? Hell, even my grandmother? Or Noah, for that matter.

My pulse pounded in my ears as the stillness in the large space seemingly echoed, pounded, and crawled along my skin, giving me the vibe that they'd left me for dead. Maybe the concoction had done something to me, and I only had hours to live. After all, the bloodstained sheets on the empty beds gave me the impression that the patients had bled to death.

I jumped up and stumbled, grabbing the IV pole to catch my fall. The dizziness came out of nowhere. I took in slow and steady breaths, zeroing in on the far wall. Sometimes looking past my immediate surroundings helped rid me of the spinzies, as my mom liked to call them anytime my sisters and I were dizzy. I blinked to orient my vision, and a door with an exit sign came into focus.

Freedom. That word packed an excited punch, my pulse racing like a greyhound at a dog track. Time to blow this joint. I put one foot in front of the other and was skirting the bottom of the bed when the door squeaked open. I froze, afraid to look, afraid to move. Afraid freedom was a pipe dream and I would never see Sam or my sister Jordyn again. I heaved out a ragged breath and saw Rianne sprinting toward me.

I laughed only to keep my nerves from making me pass out. Well, that and at the fury on Rianne's face. She was probably mad that I'd almost strangled her to death. Or maybe Sam was in the building, and she was about to finally do as my vision had warned—

kill my babies to punish him, since she believed the only way to see Sam suffer would be to hurt me.

That panic I felt a minute ago turned into rage followed by the familiar fluttering and swirling sensation right before I unleashed a banshee scream. I opened my mouth—but nothing came out. Instead, an electrical charge zipped down my arms and vanished when my gaze danced past Rianne.

My grandmother bounded into the room behind Rianne as if she was chasing her. Maybe she was trying to stop Rianne from doing something stupid. Or Harriet Aberdeen had come to her senses. Nah—miracles didn't happen in my family.

Rianne skidded to a halt, breathing fire like a dragon about to burn me to ash. She dug her nails into my arm. "When will you ever learn?"

My gaze took a slow hike down to her waist to the dagger on her hip. "I should be asking you that question." Then I remembered her panic right before I passed out. She'd sounded as if she didn't want me to die. Maybe I was imagining things, though the dichotomy of her emotions was telling me my sister was still in that brain of hers. The sister who loved me. The one who would've died for me.

Don't get your hopes up.

"You're not ready." She quickly looked at something beside the bed.

I took the opportunity to grab the dagger, ignoring whatever the fuck she meant by that statement.

The little witch was quicker, and her hand went around my neck. "Nice try." She scraped the tip of the blade across my cheek. "We are going to have so much fun when we're reborn."

Then my brain began to understand what she'd meant by saying I wasn't ready. I couldn't panic. Not yet anyway.

That feeling of electricity in my arms vibrated again as I choked out a laugh. "Go ahead, Rianne—kill me now." If that yellowish liquid was the crazy juice, then I was already dead.

Still, I knew she had the female balls to drive the dagger into me. But she wouldn't. She was too overly excited for us to be reborn together—to rekindle our relationship.

"Where's the fun in that?" she asked. "Sam isn't here to see you suffer."

Nope. Evil Rianne Aberdeen is still in that pea-size brain.

My grandmother pried Rianne's hand from my throat. "Girls, there'll be plenty of time to see who will lead my army."

She'd been lingering and watching, taking mental notes, no doubt. Or maybe seeing my stomach had her frozen in disbelief or elation. Since she'd been standing in my peripheral vision, I couldn't exactly see her expression.

Regardless, my choked laugh could be heard around the world as I whirled on sweet old Granny. "What happened to you in Fiji?" After my father passed, Harriet Aberdeen jetted off into the sunset as though she didn't give a rat's ass about her family. Then she returned home and thought we would bow down and kiss her feet. I, for one, wasn't jumping on her bandwagon.

Harriet pursed her red lips, her beady blue eyes rounding on my belly. "It seems to me, Layla, I should be asking you a similar question. Your father is rolling over in his grave right now. Pregnant by the very creature that has torn our family to shreds for centuries. I should kill you just for that."

I angled my head, wearing a patronizing smile. Granny didn't show any signs that she'd collapsed recently. In fact, she looked as if she'd just walked out of a spa. Her short reddish-gray hair was perfectly styled. Her cheeks were rosy. Her nails were well manicured and painted red. Then again, she could be dying, and no one would be the wiser. She always dressed to impress, and today wasn't any different. She wore a crisp white shirt beneath a navy-blue pants suit.

"I heard you collapsed. Are you sick, Granny?" I asked. "Is that why you're on a crusade to—" The damn light bulb switched on as I gulped in air. Noah and Rianne were brazen and stupid enough to alter their DNA. My grandmother was a lot of things, but I wouldn't call her stupid. She always had a reason for doing things. "That's why you rushed back to the States when Uncle Ray called you. You're sick. You're trying to find a way to live."

I might be talking out of my ass, but her resigned smile

confirmed that I was right. Her expression said that she was proud of me for figuring it out. I wasn't sure if my hatred toward her had changed, but there was another thing I had now for her—pity.

Rianne reared back, rounding her startled gaze on Harriet, her jaw on the floor. "You're sick?" Rianne sounded as if she'd lost her best friend.

"Now, now, Rianne," Granny said with a loving smile. "It doesn't change the goal. I still believe in fighting fire with fire. That means we stay the course with Adam Emery. The only way to rid the planet of vampires is by building an army we can control."

"Answer me!" Rianne shouted, clearly on the verge of using the dagger on our grandmother.

She ignored her belligerent granddaughter and turned to me. "You were always the intelligent one, Layla. You always saw right through people. But sadly, you missed the mark with Sam Mason."

I snorted. "No, I didn't. You're happy I'm with Sam. I mean, the stars aligned for you. You want to use me to draw Sam out. You need him if you want to find a way to become immortal without looking like Noah. I'm right, aren't I?"

My sister's nostrils were flaring rapidly, anger and hurt swishing around in her brown eyes.

I held on to the footboard. "Each of you have different motives." I flicked my chin at Rianne. "Her hatred for Sam is jealousy, so she wants to see Sam suffer because she thinks he took me away from her. And you, Granny, need to find a cure for whatever it is you have. The only one you can think of is to become immortal. As far as Carly goes, I have no idea what she's after. But as she's a scientist, I would guess it's simple curiosity. Then there's Adam Emery. He wants control. If anyone wants to build super soldiers, it's him, not you two. And you will never convince me, Granny, that you believe creating vampires is the way to kill other vampires. You're just going along with Adam because he has the resources Dand Carly to help your personal agenda."

Harriet clapped. "Bravo, Layla. But now that you're carrying Sam's baby, I don't need him."

A chill skittered up my spine. "What have you been diagnosed with?"

"A rare type of blood cancer that has no cure," she said quickly and evenly.

Rianne snapped out of her funk. "She *cannot* have that baby." She aimed the weapon at my belly.

Rage ignited inside me, causing that electrical charge I'd felt minutes ago to career down my arms and legs and encompass my entire body. It felt like a million goose bumps popping out of nowhere. Suddenly, an image of Rianne stabbing herself flashed before me.

As if I willed it so, she turned the blade inward, her hands shaking. "What's happening? I can't stop myself."

Harriet sucked in air. "First your banshee scream. Now mind control."

Her giddiness angered me, increasing my need to see Rianne bleed out.

18

LAYLA

These two women clearly shopped at a different mall—one that catered to crazy people who needed to be in straitjackets. But I could somewhat understand Harriet's reasons for what she was trying to do, although I didn't agree. On the other hand, Rianne was pathetic, letting her ego cloud her judgment.

"Layla, she's your sister. Snap out of it." My grandmother shook me. "Layla." Her voice hitched.

The blade was barely a half inch from Rianne's throat when someone behind me screeched, sounding like nails on a chalkboard.

I blinked, breaking the trance I'd been in, and the dagger clanged to the floor.

Rianne lunged at me, but my grandmother slid between us. "There will come a time and place where you and Layla can air out your differences." Harriet tugged Rianne away from me.

As far as I was concerned, Rianne was dead to me. We could never repair our relationship or trust each other again.

Carly rushed up to me, her brown eyes as big as golf balls. "What's going on? Layla, you shouldn't be out of bed."

"I shouldn't be here at all," I spat venom at my cousin-in-law. "Tell me what's in that IV bag."

Rianne laughed derisively.

Carly went over to the IV, hunching her shoulders to stare at the bag for a mere second, then she stomped over to Rianne. "What the fuck have you done? Rianne, please tell me you didn't inject Layla with that IV liquid."

Terror rolled through me, and my worst nightmare took shape.

Rianne shoved Carly. "Get out of my face. And it's Layla's time. I thought I would go first, but I want to be in my right mind to witness it when *she* changes."

Fuck me and the floor I was standing on. Talk about being an ice sculpture. I couldn't feel my limbs. I wasn't sure I could even speak. What did this mean? Would I turn into someone like Noah? Holy fuck. I would become a deformed monster. Maintaining the ability to breathe was a challenge.

My grandmother scolded Rianne, but I only heard mumbling. I was in panic mode, holding my stomach, sweat sliding down my back. My breathing became labored.

"Carly." Her name came out as a whisper. "What will happen to me and the baby?" Oh God. The babies.

My grandmother's voice catapulted to shouting at Rianne.

I was a second away from hyperventilating.

Rianne puffed out her chest, glowered at me, and marched out like a stubborn child who hadn't gotten her way. But that was her MO. She would always pout and stomp anytime Mom or Dad scolded her.

"Harriet, you were supposed to keep Rianne in check. From here on out, neither of you is permitted in this lab. If you disobey, I'll have both of you imprisoned in the dungeon."

The word *dungeon* seemed to clear the haze.

"You don't have that authority," Harriet said. "Only Adam does."

Carly rounded on my grandmother. "How blinded are you? Adam Emery is only tolerating you because of your money. But don't think for a second we can't find another investor." Her take-no-shit attitude made her seem taller than her five-foot height.

Harriet huffed, considering me. "Will Layla be okay?"

I rolled my eyes. "I'm not the cure you're looking for, Granny, so take that phony caring attitude and shove it up your ass."

If she knew I was having more than one baby, she would go to great lengths to throw me in that dungeon Carly had just spoken of until I gave birth.

"Cure?" Carly asked, her eyebrows squishing together.

Wearing an arrogant grin as if she'd already won, Harriet marched out.

Once the door snicked shut, Carly helped me to the bed.

"Please tell me I'm not about to become something like Noah," I said. The excruciating chest pains that caused me to black out were on the precipice of returning.

Carly stood in front of me, slipping her hands in the pockets of her lab coat much like Dr. Vieira did when he was about to explain something or answer a question. "The good news is—the bag isn't empty. To alter human DNA, you'll need a thousand milliliters or more of what I've developed. From my calculations, you only consumed less than five percent of the SS2. It shouldn't have any ill effects on you or the baby."

"SS2?" I asked.

She curled shorts strands of her dark hair around her ear. "Supernatural Serum. Anyway, my bigger worry is your heart. You almost coded when Barnes brought you to me." She glanced at my belly. "You look like you're four months pregnant, and I know that's not true, since I saw you five weeks ago. I'm guessing you were pregnant when you showed up at Intech in Chicago."

"I was about month along then. But that isn't my concern. What's wrong with my heart?" I rubbed my chest as if that would help lessen the panic.

"I don't mean to scare you. I'm sure the stress of what you've gone through the last few days contributed to your low blood pressure and dehydration, which led to you passing out. But... I understand the genetic makeup of the vampire species. They're human until they reach puberty and activate their recessive gene. Which means that mothers of those babies go through a normal human pregnancy. Unless you're carrying twins, which runs in your family

—then the size of your belly would make sense." She paused as if she was waiting for me to confirm or deny twins.

"And?" I tangled my hands in my lap.

She removed the stethoscope from around her neck. "A body of a pregnant woman undergoes dramatic changes. Blood volume increases forty to fifty percent, heart rate goes up ten to fifteen beats per minute, and the amount of blood pumped by the heart each minute can jump thirty to forty percent. In essence, gestational stress on the body." She rubbed her lips together. "Say, for example, your fetus is nonhuman and is growing fast, which I believe is the case. That means those numbers I just explained go up greatly, and your human body will struggle."

"What you said makes sense. But I also haven't eaten, except for a bowl of soup. I've hardly had any fluids, and you're right about the stress." I took a breath. "It's your fault, Carly. You're the master-mind behind this fucked-up scheme to create monsters like Noah. Is that what you want the world to come to?"

She swallowed, licking her lips. "I didn't sign up to test or alter a pregnant woman's DNA. In fact, I didn't recommend any of the Aberdeens as subjects. If I had my way, I would send your family packing." She sneered. "For me, this is all about the science, Layla."

I snorted out a laugh. "But you're okay with killing humans for the sake of what? A mission that will only erase humanity? All you're doing is creating monsters that you'll never be able to control."

She opened her mouth to speak.

I held up my hand. "The chip won't work, Carly. You're in over your head. Once my sister turns, you'll be her first victim unless Noah gets to you before Rianne."

She shuddered. "I know you're right. And I didn't inject Noah. He and Rianne stole a batch of the SS2. She did that to Noah."

My jaw dropped. "What about all the blood on those beds? *You* did that?"

She nodded. "I'm not innocent, Layla. I accept that. I'm a scientist who is after something far greater than I'd ever imagined." She was sounding like Dr. Frankenstein. "Ever since I began studying

Patrick Mason's notes and learned of vampires and the like, my one purpose has been and continues to be to find a way to erase the sickness that plagues humans. Think about it. What if we could find a cure for cancer or any disease? Vampires don't get sick."

My eyebrows pinched together. "That's what your motive is? I gather you know that Harriet has a rare form of blood cancer."

Her mouth parted. "I didn't know. I knew she'd collapsed, but her blood pressure had been low."

"Harriet tends to keep things to herself, although she was quite giddy about finding out I'm carrying Sam's baby. Anyway, I'm confused about one thing. If you want to find cures for diseases, why are you helping to build armies?"

She glanced around as though she was making sure no one was listening. "I don't have the money or resources. Adam does. If I help him, he helps me."

"But you were the one who set up the deal to capture Sam," I said.

"I admit that. From his uncle's notes, I understood that Sam's DNA is the key. I don't care about the chip. I was only doing what I was told. Adam knows what I'm trying to do." She pointed at the bloody sheets. "Those patients I tested were dying from cancer or another type of disease. They accepted the risks and knew what they signed up for. I have contracts to prove it."

I was blown away. Maybe she was redeemable. Sam believed she was.

"How does a shifter play into your scheme?"

"Again, from what I've learned, shifters hardly succumb to sickness. They heal quickly but not as fast as vampires. It's worth looking at their DNA makeup."

"If what you say you're doing here is true and you don't want to use me for testing, then let me go. I need Sam, Carly." Given what she'd just spilled, I figured I could share something with her that wasn't that big of a deal. She'd already put two and two together about my pregnancy—or partly anyway. "The baby needs his blood. That might be another reason I passed out."

She studied me with a quiet fascination, not responding. Instead, she finally proceeded to listen to my heart and lungs. After she finished, she hooked the medical instrument around her neck and again looked around as though we were being watched.

My pulse sped up. "Has anyone been listening to us?" Not that I'd said anything worth its weight in salt.

"No one is. I cut the wires on the cameras earlier. Your sister and grandmother are out of control, though this surprising news about Harriet makes sense of why she's here. Your sister and Noah though—they need to go. Look, I need you to stay in bed. I want you to act like everything is fine. Don't try to leave. There are guards patrolling the grounds. We have a plan."

My stomach fluttered. "You're letting me go?"

"Layla, you don't belong here. I talked to Sam."

An excited chill shook me. "Where is he?" My voice hitched.

"He's close by. You have to stay put."

She wouldn't get any argument out of me except if Rianne or Harriet returned. Knowing them, gaining my freedom might be an impossible feat.

19

SAM

I dug around in my duffel bag on the floorboard between my feet and snagged a two-ounce bottle of the special antidote Dr. Vieira had developed to counteract a sedative Edmund had used to knock out his enemies to easily abduct them. I was convinced the antidote blocked the gelsemium—the drug Carly had used on me to stop my elemental powers from working. If she was helping me, she had no reason to inject me with gelsemium. But the key word was *if*.

After I knocked back the contents of the vial, I dumped it back into my bag. "This has to work, man."

Tripp slowed as he approached the one-mile marker from Intech's facility. "It will. Like any other mission—in and out."

But this wasn't any other mission. The stakes were higher, and my mind was fucking with me. I couldn't stop worrying about Layla. For fuck's sake—her heart was weak. What did that mean? Could she not carry the babies?

Tripp wheeled off the main road and onto a narrow dirt path that wasn't wide enough for the SUV. Tree branches slapped the windshield and scratched both sides of the vehicle as he drove deeper into the forest.

I pushed out a long-suffering sigh. "I got this." I pitied anyone who got in the way of me reaching Layla.

He chuckled as he came to a stop beneath a cluster of trees. "I know you do."

I shoved both hands through my damp hair and glanced out the windshield. The storm was moving out. *Thank fuck.* Torrential rain made it difficult to see despite my excellent vamp vision. I needed the path clear without any obstacles in my way.

"A piece of advice regarding the chip," Tripp said, cutting the engine. "I know your father counseled you to fight through it. One way to do that is to concentrate on Layla's scent. That's how shifters distinguish friend from foe."

Maybe that was the reason I hadn't attacked her in my hospital room when Peter had messed with the device in his efforts to shut it down.

I filed his advice away, not wanting to linger on the topic anymore. We had twenty minutes until showtime. "I need to move." I tightened my flak vest, pressed my earpiece to make sure my comm was tucked deep inside my ear, grabbed my backpack, and jumped out.

Pine, earth, and a hint of oak carried on the light wind. Clouds slid over the moon like a slow dance on a starry night. The energy I'd absorbed from the lightning show pulsed along my arms, promising reprisal against those who wronged me or got in my way.

Tripp and I exchanged a bro hug.

"Watch your six," I said as I darted to my right while he headed straight.

Rebekah's voice came through my comm. "Sam, you're slightly off course. Turn east by an eighth of a klick, then go straight ahead. The greenhouse should be behind the wall."

"Copy that," I said into my comm.

I made the correction and took off at vampire speed. The wall came up fast. I made quick work of preparing my climbing gear. I might have immortal skills, but jumping ten feet upward wasn't one of them.

"Layla, I'm coming for you, baby doll," I said out loud before scaling over the wall.

Once on enemy grounds, I ripped off the harness, keeping an eye on the camera pointing at the three-story lab building.

I touched my ear. "I'm in. Setting my timer for fifteen. Rebekah, make sure you're in position for us."

"Copy that," she said. "Good luck."

I hurried into the greenhouse and stalked down the aisle between the rows of lush green plants with yellow flowers. "Carly," I called out in a low voice.

The petite Aberdeen emerged from around a table halfway down. She wore a dour expression as doom and gloom oozed off her in waves.

Well, fuck. "What's wrong?"

Her short shiny black hair had a blue hue beneath the moon's rays spilling in through the glass roof. "We have a problem."

Of course we did. "Fix whatever the fuck it is. I'm under a time constraint."

The power would be out momentarily, then the fireworks would begin. And once the explosions rocked the house, I was sure the sound would echo, power on or not, rousing those within a good distance—so time was limited, particularly since Wyman wasn't sure how long he could control the power company's system. We figured we had twenty minutes at most.

My fangs slid out. "Unless, of course, you lied to me." That electricity pulsing in my arms was now in my hands. I wouldn't be throwing fireballs but bolts of lightning charged with a shit ton of electricity that would kill a human in an instant.

She rolled her shoulders back. "Everything I told you is true. Except when I got off the phone with you, I learned Rianne had injected Layla—"

I had her by the throat in a flash, lifting her so her feet were dangling off the cement surface. "If you say your serum or whatever it is you're calling it, I will end you." I actually liked Carly, but I was serious. I had no problem snapping her neck. Her push and pull between good and evil would be her downfall for sure.

Her brown eyes bugged out, her pulse beating rapidly against my fingers as her fear invaded my nostrils. I lapped up every bit of it.

"I'm sorry. I had the SS2 locked up." Her voice was strained. "You know Rianne."

Rianne's name brought out the animal in me, and I growled, deep and loud.

"The power will be down in five seconds," Rebekah announced in my comm.

I released Carly from my clutches, then waved my hand down the aisle toward the door. "It's time to pay up."

Fists clenched at her side, lips pursed, Carly brushed past me.

Just as we left the greenhouse, the facility went dark, followed by a series of explosions.

Excitement and nerves swirled together. I lived for missions but was also itching to see my huntress.

Carly came to an abrupt halt. "What have you done?"

I pushed her. "You didn't think I would only rely on you. Is Roman on-site? Where's Adam?"

"They're not here." She rushed inside the lab building.

I relayed that to the team in my comm, followed by, "Heading to the target now." I flicked on a light attached to my flak vest, though I could see just fine in the darkened hallway.

"The emergency generators should turn on," Carly said over her shoulder.

"No, they won't," I returned. Dane's role was to take them out.

I held my arms at my sides as the prickly feeling began to pulse. It had been a while since I'd used an electrical charge to zap my enemy. Oh, I could burn down the building, but I wouldn't with Layla inside.

Heavy footsteps pounded in the distance, causing me to jerk my head. Did I have my vampire hearing back?

The question vanished when a man—or rather, beast—dove at Carly as she was passing the adjacent hallway that veered off from the one Carly and I were in. She hit the wall with a loud thud as air whooshed from her lungs.

The monster, tall and ugly, rose, pivoted my way, and bared his fangs.

I laughed through the shock that had me rooted to the floor, especially when claws grew out of his fingernails. "Noah Aberdeen? Is that you?"

He smirked, damn fucking proud of what he'd become.

"What are you?" He looked like a blend of vampire, shifter, and something else I couldn't put my finger on, though I'd seen someone similar. My uncle Patrick's first experimental victim—Blake Turner—had bloodred eyes as though he'd risen from the depths of hell. Noah's irises were a lighter color than Blake's, but they were ugly just the same. "You were born without a brain. Weren't you?"

He marched toward me, fists at his sides, nostrils flaring, his fangs covered in blood.

I stayed in one place. If the fucker wanted to take me on, I was more than ready. "Come on, man. You don't know what you're in for."

He smirked like he had the upper hand. Maybe he did. Maybe he had more strength and abilities than I did. Only one way to find out.

He bowed his head and charged.

Laughing, I discharged the energy writhing through me. As if he'd been tasered with fifty thousand volts, his body jerked uncontrollably before dropping to the floor.

Die, motherfucker.

Carly stared at Noah with a mixture of concern and curiosity.

I grabbed her by the arm and dragged her. "Move." We were wasting time I didn't have.

Before we entered the lab through the double doors, I could hear two heartbeats aside from Carly's.

Halle-fucking-lujah! My vamp hearing had returned. Did that mean the chip shifted? Since the power was down, I guessed I didn't need to worry about it unless someone had access to the program on a phone or tablet. The device became a distant memory when two racing pulses beat loudly in my ears. Two people breathing heavily—nervous and scared.

The moment I stepped into a room that reminded me of the one in Chicago, Layla's cherry scent wafted through the cold, stale air. My cock jerked for the first time in what felt like ages. I was ready to scoop my huntress into my arms and carry her out and away from this hellhole.

But fate wanted to fuck me sideways.

Harriet Aberdeen was holding Layla hostage with a syringe the size of a horse needle that was an inch away from her arm. Whatever was in it wasn't good.

Image after image played out like a slideshow on repeat. I saw death and destruction. Fire and brimstone. I saw Harriet Aberdeen nailed to a wall, suffering in pain and bleeding out infinitesimally slow. Rage consumed me as my fangs embedded in my bottom lip, drawing blood.

Then a disturbing and gut-wrenching thought hit me. Where the fuck was Rianne? The bitch had to be lurking in the shadows. She wouldn't miss the chance to fuck with me or take me on. Her ego was larger than Noah's, and I was curious if she'd jumped on the crazy train with him. She'd bragged that she wanted to best me, and the only way she knew how was to become a deadly creature like me.

To make matters worse, my beautiful baby mama had dark circles beneath her dull and tired electric-blue eyes. Her skin was as white as a fucking ghost, and she was dripping with sweat. Yet, she was still beautiful, especially when she delivered a smile that mended my cold black heart.

Fuck this shit. I started for Harriet. The old lady had gotten on my last nerve. What was wrong with the Aberdeens? Did they not believe in the sanctity of family?

"Sam!" Carly yelled. "Don't." She scrambled over to me. "That syringe is filled with a toxin that will kill Layla."

"The fuck," I bit out, my voice deep and caustic. "Baby doll, are you okay?"

Layla smoothed a hand down her pink pajama bottoms. "Peachy, vampire. I'm ready to go home."

Harriet snorted. "You are home."

Layla whipped her head around to look at her grandmother. She stared at Harriet for a long second. "Have you not learned yet what else I can do? Besides, you need me."

"Not if I have Sam," she said.

Suddenly, Harriet began to turn the needle on herself.

I watched in awe as words escaped me. That the babies must be helping Layla control the needle was the only reason that made sense. If I didn't believe our kids were supernatural, I sure as fuck did now.

The syringe was barely an inch from Harriet's neck, and her hand was shaking, her blue eyes swimming in fear.

Although I wasn't one to interfere with family quarrels, I also salivated to see Harriet Aberdeen six feet in the ground. But Layla shouldn't be the one to take on that burden. She would never recover.

I fled to Layla's side. "We need to go. We can deal with her later." I snatched the needle from Harriet, breaking Layla's trance. When I killed Harriet, I didn't want Layla to witness her grandmother's demise.

Harriet staggered. "Today might not be the day, but I will get what I want."

Layla tensed. "I feel sorry for you, Harriet. If I were you, I would return to Fiji and live out the short time you have left on this earth."

Harriet lunged for Layla.

Maybe Layla would see her grandmother bite the big one, after all. I reached out, snagged her by the neck, and squeezed.

Her face reddened as she smiled.

Layla touched my arm. "Leave her, Sam. She's dying. It doesn't matter."

I cocked my head. "So you think immortality will heal you?" I set her on her feet, then shoved her.

She stumbled. "It will work."

"No, it won't, old lady. My DNA or any vampire's won't heal you or anyone." I kind of lied. Abbey's blood mixed with shifter blood had healed Ben. No one could know that though. "You've been watching too many fantasy shows."

"Layla, if I were you, I would protect that baby at all costs," Harriet said.

I whirled on her. "Is that a threat?" I was seething and fucking tired of people thinking they could find the Holy Grail in my family's DNA. "The next time you come near Layla or me or anyone close to me, I will literally nail you to a wall, slit your veins open, and watch you bleed out. If you think I'm kidding, try me. You can relay that message to Rianne, Adam, and Noah."

"Sam, we need to go," Carly said.

I spun around and took Layla's hand. Instantly, a bolt of electricity crackled along my arm, rivaling the supernatural charge Jo and I experienced when we joined hands.

A crease formed between Layla's pretty eyebrows. "Did you feel that?"

I couldn't tell if the power was all me or partly from Layla. The same thing had happened once before when she and I were in the back of the SUV in the loading dock at Intech. This connection was much stronger, maybe because I had absorbed a ton of energy from the storm.

Carly whipped out her phone from her lab coat. "Barnes, it's time. Make sure the path is clear."

Layla and I hurried out with Carly in the lead.

"Baby doll, are you okay to run like the wind?" With her weak heart, she might not be able to.

She batted her big blue eyes. "Vampire, do pigs like mud?"

I laughed, and it felt fucking good until I glanced at my watch. One minute left before the power came on.

"Sam, we have a small problem," Tripp said into my comm. "We had to divert Rebekah. That door didn't blow like we wanted it to. We're working on another. Head around the back of the building and go east. You may encounter some hostiles."

"Copy that," I returned.

When we reached Noah, Layla sucked in air. "Is he dead?"

"Sadly, no," I said. His ticker was beating extremely fast.

If she was relieved or not, it didn't register because once we plowed through the exit, fate decided to fuck me again.

I took one sniff, and my brow furrowed. Rianne was holding a cup of blood, leaning against the greenhouse as if she were hanging at a party, and next to her was a short thin-framed dude wearing a bow tie with a tablet in his hands.

Maybe Rianne had changed like Noah. Maybe she was drinking blood to keep her thirst at bay—but she didn't look grotesque like her cousin.

Carly glued her hands to her hips, assessing the situation. "Felix, what are you doing out here?"

The short dude looked up from the tablet. "Rianne said you needed me."

The spotlights came on. The power was restored.

Motherfucker. We were out of time.

Carly flinched, then flicked her head to her right. "Sam, my guard, Barnes, is waiting for you around the back of the building. I'll take care of Rianne. Go. Now!"

Rianne laughed like a maniacal freak. "Sam isn't going anywhere. Do it, Felix."

On her command, two things happened at once. Felix tapped on his tablet, and Rianne lobbed the contents of her cup at Layla.

Suddenly, a banshee scream pierced my ears, and bright lights flashed, followed by darkness and ending in a blinding pain throbbing in my head. I glanced around, disoriented, unable to identify the people around me. I squeezed my eyes shut, the scent of blood sending me into a frenzy. Sniffing the delicious sweetness of the woman beside me, I licked my lips, and let out a guttural roar.

20

LAYLA

Blood dripped into my eyes, slid down my cheeks, and dribbled into my mouth. It tasted like ass, and if I knew my lunatic sister, she'd probably used some type of animal blood. I had to hand it to her though—the only way to draw a vampire out was with the sticky red stuff. But Sam wasn't a monster in the sense that he killed for blood. I wasn't worried until I realized Felix's role. He'd turned on Sam's chip. I was sure of it.

I wiped my face with my fingers as fast as I could. On a blink, I found Sam baring his fangs at me with hunger, raw and pure, steeped in the depths of his silver eyes. I'd been able to penetrate through to him once before but not when covered in blood. While maybe not impossible, it was a feat that might take time we didn't have.

He grimaced and grabbed his head with both hands, then pulled out his earpiece and examined it, curious yet confused.

My stomach dropped dangerously low. "Whoever is listening, Sam's chip is on!" I shouted.

Yanking the comm from Sam, Rianne dropped it on the ground, then smashed it with her booted foot. "They can't help you. So, dear sister, you're screwed." Her sarcasm was wrapped in hard spikes.

Sam studied Rianne and me with a predatory glare, the air around him crackling with hunger.

"Attack," Rianne said in a deep and commanding tone.

The soldier in Sam obeyed as he flashed sharp teeth in a snarl.

I ducked and darted away. With Carly out cold from my banshee scream, she was of no use. My only other option was Barnes. Supposedly, the blond giant was waiting for Sam and me behind the building. Sam had been talking to someone in his comm, which meant some of the other SEALs were here. I couldn't scan the area around me, afraid he would pounce.

Rianne followed alongside Sam as if she was his coach. I was sure my bitch of a sister had earplugs in. "That's it, Sam. Show her the monster you really are."

Backing away from the vampire I loved, I trampled through the wet grass in my bare feet, the cold ground keeping me alert until I stumbled over a rock, and pain shot through my foot. Several swear words spilled out of my mouth as I continued to put distance between Sam and me, ignoring the throbbing in my foot. When I cleared the edge of the building, I quickly looked to my left. A spotlight sprayed down from high up on the building, illuminating the swath of grass broken in two by a cement driveway that jutted from the building midway down. But not a soul was in sight.

Rianne whispered something to Sam, and whatever it was had him growling at her.

Her creepy laughter confirmed that I was in hell.

Planting my feet, I locked my knees and held up my hands as if Sam was about to arrest me. I filled my lungs with mountain air and screamed to high heaven.

Sam froze in place, flinching. Even Rianne came to an abrupt halt.

I had probably cracked her earplugs.

Sam and I stood about five feet apart, facing each other. "Sam!" I called out. "Listen to me. I love you."

He cocked his head from one side to the other.

Rianne belted his arm with the back of her hand. "I said to attack." Her guttural tone sounded inhuman and manly.

Sam snarled, flashing deadly canines at her, and she jumped back.

I had no time to bask in her fear as he stalked toward me with a sense of purpose and a ravenous interest. The hairs on my neck fired to attention, then burned when Rianne handed him a knife. She barked encouragements that I assumed comprised words like attack, kill your spawn, or something equally fucked up.

My heart pounded in my ears so loudly I couldn't hear my own thoughts or think past how terrifying yet captivating Sam looked. His silver eyes shone like diamonds in black sand. His shoulder-length hair was pulled into a low ponytail. His angular jaw was hard. His fangs were sharp and deadly. His biceps bunched through the sleeves of his T-shirt, and his legs, thick and powerful, were built to move mountains.

He regarded the blade in his hand and flung it away as if the dagger wasn't sharp enough.

I was consumed by rage for my sister. I was so tired of her antics and her corrupt desire to do everything she could to pulverize Sam and me.

My mind rioted for a split second over why he didn't lunge or attack me. He had the reflexes, the quick speed to do just that. Maybe he knew me. Maybe he was battling his own demons.

He lifted his chin, sniffing, never taking his otherworldly eyes off me.

"Vampire," I pleaded as I held up my quaky blood-covered hands. "You have to come back to me. Fight through it. Please." My voice wobbled, keeping time with my knees knocking together.

Rianne let out a scornful laugh. "You'll never be able to break him. Can't you see he's a true monster? We've killed them for centuries, Layla." The desperation in her voice was heartbreaking.

Still, I didn't need a reminder that the Aberdeens were vampire hunters. That the bloodsuckers had taken the lives of my family members over the years. Most recently my father, if my uncle Jack was right. Kendra came to mind and faded again when Sam moved toward me.

Stumbling backward, I dug deep for more adrenaline to fight through the sheer craziness of what was happening. My problem was—I was extremely tired. My emotions were on a roller-coaster ride, and even though Carly assured me I wasn't on the verge of becoming like Noah, I worried she might be wrong. I mean, how many tests had she done? If the empty, bloody beds were any indication, I could conclude that she didn't have a clue.

I stomped my foot, gritting my teeth. I was completely over this shit. If Sam wanted to devour me, then so be it. I opened my arms. "Come and get me, vampire."

"That's it, Layla. Give in." My sister's voice sounded like nails on the chalkboard. "You can't fight him off."

Maybe not, but I would give it my best shot.

Sam's gaze traveled the length of my body before lingering on my belly.

Bingo! He was in there.

"We're having a baby," I said softly. Those words had worked the last time his chip was engaged.

As he fixated on my stomach, I held out my steady hand, even though it felt like piranhas were eating my insides. "Do you want to feel your son?"

I didn't know if any of the babies were boys, although if my dreams were true, at least one of them was. Regardless, Sam wanted a son.

"Another Mason boy?" Disgust bled through Rianne's tone. "All the more reason your pregnancy needs to be terminated."

If she knew I was having quadruplets, she might murder me now. Or maybe that was her plan all along. If Sam didn't end me, she would.

She disappeared, searching the grass, probably for the dagger Sam had thrown.

"I love you, vampire." I'd cracked through a thin wall, and I had to keep chiseling through his predatory armor. I closed the distance between us and took his hand, intent on having him feel my stomach. Instead, that electrical charge that I'd felt earlier pulsed along my arms, then down my legs, making me feel as if I'd been electrocuted.

He blinked in confusion as that distant look in his eyes waned.

When I grasped his other hand, the vibration of energy multiplied. I squeezed his hands tightly, inhaling the damp night air, feeling the cold grass beneath my feet. My nerve endings came alive. The sounds of our breathing sharpened, and I could hear his heartbeat as if it were my own.

Call me crazy, but I think we were channeling each other.

"Sam," I whispered. "Come back to me."

As if those words were the code to scramble his chip, he closed his eyes for long seconds as the energy pulsing through us increased.

A glint of light shone in my peripheral vision.

Sam's eyes flew open, and he whipped his head at Rianne, who was sprinting toward us with the dagger, ready to stake me.

She looked crazed and outraged, her nostrils flaring, reminding me of bull in a ring. It would be comical if I wasn't the target.

Sam trudged through the grass, opening his arms, readying his elemental powers. But when he reached Rianne, he yanked the dagger from her and drove it into her stomach.

She bent over, swearing like a sailor.

But he wasn't done with her. He removed the blade and drove it in again.

I should have stopped him, but I couldn't. My legs were locked, and my tongue was glued to the roof of my mouth. I was equal parts shocked that I'd been able to bring Sam back and that he was on the verge of killing Rianne. I had no words or feelings at the moment. My sister deserved to feel agonizing pain. But death? I was torn.

I didn't have a chance to react when Rianne screamed almost as loudly as my banshee. "I will fucking chisel out your fangs and burn you alive. I won't fail next time."

"There won't be a next time," Sam said before he picked her up and flung her.

Her body slammed into the brick building, then crumpled to the ground.

In a flash, he was at my side. "Baby doll." Slowly, his dimples emerged, giving him more of a boyish look than one of an inhuman creature with fangs.

His husky voice snapped me out of my haze, and as I peered around him to check on Rianne, rapid gunfire peppered the air in the distance. A second later, a loud boom rocked the ground.

Sam covered my body with his, tucking me into him, holding me tightly. He smelled like pine and wood, as if he'd been the one to trek through the forest for days on end. Regardless, his scent was calming, his strong arms protective.

After holding me for a long minute in his embrace, he said, "We need to find a way out. Tripp said to go east." He untangled his arms from around me, scanning the property.

Tons of dust floated in the air, making it difficult to see.

"Sam!" a familiar male voice shouted before Steven Mason emerged through the cloud of dust.

Relief was making my limbs weak. I wouldn't be surprised if I slept for days.

We followed Steven through the dust, then through a gaping hole in the cement wall.

"Rebekah will take you to the rendezvous point," Steven said to Sam.

Sam stopped Steven as he started to return inside. "Where are you going?"

His lips thinned. "Olivia and Dane are missing. Go, son. That's an order."

Sam hesitated until Rebekah ran up out of the shadows and said, "We don't have much time."

Sirens trilled in the distance.

"Pops, we need Carly," Sam said just as Steven climbed through the hole in the wall.

"I'll do my best, son," Steven returned over his shoulder.

Then Sam and I followed Rebekah into the forest.

For fuck's sake. Really? I couldn't handle another jaunt through the woods. But my panic was short-lived when I spotted an all-terrain vehicle.

Once Sam and I climbed in the back of the four-seater, I snuggled into him.

He kissed my head. "Thank you."

I lifted my gaze to his. "For what? I should be thanking you."

"For believing I could fight through the chip. It was fucking difficult as hell. At first, I was blinded by the pain, darkness, and confusion. Not to mention, I was drawn to the blood. But the more you talked, the more I began to register the familiarity. But it wasn't your voice or scent. If you hadn't touched me..." He gulped in air and squeezed me to him, his heartbeat off the charts. "The electrical charge between us is what I think short-circuited the chip."

"All that matters," I said, "is that it worked."

Rebekah expertly maneuvered the ATV between trees and over dead wood and branches. No doubt she'd been in a similar situation before. After all, she was military.

Sam tipped up my chin. "I would've died if I lost you." He bowed his head slightly and brushed his lips over mine. "I fucking love you, baby doll."

"I love you, vampire. But, Sam..." How did I tell him I had a weak heart or that I might not be able to carry our babies or that fatal complications could happen? Or that I was injected with Carly's crazy juice?

"Shh," he said. "We can talk about everything after you rest. But first, you need my blood."

My belly perked up with that fluttering sensation as if the babies heard him. I needed more than a mouthful. Maybe then my heart would strengthen.

21

SAM

The heart monitor beeped every now and then. I hadn't left Layla's room in four days. She'd been in and out of consciousness but was on the mend. She needed sleep and lots of it, according to Doc. He urged me to do the same, but no one could pry me out of here. My sister, Jo, tried. If my dad were here, he would give it his best shot. The only one who hadn't attempted to say a word to me about rest or sleep was Webb. He knew damn well it would take an army to pull me away from Layla's bedside. Even then, a hundred troops couldn't complete that task. Webb had been in my shoes once before when Jo was fighting for her life. She'd had a cobalt blade driven through her immortal heart by a former pissed-off girlfriend of Webb's.

Layla's circumstances were different but, in my mind, worse. After all, she was human and had been through an ordeal far worse than hell. A car crash, then being lost in the mountains for three days with no food, hardly any water, no blood, and dealing with her depraved grandmother, sister, and cousin. If that wasn't the bowels of purgatory, then being injected with a genetics-altering concoction sure the fuck was. I didn't even want to think about the ramifications of what Carly's SS2, as she called it, would have on Layla. *Fucking Rianne.*

I was anxious to know how Layla felt about me stabbing her sister. During the short bursts of time when Layla was awake, we'd talked about her ordeal, but she'd never asked about Rianne. Part of me sensed she didn't want to know. I hated that she'd witnessed what I'd done to her sister, but the bitch left me no choice. When I'd seen her going for Layla with that blade, I'd lost my shit.

Was Rianne alive? I had no clue. Her heart had been slowing down when I threw her into the building. I didn't care one way or the other if she'd lived or died. If she'd survived, I was confident that sometime in the future, Rianne would meet her maker.

I shucked the bitch from my mind, unfurled my fisted hands, and switched gears to something happier. I swiped the sonogram from the bedside table and grinned like a proud bastard—a soon-to-be father. Me? A dad? It had been exactly eight days since Dr. Martin dropped the wonderful bomb on Layla and me in the ER exam room that she was carrying four fetuses. I hadn't had time to process the idea of quadruplets. Or what I would be like as a dad. Would I be overprotective? Suffocating? Nervous? Fuck. If we had girls, I had to teach them how to fight as soon as they were old enough, just like Webb and Jo had been training Abbey.

I glanced at my sleeping beauty. The color had returned to her cheeks. Her hands were no longer clammy. Her full lips weren't as chapped as they'd been when I found her. Her auburn hair was oily but nothing my expert fingers and a bottle of shampoo couldn't fix. I grinned at the remembrance of washing her hair once before. She'd giggled the entire time.

Nevertheless, she looked peaceful and gorgeous. Her eyes darted back and forth rapidly beneath her eyelids, indicating she was in a deep REM sleep and possibly dreaming.

I returned my attention to the sonogram. Layla had cried happy tears when Dr. Martin told us the babies were fine. I might have also shed a tear or two. Then Layla mentioned the nursery. I didn't give it a passing thought at the time. My main concern was her.

"Sleep," I said. *"We'll talk about that later."*

She hadn't protested. But as I sat there now, an overwhelming feeling washed over me at what lay ahead. We had to start thinking of cribs, names, and everything else that babies needed—four of everything. I shoved both hands through my hair as I leaned my elbows on my knees and sighed. I'd had a dull headache since the chip had shut down.

Jo's lavender scent announced her before she sashayed in, wearing a light-purple top that brought out the streaks of purple in her black hair. She sidled up to Layla's bedside opposite me, sporting a loving smile.

I straightened in the chair. "Spill, sis. What are the results of the DNA comparison?" That was the only remaining question hanging in the balance. Carly had assured Layla that the small amount of SS2 that was injected into her wouldn't have any effect. Carly might have helped us, but that didn't mean we could trust her. When it came to drugs or anything of the like, each person reacted differently to the type and the dosage.

"There's no change between her original DNA results we ran in Boston to the tests we recently ran. Layla and the unborn babies shouldn't be effected by the SS2," Jo announced with a beaming smile.

Dropping my head, I mumbled, "Thank you." Then I was on my feet and hugging the crap out of my sister.

Easing away, she flattened her hand on my scruffy jaw. "You look like shit, Sam. You need a shower, shave, and sleep. I'll watch over Layla. Nothing will happen to her. She's safe now."

Safe was a word that didn't mean shit in my world. Layla and I would always be exposed to danger, harm, and whatever the fuck our enemies were after. Even more so with Mason kids on the way. I shoved those thoughts into a file drawer for now. Layla was home, and I had other plans in store for my baby mama.

I kissed Jo on the forehead, then tucked the sonogram into my back pocket. "I love you more than anything. I know you're concerned about me, but you wouldn't leave this room if Webb were lying in that bed. Come to think of it, you didn't when he was rushed in on a stretcher after a mission gone wrong, and even when he was recovering, you didn't either."

She gave me a weak smile. "True. But you're her protector, Sam. You're no good to Layla if you're not one hundred percent. We might be mostly invincible, but our powers will weaken if we don't rest. You know this, brother. And if you remember, Webb took me away from base so we could both heal and relax."

I rubbed the tight muscles in my neck as a thought came to me. Layla loved the ocean. Jo's house in Maine was the perfect spot for rest and relaxation. We wouldn't be bothered, and we would be protected. The town was home to a populace of one hundred percent vampires who watched over each family with a keen eye and would know in an instant if any strangers were lurking around.

"Great idea," she said, reading my mind. "Stan can assign a couple of his deputies to guard the house."

Butterflies finally came alive inside me. "I want to officially propose, and Layla loves the ocean."

Jo couldn't contain a smile. "I'm dying to plan the wedding, the baby shower, and I'll help with the nursery."

Her giddiness was contagious, causing me to laugh, and it felt out of this world. "Slow down, Jo. One thing at a time." That overwhelming feeling returned at the mention of the nursery.

She fastened her hands on her hips. "Sam Mason, things are moving fast. Before you know it, Layla will be delivering. And once my nieces or nephews are born, you will not have time to breathe."

"Maybe we should elope," I mumbled.

She pursed her lips. "Over my dead body."

Webb cleared his throat as he waltzed in.

Perfect timing. I didn't want to argue with Jo over a wedding. If it was up to me, we would definitely elope.

"Hey, angel." He kissed his wife on the lips. "Can I have a minute alone with Sam?"

The veil of tension enveloping him said he had bad news, but if he did, Jo's loving smile that was reserved only for her husband said otherwise—unless she couldn't read his thoughts. Webb seemed to live on the mind-blocking potion we kept stocked because of Jo and my father's abilities. I hadn't touched the stuff in a while, but I made a mental note to start again because I didn't like anyone in my head.

"Of course," Jo replied. "I have to meet Alia in the library. She's been helping Doc research our archives on pregnant woman who might have given birth to a vampire baby. She's found something."

My breath hitched. "Huh. For real?" Maybe we would have more insight to help Layla through this pregnancy and shed some light as to why Layla craved blood or needed it. "By the way, how's Alia holding up?"

Her son, Matthew, Ross Gray, and Tucker Whyte were nowhere to be found. Even Sierra Dupont was still missing.

"She's trying to keep her mind occupied." Jo gave me a hug. "Think about Maine, Sam. I won't say anything to Layla about wedding plans until you propose." After she kissed Webb, she bounced out like a schoolgirl skipping to her next class.

I loved that my sister was happier than ever. She and I had a rough childhood, Jo especially. She'd gone from a timid, shy girl to a beautiful, independent woman who wasn't afraid of her own shadow anymore.

Webb chuckled. "Maine? Proposal?"

I quickly filled him in.

He settled at the foot of the bed. "Not a bad idea to head up to Maine."

"Are you sure? We have a ton of shit going on. I don't want to leave you hanging. Although Doc needs to approve first." Layla's condition was improving, but if Doc thought Layla couldn't travel, then I would find a place here, since the naval base butted up to Mount Hope Bay. It just didn't give off the beauty and serenity of the Atlantic Ocean that Layla loved.

"For the time being, we should be fine. Olivia and Ben will remain in West Virginia and monitor Intech's activities. Dane has decided to help us because of his brother. We also have help from Sergeant Whyte's team. Her captain and the rest of their Special Forces unit should be arriving in West Virginia today. And Viking II is positioned around the city, watching for any signs of Roman."

I'd been relieved when I heard Olivia had been found. She'd

been shot with those drug-filled darts, but Dane had been able to rescue her from the clutches of the two guards.

"Great news that we have Special Forces helping us," I said, feeling better about whisking Layla away for a few days. "A group of shifters with military training and our Vampire SEALs were a force to be reckoned with."

He sighed. "For sure."

"Any signs of Carly?"

Webb had been keeping me abreast of the situation in West Virginia. My father hadn't been able to snatch Carly. I'd been trying to call her off and on with no luck. I owed her one for helping me. I wouldn't put it past Harriet, Noah, and Rianne to have done something to Carly. Or maybe Adam did when he found out his star scientist had sided with the enemy.

"Negative," Webb said. "But I spoke to Victor this morning about Sierra Dupont. She was found hiding at a friend's house. According to Victor, she got spooked when she found her father's dead body." He dipped into the pocket of his cargo pants. "This was delivered by courier today. It's Layla's." He set the phone on the bed.

It wouldn't shock me if Victor joined the team in West Virginia. The man had been ready to storm into Intech with us on the night we infiltrated it.

"Take a walk with me." Webb tipped his head at the door.

"Anything wrong?"

Webb was one of those people who I occasionally had a hard time feeling his emotions or reading his expressions. His guarded blue eyes weren't giving me any clues. The stoic vampire was a rock. Drama wasn't in his vocabulary. The only times he lit up like a Christmas tree was when he was with Jo or Abbey. I didn't expect him to wear his feelings on his sleeve. As the commander of our SEAL team, he had no room for feelings other than courage, determination, and resilience.

I was tempted to stand my ground and not leave Layla's bedside, but he was my superior officer, and the fleeting look he cast Layla gave me the vibe that whatever he had to tell me concerned my huntress. Then the light bulb brightened. *Jordyn?*

We still didn't know where Junior or Jordyn had taken off to. We'd assumed they would show up in West Virginia—but they hadn't. We had eyes on Intech, watching who was going in and coming out. Webb had called Junior's father, Jack, and he hadn't heard from his son. Our team had been trying to call Jordyn repeatedly and struck out.

Once we were in the lab area, he closed the door to Layla's room, then he tucked his hands into the pockets of his cargo pants. "Jordyn and Junior have been in an accident." He kept his voice low. "She's in a hospital in New Jersey. She called your father late last night. She's banged up pretty good, but she's okay."

"And Junior?" I didn't need to hear him say it, but I waited just the same.

Blinking, he shook his head. "I'm afraid he didn't make it."

I rubbed a knot on my shoulder. "Fuck."

"Tripp and your father rented a car in Morgantown this morning. After they pick up Jordyn, they should be here later tonight."

I understood why he wanted me away from Layla. If she woke up and heard him, she would freak the fuck out.

Frustrated, I was combing a hand through my hair when Layla screamed.

22

LAYLA

Blinking rapidly, I clutched my chest, hoping beyond hope that the dream I just had of my daughter wouldn't play out in real life. I inhaled and exhaled, attempting to regulate my breathing as the machine behind me went haywire, the sound annoying as hell.

The door burst open, and Sam flew to my bedside. "Layla, another nightmare?"

I flinched when he moved strands of my sweaty hair off my cheek. "Something like that."

He jerked away, a cavernous dent marring the space between his eyebrows.

I reached out for his hand. "I'm sorry. It's not you. Just a wicked-bad dream." Oh, God. I didn't want him to think I was afraid of him. On the contrary, he was a sight for sore eyes.

His black hair was tied at the nape of his neck. He was sporting a beard. His long lashes contrasted with the ruggedness of his strong jaw, and his black SEAL T-shirt stretched across his broad, muscled chest. If that wasn't enough, the love pouring off him wrapped around me like a protective blanket.

"Breathe, baby doll. I got you." Sam's husky voice was soothing and warm, adding another layer to the cover of safety.

Webb stood in the doorway with a smile in his sharp blue eyes. "I'll call Dr. Vieira," he said, then left.

The familiarity of the room took the edge off my frayed nerves. I shouldn't be nervous, but the dream felt real and gut-wrenching. "You know, we need to stop meeting in places like this," I teased, yawning.

A lopsided grin lit up his face. "How about we find a better spot? Maybe Jo's house in Maine."

I squealed. "Really? When are we leaving?"

He chuckled. "Soon. We need to clear it with Doc first."

Suddenly, I frantically examined myself, checking my teeth to see if I had fangs, then my fingernails as Noah's hellish features danced in my vision, nail-piercing shivers crawling along my spine.

"Did I, or am I…" I couldn't bring myself to ask the question.

He held in a grin. "Are you like me?"

I blinked once, nodding.

"You are one hundred percent Layla and my baby mama. The shit didn't damage or alter your DNA or affect the babies."

I pushed out a sigh of epic proportions. "I told you not to call me that," I said playfully.

He dipped into his back pocket and handed me the scan of our little ones. "This says you are." He laughed.

Goose bumps galore popped up on my arms as I obsessed over the image. I could barely keep my eyes open when Dr. Martin had been performing the ultrasound. "We need to think of names, Sam. Oh, and the nursery. Shit. Furniture, clothes, diapers."

He ghosted his nose over mine. "I know. We can discuss names while we're in Maine, sitting on the sand, watching the waves roll in." He kissed my eyes, my cheeks, then dragged his lips to my ear. "And maybe I can devour that beautiful body of yours as we fuck under the stars. If you're up for it."

I swallowed the dryness in my throat, my body humming as arousal hit quick and fast. "Anywhere and anytime, vampire." I was ready *now*. "Skinny-dipping too?"

He straightened and belted out a laugh. "I doubt the water is warm enough in April."

How time had flown since that day at the nightclub when I tried to capture him. I shuffled through the events of that night like a deck of cards until I landed on Rianne, then the cloud of lust around us skated away.

"Rianne," I said in an unsteady voice. "Is she dead?" The heart monitor sang behind me. I sliced open the box of my feelings to discern how I felt about her. Sifting through my emotions, I couldn't find anything other than disappointment and retribution. Did I want her to die? Absolutely not. Then why didn't I stop Sam? Maybe I was lying to myself. She wouldn't stop coming after me until she took my life or that of my babies. Regardless, I wouldn't fault him for what he'd done.

Sam chewed on the inside of his cheek, debating on what or how to tell me. "Honestly, I don't know. Her heart was slowing down when I threw her."

I closed my eyes briefly and sighed, even though my emotions were suspended between Rianne as my enemy and Rianne as my loving sister. "If she is still alive, she'll keep trying to come after us." Then something occurred to me. "Your dad told me the other day that if I know what's coming, I can stop it. Since we know about Abbey's vision of Rianne killing me, we've been able to prevent that from happening. But how many more times will we be successful?"

He dragged his fingers over my cheek. "I can't say I'm sorry about what I did to her. And I know you're struggling with your feelings for her. I can feel it, baby doll. Please remember that my actions will always be to protect you"—he rubbed my belly—"and them."

"I would never fault you for putting your family first. I just wish Rianne would come to her senses. But I don't think she ever will."

He straightened, staring at me as though he was struggling with what to say next.

My stomach pitched. "What is it?" I couldn't think past my question.

He plucked the sonogram from me, set it on the table beside the bed, then grabbed my hand. "Jordyn and Junior bolted out of here the night I was on my way to you."

I gnawed on my lower lip. "Don't tell me my grandmother has

them." Knowing Jordyn, she would do everything to rescue me. As far as Junior went, he wanted answers from Carly. So both of them had reasons to help.

"No. I don't know the details, but Junior and Jordyn were in a car accident in New Jersey." He squeezed my shaky hand. "Jordyn's okay." He gave me a sorrowful smile. "Junior didn't make it."

Shock sliced through me, and the medical machine I was hooked up to beeped endlessly. I shuddered out a breath, grateful that fate had my sister's back but devastated that Junior was dead. He was irritating, stubborn, and got on my nerves like his father, Jack, but Junior had been an overall good person.

Tears slipped out one by one. "Does Jack know? This will destroy him and my aunt Tab."

"Webb doesn't have all the facts. My father is on his way home. He's stopping in New Jersey to pick up Jordyn. They'll be here tonight."

"When will any of this end, Sam?" I asked, heartache steeped in every word. "Why is part of my family evil and the other half good? We can't keep losing loved ones. I'm so frightened for our children. I'm frustrated, too, that I can't contribute and fight like I want to. I feel helpless. These people have to be stopped at all costs." I shivered, wiping my nose with my free hand.

He dashed tears away with the pad of his thumb. "They will get what's coming to them. I promise. But it won't happen overnight. Right now, we need to take care of you and the little tykes. Your health and safety is *our* number one priority."

I sniffled. "Then do you think Maine is wise?" I wanted to go more than anything. A conversation I'd had with Steven came to mind. "Your dad believes the naval base is the best place to protect me."

"Yes, but… your grandmother knows where you are, as do others, like Roman. As long as they know that, they won't be looking elsewhere for us. We'll let them think we're here, and if they declare war and storm the base, they won't find you."

That made perfect sense. Maybe we could relax and leave our worries behind. "Can Jordyn come with?"

I hated to ask, since Sam and I had been constantly torn apart. Spending time with him was crucial to our relationship from a physical and emotional aspect. Not to mention, we didn't know a great deal about each other, and we had a list of items to talk about and agree on before I delivered.

Yet, I would hate myself if another thing happened to Jordyn. She'd been beaten by Fred Emery and now the accident. I needed Sam but also my sister.

"Of course, baby doll." His loving and lustful gaze caressed the length of my body.

Heat and tingles snaked along my skin as if he was licking every inch of me. "Horny, vampire?"

The question was swept out of the room as Dr. Vieira came in, wearing the usual—a lab coat hanging over a collared shirt and a pair of dress slacks. "Nice to see you're awake. How are you feeling?" He checked the empty IV bag that looked like it had contained blood.

"I feel great." Physically, I did, although the truth would be revealed when I stood. My muscles had gotten a workout of epic proportions from traipsing through the mountains. "I *am* hungry. I could go for a juicy hamburger. Oh, and a long shower." I didn't have to feel my hair to know it was dirty and matted to my head. "How long have I been home?" Home. I hadn't felt like I belonged anywhere since my dad died, and it sounded odd to refer to a naval base with vampires as home.

"That's right. You are home," Sam said, probably feeling or seeing some type of emotion from me.

Human vampire hunter meets vampire. Falls in love and has four babies. Now that's a story waiting to be told.

Dr. Vieira flashed his brown eyes at me as he readied his stethoscope. "You've been in and out of consciousness for four days. Do you remember much?"

Sam threaded his fingers through mine.

"Aside from talking to Sam, I only remember the ultrasound," I said, giddy.

Dr. Vieira listened to my heart and lungs. When he was done, he wrapped the stethoscope around his neck. "Definitely a vast improvement. You had one hell of an experience."

"It *was* hell," I agreed. "But I have questions. Carly figured out I'm carrying a supernatural baby, although I didn't share that I had four growing inside me. Still, she believes it's growing faster than a human one. I've been thinking that I'm big because I'm having four—but is there any truth to her theory? She seemed worried I could have severe complications, especially with my heart." I paraphrased what I'd heard and remembered.

"Did you find a case like ours in the archives?" Sam asked. "Jo told me you did."

My eyebrows lifted. "That's great news, right?"

Dr. Vieira pinched the bridge of his nose as he regarded Sam.

A heart-punching-against-a-rib silence filled the room.

My guess was that they were speaking telepathically. Sam and I had done that a couple of times.

The longer Sam and Dr. Vieira exchanged pensive looks, the more Sam lost the color in his face.

"Well, someone tell me." My voice hitched.

Dr. Vieira slipped his hands into his lab coat pockets. "The woman gave birth to twins—one witch, one vampire. She craved blood and developed magical abilities, which aligns with what we're seeing with you."

I wondered if she had the same abilities I had—like mind control, which I found freakier than my banshee scream. Nevertheless, it was nice to know someone else had gone through what I was experiencing.

"I hear a *but* coming," I said. Maybe I didn't want to know.

"You will deliver early, Layla," Dr. Vieira said in an even tone. "Not only because you are carrying multiples, but Carly guessed right. The woman, Emily Crawford, delivered at about five and half months. Because the babies are inhuman, they will grow faster. I want to emphasize—*if the medical case file we found is correct.*"

"What you're saying is I will be big as house overnight?" I injected sarcasm, not at them but toward myself, mainly to unpack how the fuck my body would handle that. I mean, nine months to allow the little ones to grow at a gradual rate was one thing, but five and half months… fuck! Then another question hit me. "If the babies grow faster in the womb, does that mean they'll also sprout up quicker after they're born?"

"Logically, it would make sense that they would," Dr. Vieira said. "But I don't have an answer on that. There was nothing in the medical files that explained life after birth for those twins."

My head spun as I tried to process all of this, but it was clear he was leaving something out. "Both of you are still pale. What else are you not telling me?"

Dr. Vieira rubbed a spot above his nose. Since I'd met him, I had yet to see him panic.

The only thing I could think of that would freak anyone out was death. "Emily Crawford died at childbirth, right? That's why both of you are white as a ghost. Unless I'm having demon spawns instead of vampires or witches."

"She did die at childbirth, but we don't know why. There are pages missing from the file," Dr. Vieira confirmed. "That doesn't mean you will die too. Now that we know what to expect, we can manage your pregnancy better. In addition, this case happened over eighty years ago. Technology has come a long way. With multiples, you'll have a C-section. It's too risky for you and the babies to deliver naturally. Regardless, absolutely no stress, drink Sam's blood, eat, sex is fine, and relax. Jo tells me you want to go to Maine. Best place to relieve stress, and I would do that soon. We need to assume you will deliver after five months, so that means three months from now. Dr. Martin is onboard. The new medical equipment will be delivered within the next couple of weeks. We're adding on two rooms to the infirmary. Construction begins this week. Everything will be in place for the births."

I quivered with emotion, both from the fact I could die giving birth and what my extended family was doing for Sam and me. Of course, Sam was the main reason for their help. But they could've kicked me to the curb. After all, Harriet, Rianne, and Noah Aberdeen were out to kill Sam or build him into a super soldier. I'd been included in that scheme. Still, Steven and the others could've tried to convince Sam to let me go when we'd first met. They didn't. They'd welcomed me with open arms.

Once again, I couldn't help but remember something else Steven said the night I'd woken up from a nightmare.

"I adore you, Layla. I also trust you. You're a strong woman. You'll survive what we're about to face."

Could I survive childbirth? Was I strong enough, as Steven had said? I had to believe I was. But fate had a funny way of fucking with me.

23

LAYLA

Two hours later, my mind was a jumbled mess as I stood in the walk-in shower, feeling numb from head to toe. I stared at my belly, still stuck on how the fuck my body would handle the accelerated growth. One baby, I could wrap my mind around. Four… not a chance. I knew I had the best doctors as well as Sam, Jo, Steven, and everyone on the SEAL team to take care of me and support me. But for fuck's sake, I really wanted my mom. I needed Jordyn too. Sure, my sister would be here later tonight, and I couldn't wait to see her, but I also craved someone who had experienced childbirth. Except for Alia Costner, no one else in my new extended family had been pregnant, since female vampires couldn't have children.

I would love to have Aunt Tab with me. She'd given birth to six children, and one of her pregnancies was twins. I groaned as the hot water beat down on my back and neck. Aunt Tab would be devastated when she learned her oldest son was dead. Even more so when she found out her second-oldest son was now a beast like no other.

My heart broke for Junior. The man had loved his wife, Carly. As much as she'd helped Sam and me escape, I blamed her. She'd been the one to light the match that started the inferno of hell. She'd sent Intech's men out to Montana to talk to Jack when she'd learned the Aberdeens knew Sam. Then she'd discarded Junior like he was a bag of trash.

I spun around, tipping my face up, feeling the pulse of the water droplets against my skin. I had to find a way to focus on something good in my life and send the bullshit packing.

I had a home—a penthouse-size apartment on the naval base that Sam and I could raise our children in—for now anyway. I wasn't the white-picket-fence, minivan-driving type of mom. I just wanted a small house with a decent-sized yard in a good neighborhood and school system. Then maybe one day we would have a house or summer home on the beach.

I also had Jordyn, who I believed with surety would never break our sister bond. Above that, I had a man who loved and adored me. A strong, arrogant, protective yet compassionate vampire who would die for me. All the qualities of a man who would be a great husband and father, and we had children on the way.

Steam swirled in the luxurious bathroom as my mind rewound to the idea of childbirth. I couldn't die. I couldn't leave Sam a single father. I had to toe the line and do as Dr. Vieira ordered—drink Sam's blood, eat, sex was fine, and relax. No stress whatsoever.

On that note, I wondered what was taking Sam so long. He'd wanted to join me. I left him in the family room while I started the shower. Since my skin wasn't shriveled, I was guessing I'd only been lost in thought for five or ten minutes at most.

"Baby doll," Sam called, his voice growing louder as he approached. "Are you ready?"

I poked my head around the stone wall that separated the shower from the bathroom. "Always, vampire. It's time to christen our new shower."

Sam was stripping down to nakedness. My nipples hardened at the sight of him—cut abs, chiseled jaw, power coiled in his muscular thighs—a warrior who I swore was born of a different time and era.

It felt like forever since I'd seen my hunk of a vampire naked when in fact it had only been a week. My libido awakened, sparking lust through my veins.

Chuckling, he stroked his erection, a smile playing with the edges of his mouth until his dimples made an appearance. "Shower sex. Fuck yeah."

Flutters tickled the lining of my stomach at the sound of his husky laugh, and when he padded across the long and wide expanse of the master bath, holding his cock with lust swirling in his green eyes, those flutters turned into wild bat wings.

I shuddered in anticipation of having his dick inside me, his mouth on my pussy, and his fangs embedded in that sweet spot on my inner thigh that he loved and craved so much.

"Did you find out what time Jordyn will be here?" I said, even though it wasn't a question to be asking when I wanted to wrap my lips around his beautiful long, hard cock and suck him until he came undone—a sight to behold. To know I could unravel the powerful vampire with a flick of my tongue over the head of his erection was orgasmic.

"My dad said in about an hour. Plenty of time to wash your hair and soap you up."

I giggled, feeling the weight of my problems falling off my shoulders—all that bullshit washing down the drain. "You want to wash my hair?" He'd done it one time before, and it had felt amazing.

I inched backward and under the spray while Sam stood a foot from me, his gaze taking a slow, sensual hike up and down my body, lingering on my massive tits.

I played with my nipples, lightly rolling them between my fingers as he pumped his cock, his eyelids heavy with lust.

The moment I slid my hand down to my pussy, he pounced in one quick move.

The breath shuddered out of me as he tugged me to him, pressing his impressive erection against my heated skin. "I want to do more than wash your hair, baby doll." He gently massaged my tits. "I want to suck these." He slid a hand down to my inner thigh. "I want this right here. I'm dying to taste you." Then his fingers danced between my folds. "I'm dying to feast here too. Your arousal is driving me mad."

He lifted my chin with his knuckle, bent down, and plunged his tongue into my mouth. He took control of the kiss, commanding, teasing, exploring.

A whimper rippled up the back of my throat, and in a flash, Sam had me in his arms and was carrying me to the stone-encased bench that banked one wall of the shower.

He eased me down, breaking the kiss. "Spread your legs." Sheer dominance and power dripped from every syllable, making my clit pulsate in anticipation of his tongue.

I did as he commanded.

His fangs lowered, gleaming and promising heated passion and seductive pleasure. "Touch yourself," he ordered, stroking his erection up then down.

I quivered, obeying his command, circling my clit in steady strokes as I dropped my head back slightly, sighing heavily.

"Look at me, baby doll." Again, the huskiness in his voice was doing crazy things to my insides, and I swore I was a second away from dropping into a sensual abyss.

I righted my head, opening my legs wider as I stuck my finger inside my pussy.

He groaned, pumping his cock, his eyes changing from green to a luminous silver.

I reached out with my free hand and grabbed the back of his muscular thigh, urging him forward. Butterflies went wild inside me at the thought of pleasing the father of our children. It felt like eons since Sam and I had been intimate, but it was only last week when we'd lounged in a bubble bath before we fucked like bunnies. Though the rough sex was what had me spotting and rushing to the ER. I shook that thought off. Dr. Martin gave us the thumbs-up as long as Sam wasn't aggressive. Funny though—it wasn't Sam who wanted it hard and fast. It was me.

The second I flicked my tongue over the head of his cock, he bucked and groaned, threading his fingers through my wet hair. "Fuck, Layla."

I giggled before I sucked him into my mouth and took him deep until the head of his dick was touching the back of my throat.

He let out a guttural roar and fucked my mouth like a vampire possessed, my teeth scraping his shaft in a move that he craved during a blow job. "That's it, baby doll. I need more pain." He pressed his hands into the wall above me, then stopped thrusting. "I need to be inside you." In a flash, he was on his knees. "But first—"

"I want you to come in my mouth." I pouted.

He chuckled as his fangs grazed a path over my skin, wandering lazily across my knee and along my thigh.

I let my legs fall open as wide as I could, and he moaned, peppering light licks and gentle kisses along my leg until he bit, sinking his fangs into my inner thigh. The sting was erotic, and an orgasm was ready to burst free.

I played with a nipple and circled my clit, needing a release. Just as the orgasm teetered on the edge, Sam withdrew his fangs, trading my thigh for my pussy. He flattened his tongue between my folds and dove into a rhythm until I was writhing on the bench. In seconds, I exploded, shouting, "I love you, vampire!"

Before I could track his movements, he had me on my feet. "Hands against the wall, ass in the air."

Grasping my hips, he eased his cock into my wet channel then stilled. "I'll go slow."

I wanted to protest, but I didn't want another trip to the ER.

He rolled his hips, slow and sure, moaning, then growling loudly when I squeezed around his cock. "Fuck." His breaths came in short bursts as he picked up the pace. "Are you okay, baby doll?"

"Shut up and fuck me, vampire."

He chuckled and kept up a steady rhythm—not too fast and definitely not rough. I hated that we had to be cautious. The best thing about sex with Sam was letting our inhibitions go. No worries. No craziness. Just him and me and the feelings we shared.

His hands tightened on my hips, and on his last thrust, he roared his release. We didn't move for a beat until he said, "Okay, now it's time to wash your hair."

I full-on laughed as I straightened. "You're weird. The water is probably cold."

He dipped under the shower. "Nah, it's perfect. Come here." He grabbed the shampoo from a built-in ledge on the wall.

I rolled my eyes but joined him. Who was I to turn down a head massage?

After he squirted shampoo into his hand and started washing my hair, he said, "You're the best thing that ever happened to me, Layla."

Spewing noises of pleasure, I said, "Fate got it right, throwing us together. I love you more than words can say, vampire." I anchored my hands on his waist. "We fit perfectly together."

His expert fingers worked magic against my scalp, eliciting soft moans and a blanket of goose bumps. "I want you to know that you and I are joined at the hip until our babies come. I will do everything in my power to make fucking sure nothing happens to you."

Glancing up, I blinked at him. "But… if something does happen—"

He pressed a finger to my lips. "Shh. You and I will live a long, wonderful life together, raising our kids, teaching them the value of family, and showing them what love is all about."

"You know I'll grow old, and you won't. How do you feel about that?" My stomach pitched and dropped at the thought of me with gray hair and Sam never aging. "My boobs will sag. I might not have an ass anymore, and I'll have wrinkles."

"But you'll still be beautiful, Layla. I don't care if you walk with a cane. You'll always be mine."

My mouth gaped. "Who are you, Sam Mason?"

He traced a heart on my chest above my left breast. "I'm the man who's hopelessly in love with you."

I couldn't contain my laugh or the tears. "You are my home, vampire. Mind, body, and soul."

He pulled me to him, crashing his mouth to mine. As we stood under the shower that was starting to turn cool, my throat began to burn.

I pulled away. As if he knew what I wanted, his fangs flashed before he bit into his wrist. "I'm sorry I didn't offer earlier."

I giggled as I suctioned my lips to his skin and drank long and deep. Now everything was right in our world.

24

LAYLA

I snuggled into the pillow, inhaling Sam's woodsy scent, reveling in the king-sized bed, the soft sheets beneath my skin, and the feeling of home. This was a million times better than the tree boughs with prickly sticks poking my ass. Or smelling the dirt and musky-sweet aroma of dead leaves.

Wiping the sleep from my eyes, I turned over to find Sam's spot empty. Actually, it didn't look like he'd slept next to me at all. I wracked my brain, clearing the cobwebs. After our amazing rendezvous in the shower, Sam had gone to the infirmary to meet with Peter. He'd been working on a way to remove the chip from Sam's head without surgery, and he thought he'd had a break-through.

Considering I was still feeling the effects of my time in the mountains, my pregnancy and my body's changes, and the stress of everything that happened, I'd curled up to take a nap.

"Sam," I said as I lifted my head, scanning his room. We had yet to claim the master bedroom. It needed some touch-ups on the walls and other small upgrades first.

The metal door was ajar, daylight spilled in from the window next to the nightstand, and the alarm clock blinked 11:00 a.m. *Holy hell.* I'd slept for nineteen hours. Had I missed Jordyn? She was supposed to arrive around nine last night—if I hadn't lost more than one day.

"Sam," I called again as I climbed out of bed, pulling the sheet with me, then wrapping it around my naked body.

I grabbed my phone off the nightstand and found a note beneath it.

Baby doll,

I hope you're well rested. You were sleeping when I returned yesterday, and I didn't want to disturb you. I'm having an MRI done this morning. I shouldn't be long. Also, don't panic about Jordyn. You didn't miss her. My dad called last night. Jordyn had been discharged from the hospital later than expected, and my dad wanted to talk to the state police about Junior's body. They'll be here around noon. Oh, and Jo and Harley went in together and bought you some clothes. They're on the chair by the closet.

Love, your baby papa.

I snorted and rolled my eyes at baby papa, then smiled at Jo and Harley's generosity. When we'd gotten out of the shower, I'd made a comment to Sam about clothes and how it would be impossible to have any type of wardrobe, given how fast I was about to grow in size and weight. Yoga pants would do the trick, since they were stretchy, along with an oversized T-shirt or blouse. It wasn't my usual attire of skinny black jeans and tight-fitting tops, but it would be nice to find something that fit and looked good at the same time.

I wound my way around the foot of the bed and over to the chair. From the infirmary to the apartment, I'd worn a pair of sweatpants and a loose top that Jo had lent me. I had some outfits at Harley's house and a couple here, but none of those garments would fit me at the moment.

I snatched another note off the pile of clothes. This one was from Harley and Jo.

Sam mentioned you needed something to wear, so we picked up a variety of maternity outfits in different sizes, based on what we've seen you wearing. We can return what doesn't fit.

I sifted through an array of high-end leggings, jeans, tank tops, T-shirts, and V-neck sweaters in different colors to mix and match.

Emotion clogged my throat. I didn't know how I'd gotten so lucky to have fast friends like Jo and Harley. I needed to repay them somehow and catch up with Harley especially. She was definitely my new bestie. She'd been a rock and a gracious host during the time Sam had been in a coma.

I chose an outfit, then jumped into the shower, not lingering long. I wanted to be completely alert for Jordyn. We had so much to catch up on. I hadn't seen her since I stabbed Fred Emery in the hospital garage. *Asshole.* I should pay him a visit in the base prison and finish what I'd started.

Once I was dressed in a pair of black jeans and a light-blue T-shirt, I twisted my hair up on my head, then wound my way through the apartment. A cozy feeling washed over me. This spacious open floor plan was mine and Sam's. I poked my head into the empty bedroom beside Sam's that had once been Jo's, envisioning the nursery. If my dreams were any indication of the sex of the babies, I could confidently say I was having at least one girl and one boy, so the colors had to blend. A coat of soft light-gray paint to start. I loved the grays, blues, blacks, and pinks. I wasn't a fan of yellow.

The click and groan of the front door resonated.

Three seconds later, Sam strutted in, his long legs eating up the space as he entered the future nursery. "There's my baby mama. You're awake." His gaze roamed lazily over me. "Love the new clothes."

A slow flush crawled up to pinch my cheeks, and my lips tingled at his heated but loving stare. Instantly, my lady parts awakened, my core went liquid, and my body hummed. I was ready to strip his black uniform off him, pull the leather strap from his hair, and ride him into the sunset.

"And you're officially my baby papa," I teased through a laugh.

He leaned in and kissed the sensitive spot just below my ear. "You want to hear me roar," he retorted.

I playfully pushed him, but, of course, he didn't budge. "That makes no sense."

He captured my earlobe between his teeth, his warm breath

grazing my neck. "Sure it does. I'm papa bear, and you're mama bear."

I dropped into a fit of giggles as delicious shivers pebbled my skin. "How many pet names will we have?"

"As many as possible to make you laugh, Layla. It's good to see you happy."

I angled my head, giving him access to do as he pleased. "You know what would make me happier? You inside me."

"See? I told you pregnant women were horny." He backed me into a wall before placing one hand on each side of me and rubbing his cheek against mine as if he was marking me with his scent. Then he jammed his impressive bulge into me. "That would definitely make me happy too."

I craned my neck up at him. "But?" We had about twenty-five minutes before Jordyn would arrive. That was plenty of time to fuck like bunnies.

He gave me that boyish-yet-sexy grin as he stroked my lips with the pad of his thumb. "I have something else in mind."

I arched an eyebrow, wrapped my lips around this thumb, and suckled.

His eyes flashed quicksilver, and he groaned, mashing his dick into me. Before I could track his movements, my arms were above my head, and his tongue was in my mouth, claiming what was his— my body, my mind, my soul. Our tongues fought for control as a wild need for dominance had me nipping his bottom lip, drawing blood.

That burn in the back of my throat sparked instantly.

As if he knew, he bit into his wrist. "Drink," he rasped.

He didn't have to tell me twice. I latched on to him, sucking, moaning, and tasting the sweetness with a hint of spice.

"So fucking erotic," he said as he smoothed a hand over my hair.

I agreed. I was ready to orgasm, especially with his woodsy aroma swirling around us, his erection pressed into me, and that gravelly sexy tone of his voice.

Once I had my fill, he dropped to his knees, glancing upward as if he was seeking permission.

Who was I to say no to him? I blinked once as my core went liquid and my mind became mush as I worked the jeans over my hips and down to my ankles.

Then he nudged my legs open as far as they would go.

I sucked in air, watching him watch me.

Then his next move was the deadliest as he sunk his fangs into my inner thigh while shoving a finger into my pussy.

I cried out, gripping his hair as he finger fucked me and sucked my life essence into him. The feeling was euphoric as my brain shut down and my limbs became weak. He continued to drink while he dragged a finger over my swollen clit, then pushed it back inside me. He released his fangs, lapping up the bite marks before replacing his finger with his tongue.

I purred and moaned as he reduced me to nothing but a pool of water.

He growled, suckling my clit while flicking his tongue over it.

My pulse thundered in my ears, my heartbeat on a racetrack to the finish line. When he shoved a finger back inside my pussy, I sucked in air, and on an exhale, I exploded, saying his name over and over again.

He chuckled as he kissed his way upward, stopped on my belly, then pressed his ear to it.

"Can you hear them?" I asked as I tried to regulate my breathing.

"Of course," he said. "They sound like a beautiful chorus."

Happy tears threatened as my heart opened as wide as it would go for the handsome vampire. "I love you, Sam Mason. We do make beautiful music together."

He stood to his full height, tucking his fangs away. "You're the best thing that has ever happened to me." He kissed me softly, tenderly, gently.

I hooked my arms around his neck, sucking his tongue into my mouth, tasting him and my essence as we got lost in a simple kiss that was passionate and full of love.

But our erotic bubble burst open when his phone dinged with a text. He broke away but didn't reach for his cell. Instead, he helped me get dressed, then said, "We should start painting this room."

"And think of names," I added.

"Liam if one of them is a boy," he said as another ding sounded. That time, he checked his message.

"Have you been talking to Harley? She suggested that name."

He read the text. "Not at all. I've been thinking." He returned his cell to his side pocket.

"What if we have four boys?"

His lips split into an award-winning grin that was Oscar worthy. "Liam, Lucas, Lane, and Lincoln." He rattled off the names, sounding like he was reading a nursery rhyme.

I stared at him in awe. "Lane? As in my bodyguard?"

The color drained from his face. "In memory of him. That's one thing I haven't told you. He died during the hospital chaos."

I pressed my fingers to my mouth, gutted at the sad news. I adored Lane.

Sam hugged me. "He was a great Navy SEAL." His voice was laden with sorrow.

I buried my nose in his chest, inhaling his woodsy scent that acted like a calming agent as tears pooled. "We can't keep losing people, Sam." I felt responsible, not only for Lane's demise but for so many other things that had happened and whatever else was to come.

I knew the war brewing revolved around Abbey, Sam, and me. Each of us were targets. Even if we removed Harriet, Carly, Noah, and Rianne, if she was alive, out of the equation, I would still be on the most wanted list. I was carrying Masons and was one of the most important people in Sam's life. I hated that my family played a part in this fight.

He cupped my face. "You're right. Our immediate goal is to keep you safe. So once Peter removes my chip, we'll leave for Maine."

The sorrow and anger I'd been harboring dulled for the

moment. "So he figured out a way? That's fantastic news. When will it happen?"

"The text said this afternoon. The MRI showed the chip moved again, and he tested it and confirmed it's fried—but we're getting rid of the fucker once and for all." Relief punched through every word.

A knock on the apartment door had us glancing out into the hallway.

He gave me a chaste kiss. "That's probably Jordyn."

The day was looking up for sure. No more worry about a freaking brain-to-machine control device, and I would have a chance to hug my sister.

But when Sam opened the door, my jaw hit the floor. I wasn't in the least prepared to see my sister's face covered with cuts, stitches, and splotches of red that would deepen to black and blue, a neck brace, and a cast on her arm.

She half smiled, pain evident as she flinched.

I wanted to hug her and tell her everything would be okay, but I was afraid I would break her.

Sam cupped her good elbow, helping her to the couch.

Quiet tears slipped past my lashes as I followed, saying a silent prayer to thank whoever was listening that she'd survived. I'd already lost one sister—I couldn't lose another. My heart broke to see her shuffle in, meek and fragile. She'd suffered so much from Fred Emery bashing her face against a car and now the accident.

She eased herself down onto the cushion, her features tightening. "It's not as bad as you think, Layla."

I could have sworn my eyeballs had fallen out of their sockets. "Liar." I knew Jordyn, and she was lying through her teeth.

Sam kissed me on the head. "I'm going to see Peter. I'll see you later."

I squeezed his hand. "Love you, vampire."

He blew me a kiss on his way out of the apartment.

Jordyn settled in and sighed. "I did lie. Every bone and muscle hurts. I also cracked two ribs, and as you can see, I broke my arm. I was lucky, Layla. But Junior…" Her waterworks opened as she sobbed.

I rushed to her side and grabbed her hands. "Why were you going to West Virginia?" I asked in a gentle tone. I knew the answer but had to hear her say it.

"You're not going to like this, but Granny called me. We made a deal."

Either my ears had cotton balls in them or I'd lost my hearing. "Say again?"

She quivered as she sniffled. "You heard me."

Mind blown. I thought she would say she wanted to help rescue me, not make a deal with the devil.

I pressed my fingers into my chest as a sliver of pain came out of nowhere like it had before I ended up in Carly's lab and almost died. "Are you betraying me as well?" My breathing increased as I stood on shaky legs, needing to put distance between us.

"I was trying to save you, Layla," she said in a small voice.

I jerked so hard I would probably have whiplash. I tempered my ire, walking over to the wall of windows. I had to keep telling myself she was only trying to help. I got that. I would do the same to save her. But Granny Aberdeen couldn't be swayed—not when I had Masons growing inside me.

I tipped my head back. The sun was high in the sky, the warmth of its rays beaming in, erasing the chill that had sprung up. I welcomed the heat, imagining a quieter, less stressful place with no Aberdeens present.

"Say something, Layla," she pleaded as she sidled up to me.

"I'm sorry you were in a car accident—but that was fate telling you to back the fuck away from our grandmother. You would've suffered more in her hands than the pain you're in right now." Or she could be lying beside Junior in a morgue. I left that part out. I rubbed my chest again. It was clear she was suffering from more than her physical injuries.

She cried. "I'm the reason he's dead. I coaxed him into going with me."

"Don't blame yourself, Jordyn." My tone was even. "Junior

didn't need convincing. He was so in love with Carly that he would've done anything to see her."

She heaved a sigh. "Why do you sound cold, like you're not my sister anymore?"

I stared at the prison building across the way. A sentry stood guard outside the doors. I had an urge to trudge down there and carve out Fred Emery's intestines.

"I love you, Jordyn. Out of the three of us, you're the one who is wiser and thinks before you act. You've always been the coach and referee when Rianne and I fought. I love that you wanted to save me. But leave that task for Sam. I want you around. I want to grow old with my sister. I want you to be the best aunt to my children. We need each other, Jordyn."

Crying, she reached out and held my hand. "I want all that too."

"Then promise me you won't do something like that again."

"I promise," she said through a sniffle.

"I mean it, Jordyn. Rianne injected me with that stuff that alters humans. I was lucky I woke up in time. Noah has been changed, and he's an ugly motherfucker of a monster."

She sucked in air, wiping her eyes with her fingers. "Please understand. Granny threatened your life. She said if I didn't come, she would kill you. I couldn't say no."

"Why didn't you share that with Steven? He is your boss. Or tell Webb or Tripp?" As soon as the questions left my mouth, I wanted to take them back. I wasn't a Goody Two-shoes, and I hardly asked for permission when someone close to me needed help. "Don't answer any of that."

Silence ticked by for a beat.

"Are we good, Layla?"

I hooked my arm in her good one. "Of course. I want a hug, but I'm afraid I might hurt you."

She leaned into me, resting her head on my shoulder. "Steven is making arrangements to have Junior's body brought here."

"Does he know why you went to West Virginia?"

"He does. You can't lie to him—not that I would. But he or Jo would read my mind anyway. I thought he would lash out, but he said he understood and not to let it happen again."

I was sure Steven and Webb were at their wit's end with the Aberdeens, including Jordyn and me.

"Can we sit and chat?" Jordyn asked. "I have a few things I want to tell you, and I want to hear more about Rianne and Noah."

I grabbed two bottles of water from the fridge, then we settled in, facing each other as we got comfy on the couch.

"Granny has lost her mind and is dying of some type of blood cancer." I took a sip of water, deciding on how to tell her about Rianne. I didn't even know where to begin. Like me, she was frustrated with our sister, but despite Rianne's actions, Jordyn wouldn't want to see Rianne dead. I reached over and touched her leg. "I'm afraid Rianne could be dead."

She gaped as she clutched onto my hand. "Rianne. Dead?"

I shrugged. "I don't know for sure. It guts me, Jordyn, that Rianne isn't the sister we know anymore." I filled her in on Rianne's actions and the conversation Rianne and I had in that room at Intech. "She's so far gone that I don't know if we can save her."

Tears rolled down her cheeks. "I'm sad she chose to side with Granny and Noah. But she made her decision. We have to, too, Layla. As much as I hate to say this, we have to protect ourselves and each other now."

I bobbed my head. "You know I will always have your back."

She squeezed my hand as I brought her up to speed on everything, including my grandmother's true motive, how I almost died, and everything about my pregnancy.

When I was done, she threw herself in my arms, moaning in pain. "I'm sorry you went through all that. I've never been so scared in my life. I thought I lost you. I'm furious with our family. I want to kill Fred Emery, and I just want happiness. We won't have that with Granny in the picture."

I hated to burst her bubble, but she needed to hear this. "Sis, with or without Granny in the equation, our happiness will always be challenged because I'm having Mason babies. This war is much larger than we could ever have imagined. And if Rianne is alive, she makes Granny look like a saint."

Jordyn curled her brown hair around her ear, and the act shook a detail free that I'd failed to mention, but Rianne's shorn hair didn't matter. "You said you had a couple of things to tell me?" I drank more water.

She twisted the cap off her bottled water, then started in. "To begin with, if Sam hasn't told you, his handsome face has been prime-time news from coast-to-coast. When he was searching for you at the hospital, he was in full vampire mode in front of a parking lot full of humans. A cop even accused him of killing his partner. Steven's been trying to placate the media. It's not working. They're camped outside the gate. I guess someone leaked where Sam was. If you ask me, Roman probably did to mess with Sam."

I wasn't sure how to process that except to say, "Not only are we being hunted by our enemies, but now we have the media to contend with?" Unbelievable. The news that vampires existed would spread among humans like wildfire. Vampire hunters would come out of the woodwork. Innocent humans might run for the hills. Others would be awestruck and brave enough to try to get a glimpse of a true vampire. Basically, mayhem and anarchy.

She sipped from her bottle. "It will be interesting to see how it plays out. Again, not sure if you're caught up on what's been happening here while you've been gone. That vampire lady, Kendra, who supposedly killed Dad, is here."

I could feel the creases forming on my forehead. "Sam didn't mention her." No fault of his. We had a shitload of crap to deal with, and Kendra wasn't high on my list. I was curious about her relationship with my father and whether she'd been responsible for his death. "Come to think of it, I do remember Sam saying her name when I was on the phone with you guys. Did she show up to talk to me?"

Jordyn fiddled with her neck brace. "Not exactly. Two of Roman's men are in the base prison. After Jo read their minds, we learned that Kendra had been arguing with Roman at a hotel. Ben and Olivia went to investigate and found her passed out in her room. She'd been shot with a ton of those drugged darts."

"She's involved with Roman?" I dropped my gaze to my lap, trying to work out the connection, but I was coming up empty.

Jordyn lifted a shoulder. "I don't know. When Ben brought her in, Doc said she could be out for days. When you called from the cabin, she wasn't awake yet. No clue if she is now. I left shortly after Sam did and headed for West Virginia. Now, here we are."

I hopped up. "Only one way to find out," I said, eager to see and talk to Kendra. It was time to learn more about the vampire who had been accused by my uncles of murdering my father.

25

SAM

Part of the state-of-the-art medical facility was about to become a birthing suite. Over the years, there had been a handful of human spouses living on base who had been pregnant by vampires. But either they'd given birth at one of the local hospitals or they'd already had their kids when they'd moved into naval housing.

Doc was excited that he would now be able to accommodate the medical needs of any pregnant woman coming in, although he would have to hire an ob-gyn doctor like Dr. Martin.

To my left, a foreman for the construction company Doc had hired was discussing the upcoming demolition of one wall with two of his workers. Huddled at the other end of the infirmary, Doc and Peter were finalizing the chip-removal procedure one last time before I became the guinea pig.

Lingering outside of Doc's office, I tuned out the noise, examining the rice-grain-size device in my hand. It reminded me of an oval-shaped pill, and I was fascinated that it could control the brain. I now knew why Peter said it would be difficult to surgically remove the fucker, as tiny as it was.

After what had happened in West Virginia, I didn't care what it took to take out the chip. I never wanted to be used as a weapon again. It tore out my heart to know I could've killed the one woman who made my life a fuck ton better with her in it.

The click of the double doors that led into the infirmary perked up my senses. Jo's lavender scent announced her before she breezed in.

She buttoned her lab coat, quickly searching the room until her silver gaze landed on me. "There you are. Are you okay? You left your phone in Webb's office." She wiggled it in her hand. "It's unlike you to forget things."

My mind had definitely been on the long list of crap I had on my plate.

She swiped a hand over her head, fiddling with the errant strands of her black hair that was styled in a French braid. "Are you worried about the procedure?"

"I would be lying if I said I wasn't." I hoped Peter knew what the fuck he was doing.

She rested against the lab bench across from me. "Are you sure you don't want Layla to hold your hand? Is she awake?"

I put up my mental shields despite having taken a dose of the mind-blocking potion earlier that morning. With Layla around, I had to double up security around my mind to keep my sister out. "Yeah. Jordyn's with her. By the way, where's Pops?"

She crossed her legs at the ankles, her black patent leather flats shining in the light of the room. "Dad and Tripp are debriefing Webb. When are you leaving for Maine? And I have an idea about the wedding."

I chuckled. "You're not giving up on planning the nuptials, are you?"

"You told me last night you want to marry Layla before she gives birth, so I've been thinking. Are you sure she's going to say yes?"

Cocking an eyebrow, I looked at my sister like she was insane. I was one hundred percent sure, but damn it, that niggle of doubt in the deep recesses of my psyche wiggled free. Yet I couldn't find a reason why Layla would decline my hand in marriage. "I sure the fuck hope so."

"She might want to wait until after the babies are born," Jo said, "so she can fit into a wedding dress."

My sister was rankling my grumpy side, even though she could be right. Still, Layla didn't strike me as someone who wanted a big soiree with lavish shit and expensive gowns. If she did, I would go with the flow. But if I knew my huntress, she would prefer simple and quick with family and friends. Besides, we weren't inviting the other Aberdeens. A war would break out before we could exchange vows.

"What's your idea?" I was done speculating on what Layla would say or do. As far as I was concerned, I would toss Layla over my shoulder and elope if Jo's idea steamrolled into something Layla and I didn't want.

"How about a handfasting ceremony? It's a simple ritual of tying of the hands while you exchange vows. You can set it up any way you want. No church. No priest. It fits you perfectly, Sam. I don't know if Layla's into a church wedding or not, but if you choose handfasting, George can officiate. He's done a few hand-fasting ceremonies for the residents in town in Maine. We can use the war room. That way, more of the people we care about can attend."

I wasn't into all the details of wedding planning. I would like those I cared about to witness our vows. But if Layla and I tied the knot in Maine, then hardly anyone could attend since a war was brewing and our enemies were running amok. "You've thought of everything, haven't you?" I pushed off the wall, spotting Peter and Doc coming toward us. "As soon as Layla says yes, I'll talk to her. For now, I think it's showtime." An anxious but excited shiver gripped my stomach, and I hoped like fuck I would leave the infir-mary with my brain intact.

Peter's salt-and-pepper hair was disheveled. Wrinkles rimmed his dark eyes behind his black-framed glasses, and a sheen of sweat shone on his bulbous nose. I had to hand it to him—he was one dedicated scientist, working hours on end to help us find a solution. When my uncle Patrick was alive, he'd worked just as tirelessly in his lab. Carly wasn't any different, seeking knowledge and trying to find a cure for diseases. But immortality wasn't the answer. Or maybe it was. After Layla explained Carly's true motives to Doc and me, Doc's only comment had been that anything was possible.

Doc rubbed the back of his neck, settling his brown gaze on me. Trepidation was oozing off him as he approached, which gave me reason to pause. Dr. Damon Vieira was a vampire well known in our community for his intelligence, impeccable work ethic, benevolence, and nerves of steel. He hardly showed his true emotions to a patient, but when he did, they either conveyed bad news or that he wasn't comfortable with a procedure. Doc liked to be a thousand percent sure before he tested any of his theories on us or anyone.

"Sam, are you ready?" Peter asked, approaching. "We'll use this exam room. We're all set up." The scrawny man seemed confident, rolling his small shoulders back as he passed me and entered the room.

Jo pushed off the counter and trailed on Peter's heels. "I'm eager to watch." My sister's curious mind would bode well when she officially became a doctor. Her studies weren't quite done yet.

I blocked Doc's pathway, peering down at him. "You're nervous. Anything I should be worried about?"

He grinned. "Never let anyone tell you you're not an empath. It's a new procedure for me. But I agree with Peter. It should work. We need to get started. Afterward, Dr. Martin has the MRI room at the imaging center reserved for tomorrow afternoon. Like before, you'll need to sneak out the south gate. The media are multiplying at the main one. I hope your father can do something about them."

If anyone could quell the media, it was my old man.

Once Doc, Peter, Jo, and I were gathered in the room, I sat in one of those vitrectomy chairs—or in laymen's terms, a kneeling chair.

Peter pulled on a pair of nitrile exam gloves. "I'm going to inject a small amount of sodium hydroxide into the base of your skull in the area just below where the chip is located. The chemical will dissolve the glass surrounding the chip, and in turn, the contents inside will break apart and flush into your bloodstream."

Doc pinched the bridge of his nose. "You might feel like you're burning from the inside out, but it won't be as bad as if you had cobalt in you. The good news is—sodium hydroxide won't kill you. The bad news is—it could damage some brain cells."

Jo had her mouth slightly ajar, standing in my line of sight next to Peter. I didn't need to feel her anxiety. Her expression said it all.

"Before we start," Doc continued, "we're going to hook up an IV containing your blood to help flush your system faster, and, at the same time, it should heal any damage to your internals, including your brain cells."

"Hooyah!" I bit out the navy's battle cry in a sarcastic way rather than what it was originally intended for—to build morale. "Let's do this."

Once the IV of blood was streaming through my veins, Peter primed the needle that had to be six inches in length. PTSD slapped me across the face, reminding me horrifically of the needles my uncle Patrick had used on me—and the one Carly had used more recently.

My fangs throbbed for release as anticipation scraped my nerves. I might live off the fear of my enemy but not off my own. Losing my loved ones was my number one fear. Coming in second was flying. Rounding out third was needles.

"One last thing," Peter said. "Your occipital lobe that controls your vision resides in the back of your brain. It's possible your vision could be compromised. Since you're a vampire, it might only do temporary damage, like what happened to your hearing, which returned."

I was able to hear again because the chip moved. He was about to use a chemical in my brain. That shit was completely different. "Wait one fucking second. You chose now to tell me this?" I eyed Doc. "That's why you're sweating?"

Doc donned a pair of exam gloves. "Sam, the chip is damaged, which means it can't engage anymore. We could leave it in."

Jo shook her head. "If I were you, I would remove it. You'll have peace of mind, knowing that the chip won't shift again."

I was the one sweating now. "From the start, I've wanted to take it out regardless of whether it's working or not. I should heal anyway, right?"

Doc bobbed his head. "You should, but there is always that chance you don't. I know I sound unsure. That's because I haven't dealt with the vampire brain."

It would suck the big one if I couldn't see. Man, that would mean I couldn't look into Layla's dick-squeezing electric-blue eyes or see the birth of my kids. And I couldn't be a Navy SEAL anymore. Missions would be a thing of the past. I had to stick to my guns. My gut had told me from the start to remove the fucker.

"Just do it," I said.

The three of them nodded.

I planted my face in the padded headrest and closed my eyes. Then my sister gathered my hair off my neck and wrapped it with a band.

"You'll feel a pinch," Peter said from behind me.

Jo held my hand. I would prefer Layla's, but I didn't want her with me because we were trying to keep her stress free. As I waited for that pinch, I thought of how I would propose to her. It would definitely be on the beach and under the stars in Maine. Now, I just had to string the right words together. My stomach fluttered at the idea that I would make her my wife. Marriage had never been in my sights. Jo had that dream. As a kid, she couldn't stop talking about how she would marry her Prince Charming.

"You know, Sam, one day I will marry a man who will never lay a hand on me." She'd said that many times as we watched our foster dads beat the shit out of their significant others. My response had been, *"I have no dreams of settling down."* She'd ribbed me about that, encouraging me to reconsider.

"Sam." Jo's light voice drew me out of the past. "It's done."

I sat up, opening my eyes, and my heart stopped. "I can't see."

No sooner than I said those three words, Layla's voice filtered in, and I cringed. Did she hear me?

"Jordyn, this way," Layla said.

Fuck! If she knew I couldn't see, she would shit her pants. She couldn't be in the room. This would be a boatload of stress she didn't need.

"Someone make sure Layla doesn't come in this room," I bit out. "And get her out of the infirmary until we can fix this."

"I'll handle it," Jo said with surety. Leave it to my sister to take charge.

A second later, the door clicked shut, and I heard Layla ask Jo, "Is Sam in there?"

"He is, but you can't go in," my sister said. "Peter and Dr. Vieira are running X-rays on Sam. You can't be near the radiation. Why don't we head to the cafeteria and grab something to eat? Sam will meet us there when he's done."

Silence ensued. I wasn't sure if Layla would buy the white lie or not. But bravo to my sister for reacting fast.

"Okay." Layla's tone was suspicious. "Do you know anything about Kendra? Is she here?"

"She's not," Jo said. "I'll fill you in on the way out."

"Doc, please make sure they're gone before you say a word to me," I bit out.

My gut was one big-ass knot. If my blindness was permanent, it was my own fucking fault.

"I'll check," Peter said as the sound of the door handle clicked. "Coast is clear."

Doc and I collectively sighed.

"Now fix me," I growled out. "This cannot be permanent."

"Sam, keep your head up." Doc's voice was laden with impatience. "I'm waving a penlight around your eyes. Tell me if you detect any light whatsoever."

"That's a negative." I sat up straighter in the kneeling chair, pressing the heels of my palms into my thighs.

If I couldn't see, then what the fuck would I do? It would be a struggle to learn how to help Layla raise our kids. I wouldn't see her beautiful face anymore or look into her electric-blue eyes or see the curves of her gorgeous body. Fuck, I would never see what my kids looked like.

"I have an idea," Dr. Vieira said. "I'll be right back."

I growled, shoving both hands through my hair. "I shouldn't have done this. Doc was right—the chip is fried, so it wouldn't have fucked with me again."

Peter cleared his throat. "Maybe not, Sam. But it could potentially have moved again. I'm confident that this is only temporary." I couldn't see his body language, but he sounded sure of himself.

That loosened the humungous knot in my stomach.

Heavy footsteps clattered in. "I'm back," Dr. Vieira said. "I made a mixture of leftover shifter blood and Abbey's. It worked on Ben. Sam, lower your head, please. I need to inject this into the same spot Peter used for the chemical."

I did as he instructed, praying, hoping, freaking the fuck out, actually. I needed to be whole, to be the man Layla knew me to be —strong and protective, and that required every one of my senses.

After Doc was done, I lifted my head. "I still can't see." Beads of sweat rolled down my temples.

Fuck!

My pulse was beating like the little drummer boy.

"Any signs of light?" Doc asked. "I'm waving a penlight around your eyes."

I blinked several times, nodding. "It's blurry, but you're slowly coming into focus, Doc." After another round of blinks, I reoriented my vision. "Wait, it's dark again." I closed my eyes, gritting my teeth.

"It might take a few more minutes," Doc said. "But I'll add another dose. It won't hurt."

I felt another sting in the base of my skull. I sat there, chewing on my lip, praying to the gods and fate not to fuck with me.

"Open now," Doc ordered.

His face came in and out of focus until the more I blinked, the clearer he became. "Better. I can see the sweat on your face, Doc."

He slumped his shoulders. "You might have episodes of blurriness for a couple of days."

"I'll take that over blindness."

Now that I could fully relax and not have to worry about anyone controlling me or fucking with my brain, it was time to blow this joint and have some fun.

26

LAYLA

I sat at a table in the middle of the cafeteria, eating lasagna, one of many choices on the menu. On the way here, Jordyn had excused herself. She wanted to lie down and take something for her pain. I'd told her I would fill her in later on what I learned about Kendra. Jo was currently talking to a soldier by the door who I didn't recognize. The tall, brown-haired vampire had snagged her attention when we walked in several minutes ago. It looked like she must be explaining something interesting to him because she had his rapt attention.

In between bites of bland lasagna, I was people watching. A handful of soldiers waited their turn in the food line, which had a wide selection of different meats, potatoes, vegetables, and pasta dishes.

Jo waved at the soldier she'd been talking to, then glided over with a sense of purpose as though she owned the place. She probably did. "I'm going to grab a tea, then we can chat."

We had talked a little when we'd left the infirmary, but I'd only had the chance to ask her about the chip-removing procedure. She skirted around the topic, only saying that Peter and Doc knew what they were doing. I suspected she'd said that because she was reading my mind, knowing I'd been suddenly concerned when she'd rushed out of the room and closed the door.

I had no reason to think she was lying about the X-ray radiation. I knew there was truth to that. But I'd gotten the feeling she didn't want me to see something. I hadn't probed, mainly because I wasn't sure I wanted to know. I was so tired of what the chip had done to Sam and how it fucked with our lives that I would've probably gone apeshit if the chip decided to fuck with Sam again.

Jo returned with a steaming cup of fragrant tea and slid into the seat across from me. "How's the lasagna?"

"Sauce is bland. Other than that, it's fine," I said. I'd only taken a couple of bites. "The tea smells spicy," I added. I couldn't quite put my finger on what kind it was.

She flipped her black hair over her shoulder. "It's turmeric. You should try this. It's good for inflammation, which could help your pregnancy."

Besides blood, I'd only been drinking water. "I might." I wasn't a tea drinker. My mom had been though. "So, Jordyn told me Kendra was here," I said, jumping right into the heart of why I'd gone to the infirmary in the first place.

She blew on her steaming cup of liquid. "She was. We decided to let her go the day before yesterday. She had nothing to do with Roman. She was in the wrong place at the wrong time."

"Did you read her mind?" I asked.

"Kendra blocked some parts, which vampires tend to do." She sipped from her cup. "In a nutshell, she was in the hotel bar the day you were rushed to the ER and overheard a man drop your name and Sam's, saying that you were at the hospital. Kendra was concerned. So she asked the man about you. He told her to mind her own business. Next thing she knew, Roman was knocking on her hotel door. He wanted to see how well she knew you. An argument ensued, then Ben and Olivia found her unconscious in her room."

I cut off another piece of lasagna. "Did she say anything about my father?"

Jo shook her head. "No. But she gave me her number to give to you. It's in my purse, which is in the infirmary. I'll make sure to give it to you later."

"Was Kendra here to talk to me?" I was itching to know more.

Jo set her cup down. "She knew you were with us, but she wanted my dad's help with your uncles."

My uncle Ray was the one who had been salivating to burn her, but Kendra didn't have to worry about him anymore.

"I did ask her where she'd gone after my dad asked her to wait in the plane that day." Jo scratched a spot on her neck, her wedding ring glinting in the many lights shining down from above. "Apparently, the minute Kendra left the hangar, she ran. Once she was far enough away from your uncles, she stole a car. That was all I got from her."

It would've been nice to chat with Kendra, and I would eventually call her.

Jo sat back in her chair and swept her silver gaze over me. "Are the clothes comfortable? They look great on you."

I rolled my eyes. "Stupid me. I'm so sorry. Thank you. My head is up my ass. I want to repay you."

She grinned, looking like her brother. They had the same eye shape—the outer corners turned upward. "No need to do that. You're family, Layla. Consider it an early Christmas present."

I had to somehow return the favor to both her and Harley. "Thank you again." I was digging my fork into the layers of pasta when Sam strutted in.

I slumped in my chair, relieved to see him wearing a grin as though a huge weight had been lifted off his shoulders. Hopefully, his handsome smile meant the chip was history.

Jo turned in her seat and followed Sam's movements as he came over to me. "Sam, how did it go?"

He kissed me on the cheek, then slid into the chair next to me. "Perfect, sis."

"Is the chip gone?" I held my breath.

Jo studied Sam as if she was speaking to him telepathically or reading his mind.

"It's one hundred percent gone. No more fucking chip. I am free of that piece of shit."

My muscles loosened. "Thank God." No more worries about someone controlling him or the freaking thing turning on and him becoming a monster.

Jo sighed heavily. "So, everything is good?"

I wagged my finger between them. "Okay, Jo gave me the impression you two didn't want me to see something in the exam room. What was it?"

"Just a minor complication." Sam's hand landed on my thigh. "Nothing to worry about, baby doll. And before you protest, I told Jo to lie to you. I made a command decision for your health. Remember, no stress."

I wasn't exactly enamored with him keeping things from me, but this was one situation that I couldn't fault him for it. He was protecting me.

"You didn't tell me to lie," Jo said. "I did that on my own. You just told me to handle it."

"You look like nothing is wrong," I said, "and if we're laying our cards out on the table, I didn't really want to know. Though, I'm curious what the minor complication was."

"My vision," he said. "The chemical they used fucked with it. But again, it's all good now."

I bobbed my head. "You're right to have kept that from me. I would've freaked out. Then killed your vampire ass." No lie there.

"On a better note, are you ready for Maine?" He waggled his eyebrows.

"Hell yeah." I couldn't wait to dip my toes in the sand and ocean, breathe in salty air, and sit by the fire with Sam.

27

SAM

I jogged along the rough shore of the Atlantic, the brisk wind in my face, my bare feet digging into the sand, and sweat covering my body. The temp at six in the morning was a balmy forty degrees Fahrenheit. Not as warm as Layla would like it, but she didn't care as long as we were by the ocean.

She and I had arrived late last night. We'd finally left the base after a week of dealing with shit. I would've stolen her away sooner if it wasn't for my short stint of blindness. Doc wanted me to hang around to ensure my eyesight was back to normal. I'd suffered blurriness for two solid days. The great news was—a scan confirmed that the fucking chip was history.

Peter was brilliant for coming up with the process. Granted, the risks were quite hefty. When I'd opened my eyes and met complete darkness, I practically died, especially when I'd heard Layla's voice coming toward the room. I loved my sister for reacting on her feet. I didn't want her to lie, so I'd admitted to Layla that I had. If she would've yanked out my nutsack, then so be it. But her health was important. I also adored Jo for stepping up and owning her shit.

With all that out of the way, it was time to pamper my huntress for a solid two weeks. We both needed the quietness and to reconnect with each other before the babies came. Layla wanted Jordyn to tag along, but she said no. *Thank fuck.* I hadn't swayed Jordyn's decision either. Whether Jordyn knew I was proposing or not, she wanted time to herself. She was struggling with Junior's death and her decision to make a deal with their wicked witch of a grandmother.

Activity in West Virginia was quiet. Adam Emery was up to something with his bag of tricks. Anytime an enemy went dark, they were planning. The challenge we faced was the different motives of the players involved. Harriet had her own agenda, which was mainly to find a cure for her blood cancer. Intech and its sister company, Camden Industries, developed weapons and computer software for the Department of Defense.

If the U.S. government got wind of Adam's vision of super soldiers, vampires, shifters, and any supernatural creature would be in jeopardy, especially those with special powers like mine.

The other viable and maybe lethal threat was Roman Brown. The head of the blood cartel would sell his soul to make money. Well, not his soul, but other people, including Abbey, vampires, or shifters—anyone who could bring him tons of cash. He'd said he had his own plan brewing.

I slowed to a walk about forty yards from the house. The light was on in the kitchen. George had gotten up before me. Webb's dear friend and father figure was a century-plus-old vampire who lived at the house when Jo and Webb weren't there. Normally, he wouldn't hang around, but this time, we needed the security. Besides, George was a great cook, and since Layla was eating for five, we had our own personal chef.

As I climbed the stairs leading up to the large two-level deck, my phone rang. I plucked it out of a zippered pocket on my gym shorts and swore, answering Tripp's call. He would only call if I had hostiles heading my way or about something that affected Layla and me.

"Sorry, man," Tripp said. "I need to give you a heads-up just in case Jordyn gets wind and calls Layla." He pushed out a breath. "The team in West Virginia caught Noah Aberdeen. They found him in the mountains near that cabin Layla was at. He's feral. Remember Blake Turner? Well, Noah is worse off."

"Motherfucker. Noah was the first candidate of Carly's concoction just like Blake was for my uncle Patrick. Is Noah dead?" If not, someone should put him out of his misery. According to Blake's autopsy, he'd died because the change from human to monster fucked with all of his organs, and eventually, his heart gave out.

"Negative," Tripp said. "Don't worry about this. I just needed to fill you in. Jordyn shouldn't find out. She's not working on Sawyer's team. She's been sidelined for her recent stunt. I know it's been difficult to keep things from Layla, since she's been heavily involved, but it's imperative to keep info on a need-to-know basis."

"Not a problem." She didn't need any bad news. "Also, we need to shut Carly down. I've tried calling her, but it goes straight to voice mail. I know we can persuade her to jump ship."

"That was the other thing I wanted to mention." Tripp sounded frustrated. "Olivia found Carly's phone in the wooded area along the road leading to Intech's facility. I'm not sure what that means. Don't sweat this shit. Relax. You deserve it. One more thing. Webb and I decided that when you return, you'll help out in the control room and fill in as a guard until you're cleared for missions."

He and Webb had mentioned that they would figure out a position for me to fill until after Layla gave birth. "Yes, sir. I'll check in later in the week." I would relax, but I also wanted to keep abreast just in case I needed to react quickly.

After we hung up, my phone went off again. This time, the caller ID announced my sister.

"Sis, you're up early," I said.

She yawned. "Sorry. Abbey had one of her terrifying nightmares at three this morning. They're happening more and more as of late. But that isn't why I'm calling. I forgot to tell you that Stan's wife, Gina, sells the ribbons for the handfasting ceremony in her shop in town. After you propose, take Layla to see Gina. I also wanted to check on you. How's your eyesight?"

I sat on the bottom step, watching the sun peek over the horizon.

"Back to normal. Not to change the subject, but what was

Abbey's nightmare about?" I worried about my niece. She recently had visions of Roman capturing her. A growl lodged in my throat at the idea of Roman anywhere near her.

"Abbey didn't want to talk about it," Jo said. "I don't think she wants to tell me. She's afraid she'll upset me. But I heard her that morning when you and she were talking. She's seen Roman kidnapping her. Isn't that what she told you?"

A hard wind blew, kicking up sand as my ire bubbled to the surface. "Yeah. I'll fry the bastard before that happens."

"You'll have to get in line after Webb. And I love that you want to protect Abbey, but you have a growing family to support and protect. You know as well as I do that they'll be in the same boat as Abbey."

That time a growl burst free. "You're right. But we will all protect Abbey and the little Masons. You're still teaching Abbey how to fight, right?"

"Of course. Her powers are strengthening too. While we're on the topic, you know I've been looking into Abbey's family history. It's been a challenge, but I think I found Abbey's grandfather on Rachel's side. I don't have much yet."

For a second, my heart stopped as I thought she was about to say *on Edmund Rain's side.* The last thing we needed was a Rain coming into the picture, though it was possible. Edmund had a brother and sister, according to my dad.

"Sis, if I recall, didn't Rachel's mom die of cancer and her father in a car wreck? Also, Rachel didn't have any siblings either. At least, not from what Pops told us."

"I'm trying to confirm that," she said. "And you know people keep secrets about their past for various reasons. Look at Layla's mom. She lied about hers. Not only that, Rachel was good at shielding Dad from reading her mind. Abbey will want answers about her heritage. Webb and I agree that it's best if we start now and shake the skeletons from the closet, so to speak."

I wasn't about to argue that sometimes things were better left in the past. I had my own stuff to deal with anyway.

I pushed to my feet. "Layla and I will stop by Gina's shop after I propose, of course. Also, you, Harley, and Jordyn will be painting the nursery, right?" Jo wanted to be involved, as did Harley and Jordyn.

"Yes, we're buying the paint today. Good luck with the proposal." Her excitement came through loud and clear. "Talk soon." Then she hung up.

I sat there for another minute, enjoying the sunrise, the salty cool morning air, and the sound of the waves. I wasn't one to lounge around. I would rather be on a mission or bashing in an enemy's skull—but I needed time away as much as Layla did. It had been a bumpy road for her and me, and I didn't see smooth sailing under blue skies in the near future. So we had to steal these quiet times whenever we could. I would make the most of our two-week getaway. First up was the proposal.

I bolted up the stairs. I wanted to pick George's brain about handfasting before Layla woke up.

The second I opened the accordion glass doors, the aroma of bacon made my stomach groan.

George was flipping pancakes on the griddle attached to the stove. "How was your run? I saw you on the phone. Everything okay?"

I slid the doors shut, then grabbed my T-shirt that I'd left on the barstool and shrugged into it. "Run was good. Nothing urgent. Just talked to Tripp, then Jo."

The tall, lanky vampire wiped his hands on a towel draped over his shoulder as his brown eyes appraised me. "But something. You're agitated."

"It's SEAL business," I said, commandeering a stool.

George collected a bottle of water and one of blood from the fridge, then set them down in front of me. "I talked to Stan this morning. He assigned one of his off-duty deputies to guard you and Layla. Paul is out patrolling the area around the house. If any strangers come to town, we'll know it the minute they arrive. I know you'll worry, but don't. We have your back."

"Thanks, but you know me. I'll be on alert just the same. Let's not forget that Webb's old girlfriend, Nicki, snuck past Stan," I countered.

He picked up the spatula. "That was different. The folks here knew her. She's still in prison, right?" He flinched.

I did as well. Nicki had a screw loose, but she was mild compared to Rianne Aberdeen.

"For sure. Anyway, no one followed us up here." Another reason I was stoked Jordyn hadn't come with us—the less knowledge Layla's family members had of where the house was, the better.

The oven door squeaked as George inserted a cookie sheet filled with pancakes. "I'll keep these warm for Layla. Do you think she'll sleep late?"

I gulped down the water first. "Probably. She needs the rest." I looked around the open floor plan as I sharpened my senses. Except for George's room, which was downstairs on the other side of the house, the other bedrooms were upstairs. Layla's heart rate was slow, telling me she was still asleep.

George brought me a plate of pancakes and a side of bacon. "You're proposing tonight?"

I snagged a piece of bacon, nodding. "Jo tells me you're the guru on handfasting. Can you tell me a bit about it? And would you be open to marrying Layla and me?"

He bowed his head. "I would be honored, of course. I'll explain how it works after you propose. That way, I'll have your attention as well as Layla's." He glanced out the accordion doors. "The wind should die down, and it's a crescent moon tonight, which means the sky will be darker and the stars brighter. And don't worry. I'll make myself scarce."

"A perfect setting, then," I said as my stomach knotted in a good way, especially when I heard footsteps upstairs.

George started preparing a plate for Layla as I stuffed my face.

About five minutes later, Layla sashayed in, wearing blue pajama bottoms and one of my SEAL sweatshirts that hung down to her knees. Her auburn hair was pinned up on her head, and her blue eyes looked sleepy, but her smile that was reserved only for me was breathtaking.

My pulse was on a fast train to Layla-land as my cock jerked. The woman had my balls in one hand and my heart in the other. She owned my arrogant ass—mind, body, and soul.

"Morning," she said, touching her face. "Is there something wrong? You two look like zombies." She wound a path around the couch near the fireplace.

"We're good," George said.

Suddenly, I was on a quick mental jaunt back to the day I'd brought her up here and fucked her as she stuck her ass in the air behind that couch.

She kissed me on the ear. "You're spacing out, vampire."

I snaked my hand around her waist and pulled her to me, then rubbed her growing belly with my other hand as I pecked her on the lips. "You're glowing, baby doll."

"I feel rested," she said. "It's almost like the minute I got out of the car last night, my problems vanished."

"This place will do that," George said. "What would you like to drink?"

Layla slid onto the stool next to mine. "I prefer coffee with a shot of bourbon. But since I can't have that, is there any herbal tea? Jo is starting to rub off on me. She thought I should try turmeric."

"Jo keeps that handy here. Coming right up." George went to work, preparing her tea.

"So, I thought I heard George say you're nervous," Layla said. "About what?"

The little minx might have preternatural hearing. Maybe that was another of her magical abilities to be added to her list of mind control and a banshee scream. She'd tested her hand at mind control with me a few days ago. No cigar. She thought her temporary powers only worked when she was angry or threatened.

"About being a father," I said. That was the truth. Would I make a good one? Would I suffocate our children with my overprotective nature?

Layla rubbed my thigh. "Sam, you're going to be a fantastic father. You might be arrogant and gruff on the outside, but inside, you're a big teddy bear." She batted her big blue eyes at me.

Well, fuck. I was reduced to a pile of mush. I leaned in and kissed her on the ear. "I'm your teddy bear."

She swatted at me, flirting as she laughed.

"Have you thought of names?" George asked as the microwave dinged, and he removed the measuring cup of piping hot water.

"Sam has. If we have boys. Liam, Lucas, Lane, and Lincoln," she singsonged.

"Those names kind of have a ring to them," I added proudly.

George poured the hot water into a cup over a tea bag. "I like those. If I was to ever have children, I would name my girl Luna and my boy Andrew."

"Luna is pretty," Layla said. "I wouldn't mind naming our son Samuel."

"Like a junior. Samuel Jr." I wasn't a fan of calling my kid Junior for various reasons. And while I liked my name, it would be confusing.

She frowned, no doubt thinking of her cousin. "Maybe not. I mean, I love your name, but it would be weird to call our son Junior. I did like my cousin, but the name evokes memories of things I would like to forget."

Time to change the subject for now. "After you eat, we'll take a walk on the beach. Or whatever you would like to do."

Her full lips split into a wide mischievous smile. "I have something in mind."

Her lust wafted into my nostrils, sending my cock into a frenzy.

28

———

LAYLA

Stars twinkled, surrounding the crescent moon as the sound of the waves sliding along the shore trickled in through a tiny opening in the accordion glass doors. I was tucked between Sam's legs with my back to his front on a blanket by the fireplace as he leaned against the couch. We'd decided to create our own picnic inside.

The weather wasn't as warm as I would like, but I was by the ocean with the man who meant more to me than anyone in my life. His arms were around me, and he was rubbing light circles on my large belly. I was close to three months but looked like I was six. The rapid growth aligned with what Dr. Vieira had found in the Emily Crawford medical file.

I snuggled into him, contented despite how fat I felt. We weren't fighting enemies, getting kidnapped, hanging over a firepit, running through the woods, or dealing with any stressful situation like the ones we'd both been in since we'd met. I couldn't remember a time when I felt at peace like I did now.

The fire crackled as Sam nibbled on my ear. "A penny for your thoughts."

I tipped my head slightly to the side, feeling the warmth of his breath. "I don't ever want to leave here."

The day had been surreal. That morning, when I'd told him I had something in mind for us to do, he thought I meant I wanted to fuck his brains out. I would always want to do that. But it was time to chill, hang, and enjoy each other outside of sex. We knew we had that perfected. Now, we needed to learn more about each other, breathe, and talk about our future, which we'd done when we'd walked on the beach and had eaten a late lunch at the diner in town. One of the things on my list had been to sample the assorted desserts George had bragged about. The small restaurant was famous for its pies, and not to mention its view of the ocean was spectacular.

"One day, baby doll, we'll have a home on a beach or close to it where our rug rats can play, build sandcastles, fish, surf, if that's their thing. My promise to you."

I wished he could assure me we wouldn't have to fight the war brewing or deal with my grandmother or Rianne, if she was alive. My intuition whispered that she was. I still didn't know how I felt about that.

He kissed my hair. "You're tensing up."

I hated to tell him that my mind wandered to the dark side. Any thoughts other than Sam, the babies, and us would ruin a fantastic day. So I mentally threw everything else in the ocean.

I rubbed his thick thighs encased in blue jeans. "You should wear tattered jeans more often." I hardly saw Sam out of uniform. He was handsome in anything he wore, especially when he was suited up with weapons. That look had me swimming in lust and my ovaries spitting out more eggs for him to fertilize. But the casual clothes added a softer layer to my arrogant, powerful vampire. One that projected a man who had a big heart as well as gentle hands when need be. Despite his current outer appearance, Sam was a badass motherfucker through and through.

"You're avoiding my comment," he said in a tone that seemed faraway.

"Busted. But we're not here to talk about anything except us."

I wasn't the only guilty one. Sam had been squirrelly when we'd left the house, senses sharp, scanning the area, and at times not paying attention to what I'd been saying. I didn't complain or blame him. I would be lying if I said I wasn't jumpy, even though we had a bodyguard—a brawny vampire who was built like a brick wall. I would pity anyone in his line of fire.

I reached over Sam's leg and swiped my finger through the remaining elderberry left on the plate. I couldn't believe the diner had elderberry pie. My mom loved the fruit. I almost felt her with me when I'd savored every mouthful. Needless to say, I couldn't leave the diner without purchasing more of the delicious dessert.

I stuck my goo-covered finger into my mouth and suckled, moaning as I relished the tasty treat.

Sam groaned in my ear. "Careful, Layla." He slipped a hand between us and adjusted his crotch.

I giggled. "It doesn't take much to arouse you, does it?"

"Nope. Not when it comes to you," he said in a lustful tone. "I have an idea." Using the couch as an anchor, he pushed to his feet. Then he held out his hand. "Come on." Once I was upright, he snatched up the blanket and ushered me out onto the deck.

I inhaled the salty air as a light, cold breeze ruffled my hair. "Skinny-dipping?"

Laughing, he draped the blanket around my shoulders. "Your tits would fall off, and my balls would freeze."

"I would hate that. I need those balls." I latched on to the plaid fabric as I crossed my arms, closing myself inside.

He nipped my nose, then ushered me down to the second level of the deck. "For sure, I need those sexy tits."

We stood in front of the railing, looking out for a beat.

There was a calmness about the ocean that made it easier for me to breathe. Sam, on the other hand, had his shoulders hunched slightly.

My stomach fisted. "Sam, what is it?" I moved my head in a mechanical precision from left to right, once, twice, wondering if his sharp vamp vision spotted a threat. But I didn't see anyone or anything but a beautiful scene—a million stars twinkled in the darkened sky, surrounding the crescent moon as the soothing sound of the Atlantic carried on the wind.

He glanced upward, pulling me to him. I leaned my head on his chest near his fast-beating heart.

He released a breath. "In high school, Jo and I had a space science class that took place in the school's planetarium, where we learned about the constellations." He pointed outward and up over the ocean. "See those three stars stacked on top of one another at a slight angle? That's Orion's Belt." He used his finger to trace the outline of Orion in the air.

I couldn't exactly make out Orion, but I saw the three stars of the belt. "The arrogant, sexy vampire is an astronomer. Who knew?"

He didn't respond but continued, "I never knew my mom, but according to my dad, she believed in the mysticism and symbolism of the stars and planets. That names held power. For example, the planet Jupiter, guardian and protector of the sky, signifies great fortune." He paused, squeezing me to him, and if I wasn't mistaken, he was trembling. "Since I was born with the astrological sign of Sagittarius, my mom thought it befitting that my middle name should be Jove, which is of Latin origin and means Jupiter." A somberness flitted in his tone along with something else I couldn't put my finger on.

Dropping the blanket, I twisted around until my back was against the railing and our chests were mashed together, then I rested my hands on his hips. I'd learned more about Sam in a day than I had in the two-plus months since we'd met. From his love for baseball to his rough childhood to why his father had left him and Jo in foster care.

After their mother passed, their dad had gotten orders to deploy to Afghanistan, and the only one who could care for them was their maternal aunt. She didn't want anything to do with raising kids, and she hated Steven. But she'd taken them in anyway until a heated argument ensued when Steven called to tell her his mission had been extended. Not long after that conversation, Sam's aunt turned Sam and Jo over to the Department of Children and Families in Massachusetts. When Steven returned, he did everything in his power to find his kids but had gotten the runaround with the state. The aunt couldn't help Steven since she'd died in a car accident. At the same time, Edmund Rain was on the hunt for Jo and Sam for the same reason as Intech's—genetic engineering. Steven had felt the kids were safer in the system.

I couldn't judge Steven for what he'd done because I didn't walk in his shoes. I also didn't want to think about how my kids with Sam would be hunted, but maybe after our babies were born, it would be safer for us to stay off the grid and hide. Maybe we could even live at this house in Maine.

Still, compared to how Sam had grown up, my childhood had been blissful.

I admired every fiber of the formidable immortal. It was clear to me that the stars had sparked some painful memories. "Your mom was right. The name does fit you, Sam. Protector is who you are. But you're also kind, caring, sometimes an arrogant ass but mine, and you love unconditionally. I often wonder why you and I are together. I've killed vampires like they didn't matter. You taught me that they do. The good ones anyway. Now here we are, building a family and loving each other. Given my history, sometimes I struggle with how you can trust me. Your father, sister, and the entire SEAL team didn't have to accept me, but they did."

He cupped my face in his large hands. "It doesn't matter to me that you're a vampire hunter. The moment I saw you at the nightclub was the very moment you grabbed my heart. I've been drawn to your feistiness, your strength, and your beauty, inside and out." Silver threaded through the green in his eyes. "You care for those you love, you see the good in people, and your take-no-prisoners attitude fits us." He sighed, stepping back as he slipped his hand into his back pocket.

My legs wobbled at the emotion we were pouring out to each other. Then they shook like a leaf when he got down on one knee. I brought my fingers to my mouth, just as surprised as the last time he asked me to marry him right before he went into a coma. My heart punched my ribs as he held up the exquisite ruby gem with a trembling hand.

The precious stone was round, big, at least a carat, and set in a gold band. It couldn't be more perfect—simple yet elegant.

Tears flowed out one by one.

His silver eyes shone like a beacon calling me home. "Layla Aberdeen, would you be my sidekick, the woman who will keep me sane, a partner who will stand by my side and fight for what we believe in and those we love. Above all else, will you love my arrogant ass no matter what?"

I sobbed through the tears, my stomach a whirlwind of flutters. "I would love to be your partner, the mother of your children, and to fight to the ends of time alongside you. I will always, always love your arrogant vampire ass."

He kissed my stomach. "Did you hear that, kids? Your mom said yes." He rose, swaying as if he was dizzy, and slid the ring onto my finger, but it wouldn't go over my knuckle. "This was my mom's ring. She wanted me to have this for my bride-to-be. The ruby is a such a perfect match for your courageous and fiery personality."

More tears spilled, each one carrying happiness, peace, joy, love, and affection. "It's gorgeous, Sam." I was at a loss for words. I now understood his somberness when he started talking about the symbolism of the stars, Jupiter, his middle name, his mom, and her ring. "Maybe I can wear it on a chain until after I give birth." With the way I was retaining water and gaining weight, nothing would fit me.

He left the ring partway on my finger, then once again captured my face in his hands, his eyes searching mine. "No matter how rough the seas are ahead of us, never, ever forget it's you and me and that our kids will always come first. I fucking love you, baby doll."

I couldn't stop shedding tears as emotions clogged my throat. Never in a million fucking years did I expect I would be standing beneath the stars saying yes to a marriage proposal from a vampire, but I couldn't imagine my life without Sam.

I quivered in his embrace. "Fate hit the nail on the head,

throwing us together, and I will die a thousand deaths for you and our little ones."

His mouth crashed into mine. The kiss was slow, sensual, and passionate as our tongues intertwined. I knew our journey would be jagged and rocky, but as long as I had him, I could endure anything thrown at us.

29

SAM

Our two-week getaway had finally come to an end. I'd never spent more than a few days away from my job. I wasn't the type of person to sit around, hang on the beach, or stroll through shops. Fourteen days with Layla changed all that. She'd brought out a side of me I never knew existed, and it wasn't the side of me that wanted to strip her naked any chance I had.

Hell, looking at her now as she dozed in the passenger seat, my cock pulsed to be inside her. We'd had several nights of unbridled passion. But in between them, we talked about our fears, dreams, and fantasies whether walking the beach or lying by the fire. We checked out quaint stores, ate at the diner in town, and just chilled. If my buddies saw me in a store, they would rib me until they were on the floor, laughing their asses off.

Speaking of shops, Stan's wife, Gina, was a godsend with helping Layla pick out a necklace for her engagement ring. The pretty vampire with eyes the color of the ocean had been a wealth of information about handfasting and ribbons as well. Layla sucked up every bit of detail about the intimate ritual.

As the days passed, though, Layla was napping more and more, she was walking slower, and her stomach was quite large for three months, which wasn't surprising. After all, she was eating for five, but she was also expected to deliver after six months rather than nine, given that she was carrying nonhumans.

I exited off the highway into the city's abandoned textile district, adjusting the fan speed on the air conditioner. Temperatures for the beginning of May were warmer than usual, creeping over eighty degrees Fahrenheit. Our five-hour drive from Maine to Massachusetts had taken longer, since we hit rush hour traffic in Boston.

Darkness crawled through the streets of Fall River as I braked at a stoplight amid four- and five-story stone buildings with broken doors and shattered windows. The area had been bustling at one time in the city's history with thriving yarn and clothing manufacturers.

Releasing a soft breath, Layla stirred awake. "Are we close to home?"

Her last word made my stomach flip. Home to me wasn't a place but a feeling—one that was comfortable, safe, at ease, and loving. My sister had been my home forever, but Layla was now.

"About five miles," I said, pressing on the gas after the light turned green.

She pouted, grappling to find her necklace. When she grasped the ruby engagement ring, she sighed. "Can we turn around and go back?"

I reached over the console and dragged the backs of my fingers down her cheek. "We'll return to Maine again." I couldn't exactly say when because I didn't know.

We had a ton of shit to deal with outside of her pregnancy. The big elephant in the room was Intech. But even if we annihilated Intech, another power-hungry asshole would pop up, not even including Roman.

I wasn't exactly looking forward to desk duty. I itched to fight alongside my brothers. I knew my situation was only temporary. After all, if my dead grandfather's message to my father was right, I was instrumental in stopping this war. In the meantime, my priority was Layla and the birth of our children.

"Are the kiddos still active?" I asked. She'd been feeling kicks and wiggles here and there.

"I think they're asleep." She glanced out the window at the changing landscape as we left the textile district. "Any updates on Intech or my family?"

I'd checked in with Tripp a couple of times since I was curious about Noah. "Nothing. And before you ask, no signs of Alia's son or the two shifters." I partly lied. I couldn't share the news about Noah. As far as the three missing individuals went, that wasn't a lie. Tripp had told me Dane was beside himself that his brother Ross hadn't surfaced. I imagined the alpha shifter was one pissed-off motherfucker.

Time to talk about something else. I hated to lie to her, but I believed she would understand the nature of classified information.

I grasped her hand. "In the few minutes we have before we pull into the base, we should decide on a date for our handfasting ceremony. I need to give George a heads-up. Or we could wait."

I wanted to give her an out in case she changed her mind and wanted a big blowout wedding. She assured me that she didn't want anything fancy or expensive—just simple. She'd also agreed with me that we should marry before she gave birth and didn't mind the war room as a venue, even though I'd wanted to tie the knot under the stars. If we did, that would eliminate our family and friends from attending.

"I just love that idea. No churches. No big parties. Just you and me and a simple ceremony among our family and friends. It's just perfect, Sam." Her electric-blue eyes shimmered against the dashboard lights. "We should do it this weekend. That will give us time to settle in and focus on the nursery."

Jo had texted me that the nursery was painted.

"And names." She pushed out an exasperated sigh. "So far we have Liam and Luna, but we can only use both names if we have at least one baby of each sex. We need to come up with more names for both sexes."

Layla wasn't keen on Lane or Lincoln, two of the baby boy names I'd previously suggested. However, she'd fastened on Luna for a girl after George told us he loved the name. I agreed, especially because of its meaning—Roman goddess of the moon. Same went for Liam—strong-willed warrior and protector. My mom believed that a name shaped a person, and I wanted to carry on her beliefs.

"We have time," I said. "And it might come down to seeing the babies before we decide."

I navigated a sharp turn down the dirt road leading to the back entrance of the base. I'd called Tripp about an hour into the drive home. He'd informed me that the media was still camped outside the main gate. There weren't as many reporters as there had been when Layla and I had left for Maine, but to be safe, he didn't want me to chance it. If they saw my face, it might stir up a bigger frenzy.

I called Tripp again as I approached. The gate was chained and had a Do Not Enter sign attached and below that another one declaring Property of the U.S. Government.

"I'm at the south gate," I said when he answered.

"Copy that. The guard is making his rounds in that direction. Hang tight." Then the line disconnected.

She twined her fingers in mine as we rested our arms on the console. "Sam, I feel like we're about to enter hell. Are we ready for what lies ahead?"

I brought our joined hands up to my mouth and kissed hers. "We are, baby doll." We had to be. We had no choice.

The guard opened the gate, ending the conversation. No sooner than we drove on base, it seemed like the air changed from calm to a wild storm brewing. Maybe Layla was right. Yet, if this was hell, then I would gladly find a way to enjoy it as long as I had my auburn-haired huntress with me.

By the time we reached my apartment, Layla's anxiety had waned. Jordyn had called as we wound through the streets of the base, putting Layla in a better mood. The youngest Aberdeen sister was chomping at the bit to see Layla's engagement ring.

I had the key in the lock when Layla curled her fingers around my wrist. "Sam, before we go in…" She searched my face, her eyes filled with apprehension.

I bowed my head and kissed her on the lips as a small of

amount of irritation clawed at me. I hated how the instant we arrived, her happiness vanished. "I promise this isn't hell." I kept my voice playful, hoping to garner a smile or a roll of her eyes. "If it is, we have each other." I made a mental note to start searching for a hideaway spot like Webb and Jo's. My sister wouldn't mind us using her beach house, but I wanted one of my own. I always had.

"It's not that," she said.

"Why don't we go inside first? Then you can tell me."

She nodded as I ushered her through the door.

Suddenly, the lights flickered on, and people shouted, "Surprise! Welcome home! Congratulations!"

Layla and I reared back, exchanging wide-eyed looks.

She beamed. "Did you know about this, Sam?"

I knew Harley, Jo, and Jordyn would be waiting for us but not Webb, my dad, Tripp, and Doc.

Jo dashed up to us, wearing a huge grin, her silver eyes dancing with delight. "He didn't. This was a collective decision by all of us." She stabbed a thumb behind her.

Harley and Jordyn were standing by the wall of windows. Webb, Tripp, Doc, and my dad were near the kitchen island on the living room side.

Jordyn hurried up to her sister. The bruises on her face had lightened, she seemed to be free of pain, and the cast on her arm was covered in drawings and names. "You look fab, sis. Rested, happy, and glowing."

Layla hooked her arm around Jordyn's, and the two went up to Harley. The strawberry blonde nodded at me.

While the three of them chatted, I asked Jo quietly, "Is everything ready with the nursery?"

"Of course, brother. Remember who you're talking to: planner, detail-oriented sister. I get shit done."

"That you do," I said as I hugged her, then joined my dad, Tripp, Webb, and Doc, who were standing in the living room near the kitchen island.

After handshakes, bro hugs, and more congratulations, Webb and Tripp excused themselves. They had a meeting with Sawyer and informed me they would bring me up to speed when I reported for duty the next day.

Doc went over and joined Layla, Harley, Jordyn, and Jo, leaving my dad and me alone.

My father gripped my shoulder. "Son, proud isn't a strong enough word to describe how I feel about you and what you've accomplished. You will be a great husband and a loving father."

Our relationship had been a rocky road for a few years, but we'd worked out our differences. Now, he was one of the most important people in my life. "And you'll be an awesome grandpa."

He chuckled. "I feel old."

"Pops, you are old," I said playfully. He didn't look over a hundred, but he was.

We both laughed.

"I need to run. The council is still up my ass with the media bullshit. We'll talk tomorrow." After we exchanged a hug, he zipped out.

Doc and Layla talked about scheduling an exam, then he left.

The four women regarded me. Jo, Harley, and Jordyn all gave me that are-you-going-to-show-her look.

I was dying to see Layla's face when she walked into the nursery.

Harley curled her strawberry-blond hair around her ear as she opened up a telepathic connection. *The blindfold is on the coffee table. Layla is going to freak. I hope you like it too.*

I picked up the silk fabric and sauntered up to Layla.

Lines dented her smooth forehead. "What's that for?" She pointed at the white silk fabric in my hand.

Man, I had several sexual innuendos on the tip of my tongue. "I have a surprise for you."

She flushed. "Sam?"

The ladies snickered.

"It's not what you think," I said, though the blindfold was giving me some dick-hardening ideas. "Would you humor me?" I held out the silky material.

Layla eyed the ladies. "Should I ask you three what you did?"

"Sis, go with the flow," Jordyn said, giddy.

I stood behind Layla and tied the silky fabric around her eyes, then blew in her ear.

She shivered. "Sam," she warned.

I closed my hand over hers and guided her down the hall and into the nursery. The ladies were right on my heels.

I placed her in the middle of the room and stepped away to allow her space to see the transformation.

"Okay, you can take off the blindfold," I said.

Layla lifted it off and gasped before turning around, taking in every detail.

Jo wasn't lying about her detail-oriented skills. The room was done to perfection right down to the stuffed animals sitting in each of the four cribs.

Layla slapped a hand over her mouth and cried, "It's fucking beautiful." She blinked away tears. "You three did all this?"

Jordyn padded across the room. "With your help, of course, sis. You told Sam what you were interested in and what you liked, then he fed us the information. Plus, I knew you liked elephants."

I'd learned that tidbit about Layla in Maine. She'd also given me her ideas for a nursery—colors, furniture, and theme. Then she surfed the net and picked out everything. From there, it was easy.

Layla lowered her gaze to the elephant rug between the cribs—two of which lined one wall, the other two the opposite wall.

I thought nothing could be better than the amazing time with her in Maine. How wrong I was. Seeing that smile she wore now and feeling the tension fall off her made me even happier. She'd been nervous that we wouldn't have enough time to set up the babies' room. I hoped that whatever was bothering her before we came to the base was now history.

The ladies chatted with Layla for a minute, then took their leave.

Once we were finally alone, I wrapped her in my arms. "Welcome home, baby doll. Now we have one less thing on our plate."

She playfully pinched my nipple through my button-down shirt. "You're a sneaky bastard."

"You love this sneaky bastard."

"Maybe." Her flirty attitude was turning me the fuck on as she touched her stomach. "They're going to love this room." She glanced down. "Aren't you?"

I replaced her hand with mine. "They are. I can't wait to hold them while I rock them to sleep. Or see them light up with a smile as beautiful as yours." I nuzzled my nose into her neck. "I never want you to stop smiling, Layla. I will do whatever it takes to make sure that light in you stays lit."

She quivered against me as the love floating off her wrapped around us. "I love you, vampire." Then she sighed as she absorbed everything in the room.

In addition to the elephant rug and cribs, the nursery had two rockers by the window, changing tables, a dresser, and a stack of wrapped presents in front of the closet.

Layla kept shaking her head. "I love the gray walls, the hint of blues and pinks in the curtains, and the gray-and-black elephant rug. What an awesome surprise, Sam. I'll need to find a way to thank them—and you, of course."

I picked up an elephant from one of the cribs. "No need to thank me. I will do anything for you, Layla."

She threw herself at me. "How did I get so lucky?" She pressed a finger to my mouth. "Don't say it."

I captured her finger between my teeth. "Don't say that I know another way you can get lucky?" I sucked on her finger.

Lust swirled around her as she did an eye roll. "Seriously, you're spoiling me."

I let go of her finger. "Baby doll, nothing wrong with that."

I would spoil her for an eternity. Hell, I planned to.

30

LAYLA

I was sitting in a rocker in the nursery, inhaling and exhaling, practicing my breathing exercises for more than just being pregnant. Excitement stirred low and deep in my belly. Today was my freaking wedding day. I was marrying a man I was hopelessly in love with. I was a vampire's bride-to-be—something I never thought would happen, given that I was a vampire hunter. I was also ecstatic that Sam and I understood each other. That we didn't have secrets between us, unlike my mom who had kept so many things from my father.

I frowned as I rocked in the chair. I wanted my parents here with me. They might not agree with what I was doing, but I had to believe they would've supported me, unlike Rianne and my grandmother. I shook those two from my mind. They didn't belong in my thoughts on this special day. Besides, I had Jordyn and two other women. Jo and Harley were turning out to be great friends I could call sisters.

During the last six days since Sam and I had returned from Maine, I'd spent a good chunk of time hanging out with Harley, Jo, and Jordyn. I couldn't thank them enough for what they had done for Sam and me. Sure, Sam had asked if they would take on the task, but he didn't have to bribe them. The women had been more than happy to help.

I'd also had my three-month checkup with Dr. Martin and Dr. Vieira. My pregnancy was on track, and with how fast the babies had grown, I should deliver in the five-to-six-month window—a phenomenon only recorded once in vampire history. Since I couldn't deliver naturally and to reduce complications, we'd scheduled my C-section for mid-July, which would put me at about five and half months pregnant.

Despite that, when Doc first told me about Emily Crawford's case, I heard him, and I had no reason to discount the facts, but I didn't exactly believe my pregnancy would follow the same path. Boy was I wrong. I could feel my belly stretching almost every minute of the day. I weighed more, I was eating like a horse, and I napped, which was so weird because unless I was sick, I'd never dozed during the day before. I just prayed I didn't end up like Emily —dead. I shivered at the thought before I pushed it out of my mind. I had to believe my fate wasn't a coffin in the ground. That my destiny was for something far greater than just giving birth.

To say I was overwhelmed was an understatement of the century, and not just over the fact that I would be the second woman in vampire history to have supernatural babies. It was also due to the lightning speed at which things were moving. I felt as though I was on a bullet train. One minute I was sleeping with a vampire; the next, pregnant, then engaged, and now tying the knot.

Still, below the surface of my happiness, I couldn't shake the uneasiness. My dreams of late had been messing with my psyche. I'd been plagued with a variation of the recurring nightmares I'd been having for months—dark road, the soft voice of a young boy warning me about a woman, then urging me to go with him to help his sister. Then the scene changed, and I was chasing a woman with brown hair, but I never saw her face. In the far reaches of my mind, my intuition was telling me that the woman was Rianne. She had brown hair. Jordyn did as well. But I wouldn't or couldn't believe Jordyn would betray me. Yet my stomach churned like a storm at sea at the idea that she was the woman in my dreams.

Maybe my mind was playing tricks on me. My hormones were sure as fuck on a wild roller-coaster ride. Whoever the woman was that I'd been chasing would reveal herself at some point. I was learning that my visions during REM sleep were a window into my future. Case in point: after Sam had been taken by Intech, I'd dreamt of standing in a room overlooking the mountains during a storm. That was the same room where I'd recently been held at the facility in West Virginia. I'd also seen the initials EML during one of my crazy nightmares. This logo had been stamped on Rianne's ball cap and on the wall at the Intech lab in Chicago.

Steven had counseled me to pay attention to my dreams, saying that they could save my life. It wasn't mine I was concerned about, though, but the lives of my children.

As I rocked back and forth, rubbing my belly, Sam graced the doorway with one of his lopsided smirks. "You love it in here, don't you?"

"It's peaceful," I said.

He leaned a shoulder against the doorjamb. His black hair was tied at the nape, his jaw clean-shaven, his green eyes flickering with a mixture of mischief and happiness. "Are your vows ready?"

I shrugged. "Maybe." I fought a smile. I knew what I wanted to say as we wrapped the ribbons around our hands. I thought hand-fasting was a cool way to express our love in front of our family and friends. "Are you?"

"I've never been more ready for anything."

Suddenly, one of the babies kicked. They'd been quite active, but this one was a strong one.

Sam was at my side in a flash. "What is it? I'll call Doc." He had his phone out of his pocket at the speed of light.

"Chill, vampire. One of them just kicked like an expert football punter. Feel here." I rubbed the right side of my stomach. He'd felt the movement before, but, again, never as pronounced as this one.

He set his phone on the floor, squatted down in front of me, and placed his hand where mine was. When one of them moved again, he sucked in air. "Fuck me. It must be the boy. My star NFL kicker."

He stole the breath right from my lungs at how he lit up like the sun on a beautiful summer day. Such a poignant moment that I would embed in my memory forever. "Probably is a boy." I agreed with him, and only because I didn't want to ruin this moment or erase the gorgeous grin on his face.

He leaned in and kissed my belly, then pressed his ear to it.

I smoothed a hand over his hair, his woodsy scent surrounding us. "Do you hear them?"

"All four." He raised his head. "If you can hear me," he said to my stomach, "we can't wait to meet you."

A string of tingles spread throughout me as if they heard him. "They got your message." My voice cracked with so much emotion I was a second away from bawling.

He massaged my belly lightly. "I feel their energy."

His phone rang, shattering our tender and heartwarming moment.

He grumbled as he answered. "What is it, Tripp? Here? Now?" Creases lined his forehead. "Copy that." He stood, sliding his cell into the side pocket of his cargo pants. "Jack and Tabitha are in the lobby. Tabitha would like to see you."

I did a double take. "This is a surprise, and at the same time, it isn't, I guess." They were probably here to collect Junior's body. Steven had it transported from New Jersey where the car accident had happened.

"Do you want to see them?" Sam asked.

When I motioned that I wanted to stand, he gave me his hand. "Of course. Though, what do I say if she asks about Noah?" I knew she would, particularly if Junior told them Harriet had kidnapped me.

"You don't need the stress, baby doll."

"I'll be fine." I did want to see my aunt. We hadn't had a tight relationship, but after my sisters and I returned to Montana from Massachusetts back in February, Aunt Tab took care of me when I was sick and was instrumental in taming her husband when Sam had shown up at the ranch. "She likes you. Aren't you two besties? Your words, not mine." Aunt Tab had called Sam after I'd licked blood off the knife that day in her kitchen.

"I do like her," Sam admitted. "But at the first sign of a rapid pulse from you, we're walking away."

"Fair enough, vampire."

After I waddled down a long-ass hallway and then another before we went into the elevator, I was ready for freaking bed. As I grew bigger, I also got more winded. First thing I would do when I wasn't eating for five was work out. Pregnancy was quickly becoming miserable. I couldn't find a comfortable position in bed, in a chair, or when walking. Hell, walking was a feat in itself.

The car dropped one floor, then Sam hit the stop button, and the car rocked to a halt.

My eyebrows went up as déjà vu spun before me. "Um... do you want me to kick you in the balls like I did the first time we were in this elevator together?"

He pinned me against the cold steel wall that actually felt good on my heated skin. My temperature ran hot all the time.

He sniffed my neck and hair. "One of my fantasies is to fuck you in an elevator." Lust saturated his gravelly voice.

I gripped his erection, arousal humming through my veins. "It's a date, vampire. But we have Aberdeen guests waiting."

As if I'd doused a bucket of ice water over his head, he had the elevator moving again, snapping to attention as if he was about to go into battle. A vampire needed a suit of armor to deal with someone like Jack Aberdeen. Sam and Jack's last interaction hadn't gone well. I was pretty darn sure Jack was on our side, yet from Sam's stiff posture, he didn't think so.

Cold air washed over me as I exited the elevator. The lobby had a sterile and hollow feel to it. Maybe because of the high ceilings.

Ruth, a petite blonde, looked up from her seat behind the circular desk. "Mr. and Mrs. Aberdeen are in the visitor's room." She pointed at the open door. "Your father will be down momentarily as well."

Sam rolled back his shoulders, set his jaw, and nodded at the pretty receptionist. "Thanks, Ruth." His tone was gruff, adding another layer to his soldier's armor.

Sam and I entered to find Jack pacing the carpeted floor behind his wife, who was seated at the square table.

Jack's hard glare at Sam could've started a fire. My uncle appeared to have aged since I'd last seen him at the hotel outside of Chicago. I hadn't spoken to him since before I'd stolen his rental car.

Regardless, Aunt Tab didn't look any better. Her salt-and-pepper hair was grayer, and she had bags under her dark eyes. "So good to see you." She hugged me briefly, then gave me the once-over. "You're glowing. Pregnancy suits you. And congratulations." She sounded happy, but her swollen red eyes said otherwise. "Are you having twins?"

"Quadruplets," I said proudly, standing beside my soon-to-be husband.

Jack mumbled something I couldn't make out.

When Aunt Tab hugged Sam, the air crackled around my uncle, the disgust and fury evident in his bluish-gray eyes.

Aunt Tab didn't seem to care what her husband thought or how he reacted as she touched Sam's scruffy jaw. "You are a wonderful person and will be a great father."

"Tab." Jack's nostrils were flaring to beat the band.

She whirled around. "My son is dead because of your mother not by a vampire. So, Jack Aberdeen, don't start with me."

Jack was never one to cower. At least, I'd never seen him blanch. "Speaking of my son, we're here to pick up his body and my brother Ray's."

"My father should be here shortly," Sam said, his shoulders tense, his jaw tight.

"I'm so sorry about Junior," I said to Aunt Tab. "He was a good man. He loved Carly to death."

She tightened her lips. "She was underserving of my son." She plucked a tissue from her handbag on the table. "I can't believe he's gone."

Jack kept his distance from Sam and crossed his arms over his barrel chest. "This shit with Intech and my mother has to end." His voice boomed, almost shaking the walls.

A muscle ticked in Sam's jaw. "Then consider helping instead of hiding." He dropped the words like chips of ice into a tin bowl.

Jack took one step toward Sam, then stilled, splotchy red spots coloring his face. "I have two families to protect."

"We all do, Jack," Sam fired back. "Your mother is out on a ledge, searching for a cure for her blood cancer. She thinks either I'm her golden ticket or my children are. I will stop her. If you want to help, then get on board. Otherwise, don't tell us what we need to do."

"That's why she's doing this?" Aunt Tab's voice hitched with horror.

Jack paled. "Blood cancer?"

"A rare form," I added. "Not sure what type. But she's dead set on immortality as a cure."

"Noah?" Aunt Tab asked. "Did you see him? Either of you?"

Sam placed his hands behind his back and straightened as though he was programmed to do so, not reacting to Aunt Tab's question.

I looked to him for help, but his attention was on Aunt Tab.

I thought he would say something. After all, he'd seen Noah. I expected him to tell Aunt Tab that her son had gulped down Carly's crazy juice.

I couldn't bring myself to tell her that Noah wasn't the same boy she'd given birth to—he wasn't human.

Aunt Tab brought her fingers to her mouth. "You have. Is he dead?" Tears clouded her eyes. The poor woman had already lost her eldest son to a car accident and didn't look like she could withstand the whole truth about Noah.

Somehow, I had to put her out of her misery. "I've seen Noah. He's with Rianne and Harriet. But like my sister, there's no convincing him that the quest he's on will never work."

Jack whisked a hand through his thinning red hair, then rubbed the back of his neck. "How do you propose we help, Mason?"

Steven strutted in as if on cue to answer Jack. The Sam look-alike had his black hair tied in a low ponytail like his son. He wore a white button-down shirt open at the collar, the sleeves cuffed over his forearms, and black slacks.

I couldn't wait to see Sam dressed in a suit. His dad was loaning him one for our ceremony that evening. Sam looked hot as hell in both his SEAL uniform and casual attire, but there was something about a man in a tailored suit that tickled my lady parts.

Steven introduced himself to Aunt Tab and expressed his condolences to her and Jack. Then he invited them to stay at one of the transient homes on base.

"Thank you, but we're leaving tonight. We would like to bury Junior and Ray as soon as possible," Jack said. "And my brothers-in-law, who are holding down the fort, expect us to return quickly. We can talk over video chat at some point. Any activity since we spoke?" Jack asked Steven.

"Nothing to address. But this war is coming, Jack. Don't wait long to engage. Whether you like or not, you're involved."

My uncle acknowledged Steven with a dip of his chin. "Seems you have a ton of shit to handle with the media as well."

"One of the reasons the war will be here faster than you think," Steven added. "Intech will use the media to its advantage."

"How? By recruiting humans?" I asked. It was the first thing that came to mind. It kind of made sense.

If I was right, neither Steven nor Sam answered. They probably couldn't say for sure. Regardless, with our luck, Adam Emery would use Sam's notoriety with the public as a way to capture him or… Our children also came to mind. I swallowed thickly, clutching my chest as the sharp edges of my ruby engagement ring pricked me.

Sam grumbled at his dad, "Layla and I are leaving. Her heart rate is elevated."

My lower back was beginning to spasm anyway. I didn't have much else to say to Tab or Jack. Though, it would be nice to pick Tab's brain about her pregnancies. The more I thought about that, the more I nixed the idea. She didn't have supernatural kids. Her pregnancy was nine months, not six. I couldn't compare apples to oranges.

I almost invited them to our handfasting ceremony, then thought better of it. I liked my aunt and uncle. Tabitha had a big heart, and I felt her pain over the loss of Junior. I prayed I would never have to experience anything like that. As far as Jack went, we had our differences. We both believed in the sanctity of humanity, yet he couldn't grasp how the Vampire Navy SEALs wanted the same thing as us—protecting humankind to engender a thriving world of peace for everyone, including the supernatural community. Because of those reasons, my aunt and uncle didn't fit in our circle of family and friends. Sure, Jack had a stake in the game now—his mother and son—but that wasn't enough reason to invite him and Tab to witness the love Sam and I had for each other. Jack would probably puke the entire time or continue to breathe fire at Sam. We needed peace and tranquility tonight, not hatred and disgust.

I said my goodbyes in the hopes that all of them, including Ray's wife and my cousins, stayed safe. I wouldn't be disheartened if our paths never crossed again. Although I suspected they would—if Jack truly decided to help us.

31

SAM

I paced in the hallway outside the war room, loosening my green tie that felt like a noose around my neck. How my old man wore these fuckers was beyond me.

Footsteps scuffed the floor as my father approached, looking like he'd just walked off the runway of a gentlemen's fashion show—tailored double-breasted black suit, white shirt, and burgundy tie. Like me, his black hair was tied at the nape, he was clean-shaven, and his black dress shoes had been spit shined. The only difference in our attire was the color of our ties.

"Nervous?" he asked, his grin broadening.

"I would rather wear nothing than this monkey suit."

"Son, what has you rattled? I can't read your mind. You took the mind-blocking potion?"

"To keep you and Jo out of my head for reasons I would rather not discuss." Anytime I was around Layla, my mind always wandered—her naked, me inside her, me licking her nipples, her pussy, and the list went on. I also knew that when she stood before me tonight, my thoughts would definitely lean to the erotic side. "And I'm on edge because of the comment you made about Intech using my notoriety with the public to their advantage. Layla thinks Intech will put out a contract on me."

"I'm sorry, son," he said. "She could be right."

"I know, and that pisses me the fuck off." I released a ragged sigh. "I'm tired of this shit, Pops. I might have to keep my kids locked up. What kind of life is that?" The last thing I wanted when I married Layla was to be in a bad mood.

He clapped me on the shoulder. "I feel your pain more than you know. I want you to clear your mind. Tonight is about you and Layla."

No shit! I inhaled deeply and shoved my anger into a box and locked the fucker.

"Why didn't Layla invite Jack and his wife?" Dad asked. "Not that they would've stayed."

"Too much tension between Jack and me. And she doesn't consider them close family." I was stoked that she didn't. Her pulse had skyrocketed when her aunt Tabitha brought up Noah. Then it went even higher when my old man mentioned how Intech would use the media to their advantage. Layla had that crazy notion about a contract on my head. I looked at my watch. "It's time. Layla will be here any second."

The ceremony would be simple, which was the way Layla and I wanted it. We would exchange vows and forgo the rings until she could wear jewelry. At that time, we would pick out our wedding rings together.

I strutted into the war room and up to George, who was standing below the movie screen. The tall, lanky vampire looked as if he'd just walked off Wall Street in his expensive tailored blue suit, light-gray shirt, and a soft pink-and-white-striped tie.

"Are you ready?" George asked, holding the ribbons we would use when we exchanged vows.

My stomach was a ball of nerves. "One hundred percent," I said and stood up straighter. I couldn't wait for Layla to officially be my wife.

While I waited for Layla, I nodded at our guests as I scanned the occupied seats. In the second row was Tripp, Dr. Vieira, Sawyer, and Harley. The first row consisted of Webb, Jo, Abbey, and my dad.

I would've liked more of my SEAL team brethren in attendance, like Ben and Olivia, but it was hard to plan around everyone's schedules, particularly when we were in the middle of a looming war.

The door groaned open, and anticipation sparked butterflies to flap their wings inside my stomach. Jordyn entered first, smiling at me as she eased into a seat next to my dad. Our guests were dressed for the occasion, including my niece, who was adorable in her pink dress.

As soon as the door opened again, the guests and their attire vanished as Layla's cherry scent floated in, cutting through my nerves, followed by my beautiful huntress.

My knees buckled as Layla, beaming from ear to ear, swung those sweet hips. I swore I lost the ability to breathe.

"Hey, handsome." Her siren voice melted my heart and sent heat straight to my cock.

The sky-blue empire-waist dress that hugged her pregnant curves perfectly and accentuated her massive tits was making me painfully hard. My self-control was on the verge of bursting into flames as beads of sweat dripped down my back.

Think of anything but her naked, man. I imagined ripping off Rianne's head, and that did the trick.

"You're sweating," Layla said. "Breathe."

"I can't, baby doll. You've stolen all my breath with your beauty."

"You mean my…" She mouthed the word "tits."

I swallowed down a laugh as I nodded at George. "We're ready."

George cleared his throat. "We're gathered here today to witness the love Sam and Layla have for each other. Their union will be bound, not by these ribbons, but instead by their vows."

Layla and I collectively sighed as we faced each another and joined left hands. Instantly, a bolt of electricity shot up my arm. If she felt it, she didn't acknowledge it as she took the black ribbon from George.

"Sam." She licked her burgundy-painted lips and heaved a breath. "Your ability to love me unconditionally is the most precious gift you could ever give me." She twined the ribbon, weaving it over my hand, underneath our joined one, then over hers. "I've chosen the black because it signifies your power and strength that will protect us as we build our future and raise our children together. Our journey so far has been bathed in chaos, yet through it all, our love shines the brightest and always will." Then she pressed a hand on her chest. "My heart will only beat for you. I'm honored to be your wife and partner." A tear slid down her cheek.

My pulse was banging in my ears as my stomach was on a roller-coaster ride. The emotions pouring off her were stealing my ability to think clearly.

Quiet sobs and light sniffles broke the beat of silence.

I fixated on Layla, my heart slamming against my rib cage. "Baby doll, baby mama, my beautiful bride."

She laughed through her tears.

I pushed out a nervous sigh. "No matter where we come from, who we are—mortal or immortal, human or vampire—or what we believe, love is the great unifier. *Our* universal truth. My world is a better place with you in it." I wrapped the red ribbon around our hands. "I've chosen the color red as it symbolizes your passion for those you care about and resilience in how you handle adversity." I touched my heart. "You are the yin to my yang, the brightest star in my universe, and I give you my soul. I love you."

She blinked away a waterfall of tears. I was shedding one or two myself.

The sobs from our guests grew louder.

"Sam, Layla." George's deep voice quieted the room. "Your commitment is steeped in your love for each another and represents the dawning of your new future together. Sam, go ahead. Kiss your bride."

Thunderous applause filled the room.

"I'm the happiest fucking vampire alive," I said to Layla before I mashed my mouth to hers.

I felt more powerful than I ever had—whether it was because of the magic pulsing inside me or the love in my heart, I knew that whatever lay ahead, I was ready for it—or so I prayed.

32

LAYLA

I ran under a canopy of trees as the rain pelted down. Sticks, rocks, and dead leaves embedded in my feet, the adrenaline keeping me from feeling any pain.

The woman ahead of me tossed a look over her shoulder, her red eyes glowing like the devil from the depths of hell. I skidded to a halt, gulping in the cold, crisp night air as I struggled to make out who she was or what she was.

"You need to stop her, Mom," a five-year-old boy said from somewhere nearby. "She'll kill us if you don't."

I swiveled my head in all directions but couldn't see a fucking thing. When I returned my attention to the woman, she was gone.

My eyes flew open as I lifted my head off the pillow. I squinted through the blurriness at the clock on the nightstand—1:30 a.m.

For fuck's sake. Not again. Night after night over the last two months since the handfasting ceremony, I'd been waking up at one thirty from the exact dream. Only tonight, I learned the faceless woman had red eyes like Noah. I didn't even want to speculate if I'd been having visions of Rianne.

I wiped the sweat from my brow with the back of my hand and eased out of bed, not wanting to wake Sam. He was dead to the world, sprawled out on his stomach, arms tucked under his pillow, his tight, toned ass, muscular legs, and strong back on display. The vampire didn't believe in blankets or sheets. As of late, I didn't either. My body was running hot due to the pregnancy, and with the recurring dreams, I'd been waking up in a pool of sweat.

After I threw on a robe and grabbed my phone off the bedside table, I wound my way down the hall—or rather, waddled. My belly was fucking huge. I looked like I was more than nine months pregnant when, in fact, I was just over five months. My C-section was scheduled for next week, and I couldn't wait to shed the weight. The babies had been active, my back hurt constantly, breathing was a monumental task if I exerted myself the tiniest bit, and I was constantly in the bathroom.

Dr. Martin and Dr. Vieira were elated that I wasn't bedridden. I didn't see why I would be. I hardly did anything except rest or take catnaps. In between, I'd been in the library, helping to sift through old vampire records mainly to find the missing pages in Emily Crawford's medical file. But no such luck.

Regardless, I didn't dwell on pregnancy complications. Instead, Sam and I made a list of names. We still had to come up with two more aside from Liam and Luna. He might be right. We needed to see their beautiful faces first. I couldn't wait to see what our children would look like—Sam or me or a combination. I was also curious about what types of magical powers they would have.

Entering the kitchen, I flipped the switch on the wall, squinting beneath the bright LED lights as I beelined it for the fridge. Water —I needed cold water. I stuck my head in, sighing as the coolness of the air breezed over my face. What I wouldn't give to have a walk-in freezer right about now. The apartment had air-conditioning, but it never seemed to be cold enough to counteract the heat emanating from my body.

I lingered for a long minute before snagging a bottle of mountain spring water. I set my phone on the counter, then twisted off the cap and chugged, the cool liquid erasing the parched feeling in the back of my throat. Once the bottle was empty, I was about to toss it in the trash when my phone dinged.

Kendra's name flashed with a text. I'd finally decided to call her last week when I was in the right headspace to listen to her story about how she knew my father and whether she'd murdered him. I doubted she would admit it if she had. That day in the hangar at the abandoned airport outside of Chicago, I'd gotten the vibe that she cared about my dad. My uncle Jack assumed Kendra and my father had slept together. Neither he nor Ray knew the whole story, only that Kendra was an enemy who should be strung up over our firepit in Montana and burned to a crisp.

I hadn't been able to actually talk to Kendra yet. I'd gotten her voice mail and asked if she could reach out when she had the chance.

Kendra: *I got your message. I won't be back in the States for a few weeks. When I return, I'll reach out.*

Me: *Thanks for responding. Safe travels.*

Sam had urged me not to open a can of worms with Kendra, at least not until after I'd given birth. I loved the vampire to death, but, at times, he worried way too much.

I left my phone in the kitchen and shuffled over to the wall of windows.

Darkness crept through the courtyard below, broken only by the dim glow of the light beside the sentry standing guard outside the prison building. On many occasions recently, I'd wanted to pay a visit to Fred Emery. The SEALs hadn't gotten any answers from Fred. I wouldn't mind interrogating him. According to Doc, Fred had healed from the stab wounds I'd inflicted on him. I clenched my fists at my sides whenever I thought of him smashing Jordyn's face into a parked car.

Speaking of my sister, she hadn't been herself since my return from hell. The harrowing experiences she'd been through were messing with her mind. She was having a hard time dealing with Junior's death. I'd encouraged her to talk to Dr. Vieira or ask him if he knew a therapist. I could probably use one myself. I couldn't stop thinking about Rianne and if she was dead—or even what my grandmother was up to. I had a mixed bag of feelings about them. Rianne, Noah, and Granny deserved to be punished in some way. Was death the answer? I didn't think so. Though, after what they'd put me through, I would be lying if I said I didn't want to murder them myself.

I toyed with my ruby engagement ring on my necklace, a habit I'd developed the moment Sam clasped the chain around my neck. At first, I was afraid I might lose the precious gemstone, but as time passed, I clung to it whenever I was nervous or deep in thought.

I stared up at the moonless sky, shuffling through thoughts of how my life had been quiet and vastly different since Sam and I exchanged vows.

My days began with a physical checkup. Doc wanted to see me every morning. The man was fascinated with the looming birth of supernatural newborns. I was as well. Would we have a mixture of vampires and witches or all of one species? Would they be as strong as Sam? What types of powers would they have? If they were vampires, would their fangs grow in when they were teething? No one knew any of these answers. Yet the one question Dr. Vieira and Dr. Martin had the answer to was the sex of the babies.

I was rubbing my stomach when movement below zapped my train of thought. A woman ran through the courtyard and up to the guard. I squinted, straining my eyes to see who she was.

I did a double take. "Jordyn?"

She tried to skirt the guard, but she wasn't having any luck with the big dude.

I wanted to run, but that was out of the question, so I walked to the door as my heart rammed against my chest. I had to find out what in the fuck she was doing. I mean, I knew. She wanted retribution for what Fred Emery had done to her. I had to stop her, talk to her, hold her, somehow help her.

"Where do you think you're going?" Sam's husky voice slid along my arms like melted butter, making me freeze in place.

I swung my gaze to the imposing vampire strutting down the hall in zipped but not buttoned jeans slung low on his hips, bare feet, and unkempt black hair as if we'd had a wild time in bed.

Don't I wish. Rough sex went out the window a while ago. Oral sex, on the other hand, had been our vice. I couldn't complain. His tongue worked magic on my clit, and sucking him off was my aphrodisiac.

"Jordyn is trying to get into the prison building. I need to stop her." I motioned toward the door.

He blocked me. "The guard will handle it." He lowered his voice to a softness that still held a warning. "And you need to stay off your feet."

Growling, I fastened my hands on my hips. "Husband, get out of my way, or I'll knee you in the balls."

He flashed sharp teeth in an arrogant smirk. "No, you won't. You need these balls."

I huffed, flaring my nostrils as I clutched onto his precious jewels. "I'll squeeze them off instead."

His eyes rolled back in his head.

Stupid me. I knew better. Sam lived for physical pain—at least in the bedroom. "You would get off on me whipping you?"

Silver threaded through the green in his irises, a true sign of the vampire's emotions. "I would like that." His fingers flew through his hair. "But right now, if you want to help Jordyn, you need to put on some clothes."

I swallowed an exasperated scream that desperately wanted out as I stood before him in a terry cloth robe.

Again, stupid me.

He plucked my hand from his balls. "I'll call the control room and see what's happening while you dress."

I narrowed my eyes. "Don't you dare leave without me."

He pressed his lips together, fishing his phone out of his pocket as I walked back to the bedroom—slowly, I might add.

He was right. What was I thinking? I couldn't traipse around, putting out fires.

I'll take my time, dress, and have Sam bring Jordyn up to the apartment.

Five minutes later, after I'd thrown clothes on, I returned to Sam feeling winded and clammy all of a sudden.

I inhaled and exhaled several times as I padded across the living room to the wall of windows where Sam was standing and glancing out with his cell to his ear.

Before I reached him, he jerked his head at me, eyebrows pinched, fear in his green eyes.

Did something happen to Jordyn? My pulse went from eighty to one hundred and twenty in a flat second.

"I have to call you back," Sam said to whoever he'd been talking to. "Layla, what's wrong? Your heart rate is off the charts." He helped me to the couch.

"I'm fine. Just feel weird. I need a minute. Is Jordyn okay?"

"You're not fine. You're pale. Do you need blood?" he asked, his voice bordering on panicky.

I swallowed the dryness, rubbing my throat. "Water."

He flew into the kitchen and was handing me an uncapped bottle of water within seconds. "I'm calling Doc."

I'd brought the bottle to my mouth when a sharp pain in my chest had me gasping. The bottle slipped out of my hands, and then Sam began to spin before me. I rubbed my chest, breathing in and out.

Sam's voice began to fade as he talked to Doc.

Next thing I knew, I was in Sam's arms.

"Layla," he said. "Stay with me. I'm taking you to the infirmary."

"The babies," I managed to say, laboring for breath. "Save them." The lights in the hallway began to flicker, then a swirling swath of blackness took me under.

33

SAM

I carried Layla, trying like a motherfucker not to freak out. But as her heart rate began to slow, mine went through the roof. Thank fuck the infirmary was in the same building, only on the other side, which felt like ten thousand miles as my soul shattered with each step I took.

"Layla, baby doll—if you can hear me, hang in there." My voice cracked on every word.

A huge fucking knot fisted in my stomach. A daggerlike feeling stabbed my heart, and I was dripping with sweat—or maybe those were tears rolling down my face.

The double doors loomed ahead, seemingly sliding farther and farther from me. I prayed like a motherfucker, asking whoever was listening to save Layla. The closer I got to the infirmary, the more her heart slowed. I wanted to scream, roar, and punch a wall.

You need to stay calm, man. Trust fate.

Fuck fate. All it had ever done was create chaos and pain.

"Layla, I love the fuck out of you. You cannot die on me."

A high-pitched alarm shrieked through the hallway, echoing so loudly that my eardrums were about to burst.

Then a booming sound cut through the siren. I blinked as sweat seeped into my eyes, making the hallway ahead a bit blurred.

I could make out Doc pushing the stretcher through the double doors, running as fast as he could. "You've got to be kidding me. Is there a fire?" Doc asked.

I grunted out swear words left and right. If the alarm was a distraction for a surprise attack, I would murder the bastard responsible. Roman popped into my head. The fucker had a way of playing games.

I laid Layla on the stretcher. "Her heart. It's weak."

Doc didn't seem surprised as he rolled her toward the infirmary. "Dr. Martin is on his way. The gates will be locked down. I need you to make sure he gets in."

Several footsteps battered the floor behind us in the hall. "We're here!" Jo shouted above the alarm. My sister would've made a great cheerleader, belting out cheers with her powerful vocal cords.

Three other women followed Jo.

Doc had a team of nurses from our medical facility in Boston prepared to help. They'd arrived a couple of days ago. Since the C-section was scheduled for next week, Doc was being proactive. No surprise Doc had his shit together.

Jo pushed me out of the way. "We've got this, Sam."

The three nurses—two brunettes and one redhead—dove into action. The redhead I recognized. I'd met Beverly after my father had been rushed into the Boston facility. He'd suffered injuries from Roman's great escape from the prison at our vampire complex.

Doc barked orders as they rushed Layla into the infirmary.

My sister pressed a hand on my chest. "Find out what's going on. That's the fire alarm, but I didn't see or smell anything related to a fire."

"I am not leaving Layla."

"Sam." Doc's tone was harsh. "Dr. Martin. Now!"

The nurses wheeled the stretcher straight down the aisle and through another set of double doors at the back side of the infirmary where the new wing had been constructed, complete with an operating room and a nursery for newborns, including a neonatal room with incubators. The latter was necessary with an early delivery.

I trailed behind them.

Jo blocked me. "It's imperative you let us do our job."

"I got that, sis. I'm taking the stairs." Truth. The stairwell was through a side door on the left end of the infirmary. I couldn't stand still in an elevator, or I would feel closed in. "Sis, if she dies, I will blow up this place," I said through clenched teeth. *Or burn it down.*

She flattened a steady hand back on my trembling body. "I know. I'll help you." My sister was as calm as a windless summer day.

Not me. I was about to self-combust, and I pitied the person who got in my way.

I bolted out the back entrance and jumped the stairs two at a time. No sooner than I was outside in the balmy night, the fire alarm died. We had different sounds for each threat. If our enemies were storming the base, the siren would wail every two seconds, while the recent one had been constant.

I jogged to the end of the building, scanning and sniffing. I didn't see any fire or smell smoke. That was a good sign that the infirmary wasn't compromised, yet that didn't erase my need to filet the asshole who'd screwed with Dr. Martin coming onto the base.

I called Tripp, who I'd been talking to earlier about Jordyn. As soon as the line connected, I shouted, "What the fuck is happening?"

"Jordyn pulled the fire alarm," he said. "No fires. I called off the trucks."

The headline would read: "Jordyn Aberdeen Dead at Age Twenty by the Hand of a Vampire Who Is on Every News Channel in the Country."

"Layla is in the operating room, and I need to clear the path for Dr. Martin to come in."

"One step ahead of you. He should be pulling up now," Tripp said. "His name is on the list at the guard shack to let him through anytime. I'll meet you up in the infirmary." Then he hung up.

Maybe luck was on my side.

I wound my way to the front entrance of the building. Petty Officer Cole Dawson stood watch outside the lobby doors.

"Sir." He straightened, his amber gaze flickering at me. "Is everything okay?"

The last time we ran into each other, he was guarding Junior Aberdeen's room in the men's barracks. I'd been on a mission to strangle Junior the day Layla had been kidnapped. I'd thought Junior had been part of the plan to snag Layla. Regardless, I'd been seconds away from strangling Junior when Petty Officer Dawson tried to pull me down off a ledge and pissed me off in the process. He'd only been doing his job.

Now, here we were again. Same thing. I was fucked in the head with worry over Layla.

"Just waiting on Dr. Martin," I said in an even tone. He didn't need the brunt of my wrath. Jordyn did, though.

She was the reason Layla's heart rate had nose-dived. What was wrong with Jordyn? I knew she was struggling with Junior's death and was dead set on revenge against Fred Emery, but she knew better than to go into the prison. She knew our rules.

"Oh, is your wife having the babies?" Dawson sounded excited.

The SEAL team couldn't wait to meet my kids. I couldn't either. But I also couldn't be a single father with four kids to raise. *Fuuuuck!* Layla had to live.

I nodded at Petty Officer Dawson as the sound of the engine filtered through the light wind before the headlights lit up the darkened road leading in from the main gate.

Dr. Martin had barely parked before I was at the driver's side door.

The tall, slender doctor climbed out with his hazel eyes wide. "Sam, I just got off the phone with Dr. Vieira. He's filled me in. Layla is stable."

My legs were about to give out. "She is?" I shouldn't have left the infirmary.

He placed a gentle hand on my back. "Breathe. We're going to do the C-section now." He gave me a nudge. "I need to head in."

As we walked at a brisk pace past Petty Officer Dawson, I asked,

"Is she going to make it?" I wasn't naïve enough to believe he could give me a definitive answer. I just wanted his thoughts.

"I can't answer that, Sam. What I will tell you is that in a normal pregnancy, carrying quads wouldn't be an issue. But Layla has two things not in her favor—four supernatural babies, and they're growing faster than humans. Her body just can't handle it. Though, up until now, she's done great."

After an elevator ride that seemed like we were on a slow-moving train to nowhere, Dr. Martin and I hurried to the operating room.

Before he went in, he regarded me with warm hazel eyes. "We will do our best. Try to stay calm. We'll update you as soon as we can." Then he ducked into the operating room.

When the door opened, I saw a scrub station and beyond that a window into the operating room. I was desperate to be by Layla's side. She needed to hear my voice, feel my touch, and know that she wasn't alone.

Tripp came into the hall, tired bronze eyes searching mine. "I'm here for you, man."

We exchanged a quick hug. "Thanks. I'm not sure I'll be good company."

"I'm a good listener," he said.

Tripp had always been there for me. When I first turned vampire, he'd been my bodyguard, protecting and watching over me. He'd also been my teacher, schooling me on the ways of the vampire world and what it took to become a Vampire Navy SEAL. From there, our relationship developed into a close friendship.

As we stood in the middle of a brightly lit hallway with doors punched into the walls on both sides, I filled him in on what had happened right before Layla turned pale and started having pains. By the time I was done, the anger, frustration, and heartache multiplied a thousandfold.

I was a second away from ramming my fist into the supply closet door several feet away from me. Doc would hate it if I ruined his spanking-new wing. "I want to murder Jordyn. What the fuck happened?" I had to talk about anything other than my wife.

I began pacing, a smile tugging at the edges of my mouth as a sliver of happiness overshadowed the fury coursing through me. Layla, my wife. I rolled that around on my tongue once, then twice. It was still foreign to me that I was married. I wasn't complaining in the least. What was I saying? I couldn't believe I was about to become a dad either.

"What's with the cheeky grin?" Tripp asked as I wore a hole in the white-speckled tiled floor.

I dragged my fingers through my hair. "Can you believe I'm married and about to have kids?"

He shook his sandy-blond head of hair that was bound in a ponytail. "Nope. I remember when you were green around the gills and angry as fuck when you turned vampire. Now look at you. A man who wants to conquer the world. A man of substance."

Choking out a laugh, I stopped pacing. "You have your concept of me wrong, dude. I'm powerful. That's it. I'm not rich, and I certainly don't have influence."

Tripp massaged his shoulder. "How wrong you are. When you walk into a room, you exude authority."

"You mean, people fear me?"

"And respect you," he said. "You're just like your father, and that is a compliment," he was quick to add.

For two beats, silence traveled through the long hallway.

My father and I had had a tumultuous relationship early on when I'd given up my humanity, yet I now saw a lot of him in me.

"Anyway, we got off the topic of Jordyn." I anchored myself against the wall, then slid down until I was sitting on the floor, knees high, forearms resting on them. "Layla said Jordyn was trying to skirt past the guard outside the prison." When I'd gone to the window, I didn't see her.

Tripp joined me, kicking out his legs, then he crossed his ankles. "She pulled the alarm as a distraction."

"She's been off lately," I said. "Junior's death messed with her head. Not to mention, she's itching for revenge against Fred Emery."

"We're moving him to the prison in Boston. He won't talk, and until he does, he'll have a home with us."

"You know Adam is going to come for his brother," I said, hoping I was right. "We need to take him out. That's the only way we can slow down this war." Adam wasn't the only one on our list. Roman needed to be dealt with as well.

Tripp adjusted the empty sheath around his leg. "Agreed. But he's in bed with the U.S. government. So we have to be smart about our strategy. We can't afford to have the entire human government on our asses. The war would be even bigger."

Icy claws crept up my spine. "I'm sure they've seen my mug and Hawk's on the news. I have a feeling they might be breathing down our necks with or without Adam in the picture."

He nodded. "Possible. We have work to do to prepare for every scenario. Right now, Layla is your priority along with your kids. You and I know they'll be part of this looming war."

Not something I wanted to hear, but the truth was a hard nut to swallow sometimes.

"Circling back to Jordyn—where is she now?"

"In a cell next to Fred Emery," he said. "If she wants to release her anger, she can yell at him from there."

I jerked my head at one of my best buds and superior officer, deciding if I should laugh or not. "You're serious?"

A muscle ticked in his unshaven jaw. "As a fucking heart attack. We're not tiptoeing around the Aberdeens, Sam. I had to deal with Rianne when she was here. Jordyn has been great up until she returned from New Jersey. And you're not going to like this, but I see a lot of Rianne in Jordyn. We're done dealing with Aberdeen shit. No offense to Layla. She's not like her sisters though. Sometimes I wonder if they were born from the same parents."

Layla's sisters had brown hair, not auburn, but that wasn't a reason to think they weren't blood related.

Another round of silence dropped over us until a baby's cry resonated.

I was on my feet, my pulse thundering in my ears. "Did you hear that?" I blew out a breath.

Tripp rose, eyes wide. "Boy? Girl?"

I shrugged. I couldn't tell.

Then another cry.

I slapped a hand on my chest. *Fuck! This is really happening. I'm about to see my kids.*

I lowered my gaze to my boots, listening intently, itching to plow through the door.

"Her heart rate is dropping," a nurse said.

"Come on, Layla. Stay with us." Panic colored Jo's tone.

As I jerked up my head, Tripp flew to the door that led into the scrub station. He knew me well.

He held up his hands. "You are not going in there."

"Wanna bet?" I marched toward him. "Get out of my way." My voice didn't sound like my own as nerves rattled in every word. My elemental powers vibrated in my arms, primed to wreak havoc on Tripp.

He pushed me against the wall across from the scrub station door. "Look at me, Sam. Your heart is racing too fucking fast. Breathe."

Another baby cried, and I froze. Was that the third one? But what about Layla?

I banged my head against the wall as Tripp shielded me. He was powerful, but I had him beat.

Besides, there was another way in. The patient entrance into the operating room was through a set of double doors located halfway down the hallway to my left.

"She's flatlining," one nurse said.

Shards of broken glass coated my insides, gouging into my flesh. I couldn't move. I couldn't think. I couldn't lose Layla. I would die right beside her.

"Crash cart now!" Doc shouted.

That broken glass cut deeper and deeper, tears on the precipice of rushing out like a waterfall after a hard rain as I glanced down the hall.

Tripp followed my line of sight as he pressed his hand into my chest, fastening me to the wall, anticipating my next move, no doubt. But he couldn't hold me back.

Roaring like the animal I was, I threw him to the side, then rushed over to the scrub station door. The fucker was locked. I was tearing the handle off when Tripp tackled me to the floor.

"You can't stop me!" I yelled.

The fucker sat on me, then pinned my hands to the floor. "I'm your superior officer, and I order you to stand down, soldier." Rage threaded through his bronze eyes as they shifted to vampire black.

My fangs shot out. "I'm not on a fucking mission. This is my wife we're dealing with."

"What will you do if you go in there? Think about it. You'll only prevent them from doing their job. Then Layla *will* die."

"Get off me," I snapped.

"Not until I'm sure you won't kill your wife." His tone was harsh, serious, and pissed me the fuck off.

I hated that he was right. "I would never kill my wife."

He cocked an eyebrow. "Then think before you act. Now, I'm going to stand, and if you so much as attempt to go in through either entrance, I'll throw you in the brig next to Jordyn. Are we clear?"

"Fucking crystal."

Once we were upright, he stood guard outside the scrub station, eyeing me.

I leaned against the wall across from him, interlaced my fingers, and brought them to my mouth—praying, praying, praying.

"Come on, Layla," Jo cried.

My heart stopped cold.

"She's not responding," a nurse said.

I crumpled to the floor. This couldn't be happening. Layla and I had just exchanged vows. She was my one and only true love. We were meant to build a future together, have more babies, buy a house beside the ocean, fight alongside each other, watch our kids grow, and love each other until the end of time.

Instead, I would be planning her funeral.

To be continued in The Prodigies…

ABOUT THE AUTHOR

Bestselling author **S.B. Alexander** is an independent author with over 25 titles to date. She writes paranormal, new adult, and sweet romances that feature hot heroes stealing hearts.

S.B. or Susan as she likes to be called is a navy veteran, former high school teacher, and former corporate sales executive. She's a lover of sports, especially baseball, although nowadays you can find her glued to the TV during football season.

Her motto: "Life is too short to waste. So live every moment like it's your last."

You can connect with S.B. Alexander in the following ways:

Reader Group: https://sbalexander.com/beastsandbitches
Author Website: https://sbalexander.com
Newsletter: https://sbalexander.com/newsletter
Email: susan@sbalexander.com

facebook.com/sbalexander.authorpage

twitter.com/sbalex_author

instagram.com/sbalexanderauthor

amazon.com/author/sbalexander

bookbub.com/authors/s-b-alexander

tiktok.com/@susanbalexander

ALSO BY S.B. ALEXANDER

Visit https://sbalexander.com/all-books/ to learn more about S.B. Alexander books and future releases. Please note release dates are subject to change based on reader demand and the author's schedule. Subscribing to the author's newsletter or following her on Facebook is the best way to stay updated with planned new releases.

GLOSSARY OF TERMS

Natural-born vampire: A human born with the vampire gene that, when activated, will turn them into a vampire.

Activation process: Those who carry the vampire gene can only turn by drinking the blood of their vampire father at the age of sixteen years or older.

Council of Elders – A group of five vampires who set the laws.

Genetic engineering: Turning humans into vampires through a process of restructuring their DNA.

Cobalt – A vampire's kryptonite. The metal will kill a vampire if staked through the heart. It will also burn a vampire's skin if they come in contact with it.

Reproduction: A natural-born vampire is born by a male vampire and a human female with a rare blood type of Vel negative.

Council of Eternal Affairs: The legal department of the vampire government.

Vampire characteristics: Sunlight doesn't burn them. Their hearts beat at <5 bpm. Skin temperature is ten degrees cooler than a human. Eye color changes to black except for a few chosen ones.

Steven Mason: Vampire and father to twins Jo and Sam Mason. He's dubbed the most powerful of all vampires because of his many powers, including his mind-reading abilities. He can only read minds when touching someone except when it comes to his children. His normal eye color is green. His vampire eye color is silver.

Jo Mason: Turned at sixteen. Powers include seeing the future through her dreams, mind-reading without touching a person, telekinesis, and she's an elemental with the ability to manipulate water, air, earth, and fire. Her normal eye color is silver. Her vampire eye color is violet.

Sam Mason: Turned at sixteen. Powers include feeling what others feel (Empath), telekinesis, and he can compel a person using a series of numbers woven into a magical spell. He's also an elemental with the ability to manipulate water, air, earth, and fire. His normal eye color is green. His vampire eye color is silver.

Guardians: Vampires who are equivalent to the human police.